I0630760

MURDER AT MIDNIGHT

AN AT MIDNIGHT NOVEL

JESSICA LYNN EVANS

SPARROW & VIXEN PRESS

To my husband, Daniel
Thank you for being more than my best friend and loving husband.
You're my rock. Without you, this idea would still be a dream.

CHAPTER ONE

"JUST GRAB the handle and open the door. It's not going to bite," Sam muttered under her breath, hoping no one heard her. Samantha Crenshaw breathed in deeply, the pine scent from the recently washed doors a deterrent instead of a once familiar comfort.

She straightened her back, wishing she would've changed the high heels she dug out from the bottom of her closet for a pair of flats. She wanted her first appearance back into Midnight Harbor society since her hospitalization months ago to go as unnoticed as possible.

Another deep breath, then she slowly exhaled through painted pink lips, grounding herself. She prepared for this moment. So why was she stuck in place, the simple act of opening a door beyond her ability?

She looked down at her hand frozen in midair, halfway to the metal door handle. Standing at the threshold of the room, realization washed over her like a cold shower.

All her preparations accounted for the image she needed to portray. She caught her reflection in the window. Makeup applied tastefully, a stylish dress with towering heel, she looked the part of bored housewife turned pseudo socialite.

Ha, Sam thought. Socialite was an inept description of her previous life but one that was probably closest to the world she lived in prior to the tragedy.

The reality was her life revolved around the career of her husband, Heath Crenshaw, one of the top defense lawyers in the county. Her role as socialite? Charm and delight while her husband networked to advance his career. She attended charity galas and dinner parties, hosted her own events and was voted chairwoman of the Midnight Harbor Women's Auxiliary Club. Even though it was 2020, Sam often thought her social life was an outdated dance she was forced to participate in.

Until six months ago when she fainted only to wake up on a hospital bed, rushed into emergency surgery, as her husband's scared face hovered over her.

Sam swallowed as her pulse quickened. The wives, widows and wannabes of Midnight Harbor's elite were seated inside, waiting for the arrival of Kerri Reid, actress and cookbook author, not the arrival of Sam Crenshaw, recluse. Why did she even bother attending?

She dropped her hand and stepped back from the door when she thought of her promise to her best friend, Josie. This event meant everything to her friend. She couldn't let Josie down. Sam forced herself forward by placing her palm on the cool door handle when a rush filled her head, bringing about a sense of déjà vu. She found herself caught between two possible outcomes.

She could step through the door, committing herself to reenter society and face the questions and gossip surrounding her absence for the past six months. Or she could leave, disappointing her best friend. Inevitably her absence would incite questions when this event was her way back into society. Sam cursed under her breath.

No matter her actions, Sam would fuel the fire of the ever-constant Midnight Harbor gossip mill. Let fate play out her fickle plans. She smiled, a practiced skill she learned early from her mother, and pushed open the door to whatever fate had arranged for her.

The scent of fresh scones and fruity teas rushed out of the cream-and-pink-walled room. The delicate aroma mingled with a heavy scent of perfumed women.

Tiers of delicate finger sandwiches and crusty pastries were piled precariously between dainty tea pots. White and pink flowers decorated the top of round tables arranged in front of a rectangle table near the large windows in the back of the room. Sunlight poured in through the tall windows, across polished oak floors onto the white clothed tables.

Sam admired the effort the planners placed in preparing for the event. Though she would've chosen a delectable luncheon from a local chef, not an overly pompous tea service.

Closing the door behind her, the space between Sam's shoulders twitched, as if she could feel multiple sets of eyes boring holes into her, searching out her innermost secrets.

She turned around and saw the familiar faces of Midnight Harbor's elite watching every move she made. Her smile faltered before she looked away, fingers tightened on her handbag while she walked down the aisle to her seat, heels click-clacking. A large placard with a photograph of a beautiful brown-haired woman stood next to the head table.

As she glanced around for an empty seat, the rustle of fabric and urgency of whispers increased with each step. She strode by them with faked confidence, the familiar sting of tears behind her eyes.

Sam knew the women were chatty busy bodies but, despite that knowledge, she wasn't prepared for her walk through purgatory. Her heart beat wildly in her chest, the strings of panic threatening to break free. Steeling herself against the whispers, Sam looked frantically around the room.

"Psst, over here, Sam!" a voice called out. She turned toward the sound. A young woman with an angled haircut, the tips dyed lavender, sat to her left, her hand flailing above her head.

Sam choked on a laugh, relief swelled across her body pushing away the tears she held back at the familiar face of her best friend, Josie Scarborough. She sat down, and Josie immediately took her hand into her own. "Looking beautiful as ever, Mrs. Crenshaw."

She squeezed Josie's hand. "Hey you."

She'd done it. Sam exhaled, releasing the breath she held. The walk back into a society event completed, without making a complete fool of herself. Now she only needed to stay for an hour before excusing herself from the event.

A pain in her hand forced her to look down at her handbag clenched against her chest, the white of her knuckles stark against the dark blue of her handbag. She loosened the grip, the feeling rushing back into her hands like needles pricking her palm.

"How about you place your purse under the seat," Josie suggested, her finger pointing at her own handbag under her chair. "You never know when these old biddies will take a swipe at your purse."

Sam smiled, a real smile, not fake or forced, for the first time in what felt like years. She needed humor now as she became aware of the enormous weight of emotions settled over her chest. Her breathing eased, loosening the tightness in her shoulders.

"Everything is going to be okay," Josie said to her. "Now everyone knows you didn't grow horns or a tail. The gossip will slowly subside until the next big juicy drama."

"Thank you for the confidence boost," Sam replied. With her lavender tipped hair, Josie stood out from the rest of the women gathered for the event whose tastes were conservative rather than trendy. While Josie's hair may be different colors depending on her mood, her confidence was everlasting and contagious. A trait Sam admired from when they first met as awkward high schoolers and became quick friends through college and after. Josie held her head high and gave withering glances to her critics. If only she could fake the confidence Josie had, this evening would go by so much faster. Instead, Sam's awkward attempt at sneaking in unnoticed sparked more whispers than her prolonged absence.

"Isn't it exciting to meet Kerri Reid?" Josie said, her bright green eyes gazing at the rectangular table setup in front of the room. Her body practically hummed with an energy reserved for hyperactive children bent on a sugar rush.

"Yeah, it should be fun," Sam said, forcing a lightness into her voice she didn't feel. Her presence here for Josie; a lifestyle blogger and Kerri Reid fan, Josie hoped to make a connection with the celebrity to grow her brand. "I didn't expect to see so many women here tonight."

"Umm, it's Kerri Reid. Of course all the women of Midnight Harbor would be in attendance. I told you I would drop off her latest book. Just don't embarrass me." Josie pinched her.

"Ow," she said, grabbing her arm. "I—" Sam stopped mid-thought as a hush fell over the room. A dark-haired woman in a tight-fitting red dress with black stilettos walked out to stand behind the rectangular table. Sam let out a small gasp. The woman looked out at the crowded room, her gaze studying each of the faces in attendance. Her eyes stopped on Sam and a smirk quickened at the corner of her mouth.

"When did Gia Hamelstein take over as hostess for auxiliary events?" Sam whispered to Josie, the words stuck in her throat. Sam understood her extended absence would force the auxiliary to find a new chairwoman, but why Gia?

"I'm not sure." Josie squeezed her shoulders. "You know I'm only here to meet Kerri. I'm not privileged enough to know the details. Maybe Betty or one of the other women have a better idea." Sam stayed in her seat and fought the sudden urge to run from the event. The last thing she wanted to do was cause a scene. As much as she wanted to leave and be alone in her home, she stayed seated, for Josie.

Gia raised a red painted finger to her lips, the whispers stopped as the room fell into silence. "Thank you, ladies, for gathering here on this lovely evening," her husky voice drawled on. Sam tuned out Gia as the other woman launched into a speech. Watching the other women around her, it was easy for Sam to spot the fakeness of it all. The women here gathered together not for good works but gossip and attention. The desire to one up one another in a petty game of society. How did it escape her notice before?

An unease skittered across her skin forcing her attention back to the present. When did Gia stop talking? She turned her head to discover the entirety of the room staring at her. Sam pushed back the rise of anxiety, her cheeks burning red at the blatant attention. So much for her entrance back into polite society.

Sam found herself stumbling over her words. "Umm…"

"Are you going to answer or did the cat bite your tongue, Samantha?" Gia said to the crowd, the smirk on her face growing to reveal perfect white teeth. Her remark incited a few titters from the crowd.

"She's happy to be back," Josie said loudly from beside her. "Why don't you get back to reminding everyone why we're here. Unless you want to ask Sam how Heath is doing?"

Sam bit her lip to prevent herself from laughing out loud. She watched Gia's cheeks turn pink from Josie's barb.

Josie reached for Sam's hand underneath the table and gave it a squeeze.

Thank you, Sam mouthed.

Josie winked.

Leave it to Josie to bring up the old college feud over

Sam's husband. The long-ago almost love triangle ended when Gia's heavy-handed manipulations had the opposite effect of her desired outcome on Heath. Instead of pushing Sam aside, Gia inadvertently brought Sam and Heath closer together. Though Sam and Heath later married, Gia loved to bring up the old feud. Sam wasn't sure of Gia's intentions but she wasn't sorry for what she did to win over Heath.

Gia's smile remained on her face. "I'm sure everyone would like to know about the best lifestyle blogger around. Luckily, we have her here tonight, as a guest of honor…" Gia emphasized the last words. Josie rolled her eyes at Sam.

"Welcome, Kerri Reid," Gia announced. The women around her were on their feet, clapping as the brown-haired woman from the picture at the entrance walked out to stand beside Gia. Kerri Reid practically dripped money. From her designer clothing and shoes to her jewelry, not one aspect of her image was out of place.

Sam stood with the women, politely clapping in tandem with them. Her eyes caught those of a petite blonde woman standing off to the side of the room. The young woman appeared preoccupied with something other than the meet and greet, an anxiousness etched into her face not fit for a woman her age.

Sam's attention was pulled back to Kerri Reid as she began her speech. "I'm honored to be invited to speak to you here in this lovely town. Thank you, Gia, for the invitation," Kerri said.

The group of women listened to Kerri while Sam found her attention lingering on the blonde woman to the side of the room. What sorrow etched those worry lines into the young woman's face?

It wasn't until Josie pulled her out of her seat that Sam realized she had been daydreaming. "Come on, Sam. Let's go before Betty gets a chance to talk with Kerri. Then no one will ever have their turn." Josie pushed her way to Kerri's table, pulling Sam along with her toward the front of the room, past the gawking women of the auxiliary until they were standing in front of Kerri Reid. The other woman was seated at the table, a gold marker in hand, signing copies of her cookbook.

"Hi, Kerri, my name is Josie Scarborough. It's so exciting to meet you. I'm such a fan of your work." Josie held out a hard-covered book for Kerri to sign. "I love the Black and Bleu Salad recipe you included."

Sam watched her friend gush over the pretty woman seated before them. Kerri looked to be a similar age as Sam. Her hair coifed and polished, makeup tasteful.

"It's a pleasure to make your acquaintance, Josie," Kerri said as her hand swept across the page of the book, her signature a flourish of letters and curves.

Josie pulled Sam forward to stand beside her. "This is my best friend, Sam Crenshaw. She...she, uh...likes to...do research about things."

Sam pried her arm from Josie's hand. "I'm a librarian, well, used to be a librarian," Sam managed. The desire to leave overfilled her heart at the mention of her former profession. She missed going to work. When did getting out of bed become an obstacle?

"That's wonderful. I would love the chance to learn more about Midnight Harbor. This town has a peculiar old-world charm for being so close to Charleston."

"Sam would love meet up with you," Josie said her head nodding enthusiastically.

"Great! Lilliana dear," Kerri called to the blonde woman standing off to the side. "Would you please exchange contact information with Sam so we can meet before I leave town?"

Lilliana walked over to them with a smile that failed to reach her eyes.

"It was nice meeting you ladies," Kerri said with a wave

of her hand as Lilliana jotted down their contact information on a tablet before moving to Kerri's side at the table.

Sam looked over to see Josie staring at the inside of her book. She managed a small smile at her friend. Her best friend duty accomplished, Sam knew she had been here long enough.

Gia appeared at Josie's elbow. "Lovely to see you again Samantha." Sam's skin burned as Gia eyed her up and down. She smirked, ushering them away for the table. "Don't forget to tell Heath I said hello. We've missed him at Big Pete's."

Josie stepped forward, her mouth open when Sam placed a hand on her arm. "She's not worth it." Sam waited for Gia to saunter away. "I think I'm going to head home."

"Are you sure you don't want to stay longer? We could get drinks at Big Pete's and watch all the college coeds get drunk?"

"I'll pass, but you can fill me in on the details later."

"All right, party pooper. Thank you for coming out tonight," Josie said as she wrapped her arms around her in a tight hug. "You're brave for facing these old biddies after so long. And forget about Gia. She's still jealous you have Heath."

"You're welcome," Sam said, returning the hug. "Go see what you can find out from Kerri, maybe she has a blog contact she could give you." Josie grinned at her in response.

Sam waved goodbye to Josie and walked toward the exit, past the tables of women whose attention was now on the celebrity in front of them. Once outside she leaned against the back of the door and let out a long sigh.

It was over and she still was in one piece. The queasiness in her stomach was slowly fading. Her first foray back into society wasn't as terrible as she thought it would be. Now, she just needed an excuse not to meet with Kerri Reid.

It wasn't until Sam made it back to her car that she relaxed her shoulders and settled into the driver's seat. She closed her eyes briefly to regain her composure before leaving. The attention of the ladies' auxiliary may be on Kerri Reid for now but Sam knew her presence tonight would be the topic of conversation for the next few days.

She shouldn't care what others thought of her, but it was a long-ingrained trait she couldn't shake. Sam recalled the burn of her cheeks earlier. She cared deeply what other people thought of her. She cultivated her reputation as a good housewife and society lady with expert care. Sam avoided gossip, instead choosing to focus on kindness and volunteer work. The thought of people thinking ill of her made her sick.

But none of that mattered since she become a recluse. Of course she would become the topic of conversation; this was the first event she attended in six months, what did she expect? For the ladies to still think of her as society's darling?

Sam pushed the thoughts away as she drove home through the streets of Midnight Harbor. A former busy harbor much like the neighboring port towns of South Carolina, the name was taken from the indigo color of the ocean at night. Sam rolled down her window, enjoying the breeze in her hair as she drove home on one of the back roads away from the busier streets.

She drove and drove, her destination sidetracked, as she let the stillness of being alone calm her rattled nerves. Her silent reverie only interrupted by the sudden sight of a person on the left-hand side of the road. Before Sam could slow down the person ran into the middle of the road.

Wheels screeched as she slammed on the brakes, turning the steering wheel to the right, swerving the car away from the person, hoping she was able to avoid a collision. Teeth clenched and hands gripped on the steering wheel, Sam drove off the side of the road into the grassy shoulder, the car bumping over the dirt.

Sam slid the car to a halt, barely throwing the gear into park before she jumped out of the car to check on the person.

Sam looked around and found herself standing in the middle of the road, alone. Sam's brow furrowed as she spun around in a circle, desperation sinking into her as she looked for the person. She stopped herself and looked down the yellow dotted road. The person who had been on the side of the road moments before was nowhere to be found.

"Hello?" Sam called out into the surrounding darkness. When no one responded, goosebumps broke out over her skin as the balmy spring night turned cold. She used the flashlight from her phone while she searched around her car for any sign of the person or damage to her car.

Nothing, no footprints or belongings were left behind, only the black skid marks from where her car veered off the road. She shined the light on her car, expecting to see a scratch or dent but found none. Sam held the light high above her head, retracing her steps. She knew she saw someone jump out into the road. It was as if the person disappeared as quickly as they appeared.

Sam shivered as a chill ran through her as she walked back to her driver's side door. She glanced over her shoulder for one last look around. Had she lost her mind? How did someone go missing out of thin air?

She eased into the car when a hand grasped her arm from behind. Sam screamed at the cold touch, a bellow escaping from her throat that cut through the air around her. She fumbled into the car, her hands grabbing for the door.

"I'm so sorry...I didn't mean to scare you," a feminine voice pleaded. Sam turned toward the voice, hesitation stalling her from driving away. The voiced belonged to a young woman with sandy blonde hair standing in front of her. "I wanted to get your attention." The young woman walked around to the front of Sam's car. She picked something off the ground and held it up to the headlights.

Sam caught her breath and stepped out of the car to stand beside the woman. "Is that what I saw?"

The young woman held out the light heather gray sweat-shirt and grimaced at Sam's glare. "Yeah, yeah, it was a terrible idea. I didn't think you saw me. I started waving my sweatshirt around and I lost grip of it."

"I thought I hit you," Sam said her voice hoarse and legs wobbly from the shock. "Are you sure you're okay?" She couldn't believe a sweatshirt spooked her.

"Yes. How about you? You look really pale."

Sam nodded, her heartbeat slowly returning to normal. "Why are you out here alone?" Although the moon shown bright overhead, the night washed the surrounding area in darkness.

"I had car trouble a half a mile up the road, right after the road forks. I was on my way to the train station."

Sam eyed the woman up and down. She had the appear-ance of a college coed, fresh faced and probably on her way home for spring break. Though a few years older, the young woman reminded Sam of her little sister. The train station was a few miles up the road, a short drive but long walk in the dark. She couldn't leave her out here alone.

"Midnight Harbor is a safe place, but you really shouldn't be out here alone without any reflective gear. Anything could happen to you and no one would notice unless they looked for you. If you would like, I can give you a ride to the train station," Sam volunteered.

"Awesome! Let me just grab my bag." The young woman ran back to the side of the road and picked up a bag from the ground before joining Sam in the car.

Sam drove with the young woman in silence. Every now and again Sam snuck a look at her from the corner of her eye. She wore jean cutoffs and plain white t-shirt with no makeup or jewelry, save for a small silver band on her right ring finger, hair pulled back in a high ponytail. The young woman stared out the window and occasionally pulled the phone in her hand, as if she was waiting for a call or text message.

"Do you go to school around here?" Sam asked in an effort to make conversation, the silence beginning to make her feel uneasy.

"Uh, yeah, I do."

The young woman, eager for help a few minutes ago, now proved to be less than forthcoming. Sam had a sudden sinking feeling. She hoped she wasn't helping someone commit a crime.

"I'm sorry, you probably think me a pest. I don't mean to pry."

"It's okay. I'm just...I go to Charleston College. I'm on spring break."

"What were you doing going to the train station if you have a car?" Sam said, needing to reassure herself she did the right thing by offering this woman a ride to the train station.

"I, uh, it was a rental. It's easier for me to park and ride the train back home to my parents' house than drive."

Sam didn't try to pry any more information out of her. She could sense she didn't want to divulge any more details. Everyone had their secrets, some more than others.

The two women continued the rest of the ride in silence. Within minutes Sam pulled her car up to the Midnight Harbor Train Station. The recent renovations of the station replaced the peeling paint and rickety wooden planks with an updated façade, keeping the Georgian-themed charm this area cherished.

"Here we are," Sam said, parking the car at the entrance of the station. The young woman had taken on a pallid color.

"Are you going to be okay?" Sam reached out to take the young woman's hand before thinking better of it. "I can take you somewhere else if you would prefer?"

"No, thank you, I appreciate you taking me this far." The young woman started to get out of the car when Sam placed her hand on her arm and gave her a small smile.

"I would feel much better about leaving you here alone if I had your phone number to check on you."

The young woman smiled in return as she pulled a small notebook out of her bag. As she scribbled down a phone number, Sam noticed a small rose tattoo on the inside of her wrist. Sam had always wanted to get a tattoo but her mother forbid it. Even so, Sam wasn't sure she was able to withstand the pain. She shuddered and the young woman handed the piece of paper Sam. "I appreciate your help. I'll be fine though. I've always taken the train home on holiday break. It's usually a bunch of us college students going home."

Sam tucked the slip of paper into her purse. "I'll check on you tomorrow morning. Here, let me give you my number too, in case you need someone to talk to," she said recalling the young woman's silence and glances at her phone. An uneasy feeling pricked at Sam's conscience, as if a sixth sense was telling her to look beyond. Sam shook off the feeling and opened the center console to grab a pen when she heard the car door shut. She looked up to see the young woman wave from the other side of the passenger window then she spun around and walked toward the ticket booth, her long ponytail swinging with each step.

Sam started the engine, easing her car back onto the road-way. It wasn't until she was nearly home that she realized she never asked the young woman her name.

CHAPTER TWO

THE NEXT EVENING, Sam sat alone at a dinner table, impatient for her husband's arrival. She watched the candlelight from the crystal chandeliers flicker across the faces of couples seated throughout the dimly lit restaurant. One couple, their heads close together, caught her attention. She focused on the subtle movements between the man and woman, the whispering in ears and soft touches. Sam wondered what promises they whispered to each other when the woman glanced up, catching Sam's eye. She gave Sam a feline smile before turning back to her partner. Sam looked away, feeling the blush on her cheeks and a longing inside her, unsettled and restless.

A few months ago, Sam would've engaged in a similar flirtatious game. She could picture it now. Her hair and eyelashes perfectly coiled, a slinky dress worn with a pair of killer heels as she strode into the restaurant on the arm of her husband of nearly five years, Heath Crenshaw, protégé of Rex Brown, the most sought after defense lawyer in Midnight Harbor and Charleston.

Heath would tease her over dinner, making her blush with his bawdy whispers and caresses. The anticipation of what the night held, a delicious appetizer savored throughout dinner. When they could no longer stand the temptation, they would practically fall over each other as they peeled off one another's clothes in the privacy of the townhome they shared, amongst the sheets of their king size bed.

Sam closed her eyes, forcing herself to think of anything but those memories. She spared a quick glance at her watch Heath gave her when she turned twenty-seven. He was late, again. Did he understand how much energy it took for her to come to dinner after the book signing event the night before? It was only a day later, but the exhaustion of keeping up her appearance was already getting to her. She wondered again how she kept up the charade for so many years.

Or how her life had become riddled with broken promises, late arrivals and her most disliked word, "again." Sam huffed, glancing around the interior of the restaurant. Any other time the sight of the fine china, crisp white linens and dangling crystal chandeliers would incite a happy feeling in her. Instead, the familiar threads of disappointment took over. How was she to enjoy dinner with no one to share it with?

Preoccupied with wanting to make good of this dinner and thoughts of Heath, Sam almost forgot about the young woman from last night. The thought seemed silly, but she felt a genuine concern for the young woman after she tried calling the young woman's phone twice today to no avail. The phone rang and rang each time with no answer, only interrupted by the automatic recording that the voicemail box was full.

Sam pulled her phone from her clutch and dialed the young woman's phone number for the third time. She listened to the ringing, silently counting five rings before hanging up. She didn't bother with a message. The young woman was probably screening her calls. Sam didn't blame her. She did, too.

Her chipped fingernails tapped on the table while she

contemplated walking out of the restaurant. She exercised a tremendous amount of courage leaving the house two days in a row. She felt drained of energy. Unlike yesterday though, no one appeared concerned with her. Yet, the feeling of being unsettled, out of place, was still present. Almost like she wore a skin that was not her own.

As if she was trying to be who she was before grief occupied her life.

Feeling the threat of intrusive thoughts creeping in, Sam stood abruptly, not wanting to go into full blown panic mode in public. A warm hand touched her bare shoulder.

"Leaving so soon, lovely lady?" a male voice whispered in her ear. Sam smiled in recognition of the voice. Heath. His touch a comforting distraction to her thoughts. He gave her shoulder a gentle squeeze before placing a kiss on the top of her head.

"So soon? I've been waiting for nearly thirty minutes."

"I'm sorry I'm late. Nathan wouldn't stop rambling on after court. I told him a beautiful woman was waiting for me, but he insisted I hear about his client dinner." Heath settled into the chair across from her.

Sam admired the way his gray suit hugged the wide breadth of his shoulders and his long, lean body. Heath told her appearances were a weapon for men as much as they were for women. His strong jaw and full lips were only part of the face Sam imagined as the perfect Renaissance model. Heath was classically handsome but retained a boyish charm that aged like fine wine. She watched him run a hand through his dark blonde hair, the candlelight on the table picking up the warm bronze highlights, remembering how silky his hair felt running through her fingers. His dark brown eyes twinkled, and the corners crinkled as he flashed her that boyish smile, reminiscent of the feigned innocence he used to charm her with in college. He cut a damn fine figure in his suit and the smug bastard knew it, too.

"You look lovely," Heath said as he placed his phone on the table.

Sam's face grew warm, certain her cheeks were burning bright red. She ducked her head behind the menu and peered over the top, lest he know her innermost thoughts. "Thank you. It's been a long time since we had a nice dinner together," she said before she realized he was playing her. Her pleasure quickly soured into annoyance at his attempt to dissuade her from calling him out on his late arrival. Instead, he deflected her anger with the compliment. Annoyed at herself for falling so easily for his tactic, Sam opened her mouth to respond with a snappy retort when the waiter appeared, a bottle of wine held in one hand. She forced herself to bite back her response.

"Sir, ma'am, a gift from the gentleman at the adjacent table," the waiter said as he poured the dark red liquid into two glasses with a steady hand. Sam and Heath looked over to where the waiter motioned discreetly with his arm. An older gentleman sat with a well-dressed woman. The man raised his glass to them.

Heath returned the gesture. "A satisfied client," Heath said to Sam with a wink.

She knew her husband's tricks. Despite her knowledge, Sam's earlier annoyance faded away as she looked across the table at her husband. Why bother upsetting the both of them with a snappy retort? She decided anger was better forgotten and tried to enjoy what remained of the evening with Heath. As a society wife, her mother and mentors taught her early in her marriage tactics to master her emotions. The perfect image was everything.

Like she wore a skin that was not her own. The intrusive thoughts began again. She tampered the thoughts, pushing them down inside her.

Sam shook her head, a staunch refusal of the lingering doubts. Sam asked as she took a sip from her glass, the wine a dry bite on her tongue with a sweet cherry aftertaste, "What's so special about Nathan's case that he wasn't able to let you leave?"

"Mhmm," Heath said as he continued to look over the menu, without so much as a glance in her direction.

Sam placed the wine glass down on the table with a thud, the table shaking from the impact. Heath glanced up to meet her eyes, his face softening. He dropped the menu and reached for her hand, his thumb caressing her wrist as he spoke, "I said I was sorry." He fluttered his eyes at her.

"Stop it with the puppy dog eyes. It's not going to work on me this time," Sam said looking down at their clasped hands, the pattern he traced on her wrist a distraction keeping her from normal speech. "I thought you would be here on time considering this is the first dinner we're able to spend together in months."

"Rex is beginning to take on more cases as the Firm reputation grows." Heath gave her hand a squeeze. "The caseload will slow down and when it does, I promise to take you on a nice long vacation away from here."

He leaned back in his chair, his hand dropping from hers as he moved positions and draped his other arm across the back of his chair. Sam watched him look around the large dining room at the surrounding guests, she imagined him taking their measure, honed to notice details others missed. It helped him create a reputation as a top attorney and a common trait they discovered they shared during one of their college classes. As well as undeniable attraction to one another that she wondered still existed.

"It's been a long time since we had dinner together, let alone a night in a fancy restaurant as this," Sam said as her eyes took in the softly lit room, encouragement for intimate whispers between partners. "I want to spend time with you, not Rex or your work" she said with half smile on her lips. She felt more at ease here with him than she did at the book signing last night. Was her attraction to Heath mutual? More so, was she brave enough to find out?

"Me too," Heath said as her turned back to face her. He smiled and opened his mouth but a flash of emotion across his face told her he changed his mind.

Both were silent, the silence growing between them as Sam played with the stem of her wine glass. She struggled to find a common topic to discuss. Their daily life was a series of quick hellos and goodbyes over the past six months since Heath took on additional cases at the Firm. When had a simple conversation become difficult for them?

"How is your volunteer work with the auxiliary club going?" Heath asked, breaking the silence between them.

"I haven't spent much time with the club. I attended Kerri Reid's book signing with Josie last night." Sam diverted her eyes as her voice trailed off. Despite her misgiving yesterday, the ladies did have big hearts intent on giving to others. And bigger mouths. Last night provided all the involvement she could handle for now. She didn't want to have to deal with them prying into her life or listen to any advice they cared to dish out. "I've been...busy with things," Sam blurted out. She tried to think of something else to say that didn't sound so desperate.

Heath raised an eyebrow in her direction. "Going out two nights in a row? That's a big step for you, Sam. Have you thought about volunteering at the library?"

Sam grimaced. She didn't want to think of her old job or the painful memories it brought. "No, I haven't. I'm going to take everything day by day before I make any commitments."

A vibration from the table startled her.

Heath met her eyes then glanced down to his phone. "It's probably Nathan." Heath reached and glanced at the incoming caller ID, his brows knotted. He met her eyes from across the table. "I need to take this." His voice held no question. He wasn't asking.

Sam nodded to him. Their conversation would wait. It wasn't like she had much more to share.

"Hello?" Heath's voice was brisk as he excused himself from the table.

Sam played with the stem of her wineglass, the repeated motion calming while she waited for Heath's return. For once she wished they could spend an evening without an interruption from his work. Sam occupied her wait by watching the other couples when she noticed a young woman seated alone at a table across the room. The features of the woman looked familiar, with her sandy blonde hair and big eyes, but Sam failed to recall where she had seen the young woman before.

The woman's mouth turned down in a frown, a sad expression for such a lovely face. She looked up, the dark color of her eyes black against her skin. Startled, Sam looked away, ashamed for being caught so blatantly staring again. When curiosity beat the better of her manners, Sam peered again to discover the young woman staring straight at her. Sam watched as the fine features of her face shifted from bored countenance to reveal the sun-bleached face of a skeleton, the eyes gone except for the bottomless black pits that remained.

Gasping aloud, her forehead beaded with a clammy sweat. Squeezing her eyes shut to compose herself, Sam peeked open her eyes, discovering the table empty.

The young woman disappeared. Gone with a matter of seconds between Sam blinking. How could she disappear so fast?

Sam looked around and rubbed her arms to shake off the lingering eerie feeling. Yet, she couldn't forget the ominous image of the skeletal face from her mind. Convinced it was an illusion due to her emotional state, Sam looked up to find Heath emerge from the back of the restaurant. He strode toward her, his mouth set in a grim line.

"Sam—"

"It's okay, go ahead. I know it's probably important otherwise he wouldn't have called." Sam waved her hand in dismissal. "I'll finish dinner here, then head home."

Heath kissed the top of her head. "Thanks for understanding." He placed a few crisp bills from his wallet on the table. "Don't wait up. I'm sure I'll be home late," Heath called over his shoulder as he walked away. She watched a man greet him on his way out of the restaurant, the man shaking Heath's hand before calling over another man.

Sam turned back to Heath's empty chair, now her companion at the candlelit table. A sting of tears welled behind her eyes, threatening to run down her cheek. Sam breathed in a shaky breath and looked up to battle the forthcoming onslaught of tears. Not here, she wouldn't allow herself to cry in front of a room full of people. Her mother's words were like a lance in her mind, opening the fresh wounds of tonight's failed dinner. She withheld her emotions, buried them within and recounted her mother's words. Sam held her emotions in check, the ability one of many tools in her arsenal of polite tactics when in society.

The familiar hurt and longing crept back into her heart. When had silence between them been anything but comforting? Sam felt awkwardness between them earlier, the roots of reservation planted long before tonight.

For once, she thought, wiping at the stray tear on her cheek and forcing the serene smile on her face, she would love for her husband to rush to greet her in the same way he rushed to his work.

Sam tucked her purse under her arm, grabbed her red pashmina and strode toward the exit of the restaurant, dancing around the group of men surrounding Heath. She refused to dine here alone while the whispers of other couples hung in the air.

She signaled the maître d for her car to be brought around front. She needed to put as much distance between herself and this disastrous night as possible. Sam stopped mid-stride when she caught sight of the familiar figure of Mrs. Elizabeth "Betty" Knight ahead of her in line.

Sam groaned and ducked her head. The last thing she wanted to do this evening was get caught up in conversation with Betty about the club and Sam's presence at the book signing last night.

"Samantha!" The tall, heavy-set woman walked toward Sam with both arms extended out for a hug. "It's been ages since I last saw you, dear."

"Hello, Betty. I hope you're doing well," Sam managed while she was crushed into the ample bust of the older woman. The smell of lavender permeated the air around Sam, burning her nose. Sam swallowed against the cough tickling in the back of her throat. Betty still liked to bathe in her perfume.

"I'm having a horrible gout flare up. But enough about me…I'm so happy I ran into you. I've been meaning to reach out to invite you over for the next meeting."

"That's so kind of you," Sam said pulling away from Betty. She adjusted the pashmina over her bare shoulders. "I'm ashamed to have been away from the club for so long." Her eyes darted toward the exit of the restaurant then toward Heath's figure. Could she make it out without him noticing her?

"Oh poo," Betty swatted at Sam with her hand, "I'm sure that handsome husband of yours is keeping you busy. Where is he, making friends with that devilish Mr. Brentworth? My bet is the two of them would get on fabulously." Betty winked at her. "How about I call you this week so we can plan something, dear?"

"That would be great!" Sam said with a tad too much enthusiasm. "It was nice seeing you again, Betty. Tell the other ladies I said hello."

Sam didn't wait for a response from Betty before she

walked through the doors into the night. The fresh air hit her with an unusual crispness instead of the sultry warmth this spring had brought Midnight Harbor.

"Agh!" Sam brought her hand to shade her eyes as a bright light flooded her vision from all directions.

"Mrs. Crenshaw, Abby Jones from WMZ3 News, how is your husband handling the rumors surrounding the Robinson case?"

The journalist shoved her phone in front of Sam's face, eager for an answer. "What does he know about the disappearance of Bailee Talson?" she pressed.

Sam brushed away the phone from her face, the white spots fading from her vision. "Who? No comment, Abby. Besides, you know us better than that. I'm not privy to that information."

Sam knew Abby from their college days together at Charleston College. They both ended up moving into Midnight Harbor around the same time. Abby had an uncanny gift for fretting out the current gossip or news story with a relentless drive. Sam wasn't surprised when Heath told her Abby was hired on at the local news station. She proved herself a powerhouse, always looking for the next tip or story. She also happened to be the last person Sam was interested in speaking with right now.

No doubt this news ambush, as Heath called them, was related to one of his cases. Sam peered through the small crowd of reporters to see the valet pull up in her car. It was times like these she disliked the attention being Heath's wife brought.

Using her clutch and the drape of the pashmina as a shield over her face, Sam pushed through the continuous flashing lights of the photographers gathered outside the restaurant. She weaved her path away from the crowd toward the valet, seeking the quite solace of her car from the relentless cries for more information.

Stopping at edge of the curb with her back to the throng of journalists, Sam waited as the valet opened the driver side door of her sleek black sedan. Grateful for the reprieve, she slid into the privacy of her car, handing the valet a tip as he closed the door. The warmth of the leather seat was a much-needed comfort to her hurt soul. Sam wasted little time throwing the gear into drive, desperate to distance herself from the failed attempt at a romantic dinner.

As she drove home, her thoughts wandered back to the sad woman from the restaurant and wondered if that woman left tonight with an ache in her heart, too.

CHAPTER THREE

HEATH RECOGNIZED the emotions he saw in Sam's brown eyes as he watched her leave the restaurant.

Hurt. Anger. Sadness.

Those emotions were etched into Sam's face and in the depth of her big blue eyes.

He had broken her heart.

Cursing under his breath with the type of language that would make his eighty-five-year-old grandmother blush, he slammed his fist on the dashboard of the car. Not only did he cause undue hurt to the woman he loved, he left her alone to face the swarm of greedy journalists gathered outside the restaurant. What type of husband would leave his wife alone at what should've been an intimate dinner?

He sighed. The same man who would allow her to confront the crowd gathered outside the restaurant without his support.

The temptation to turn around for her licked at the edges of Heath's conscience. Despite his inner turmoil and self-doubt, Heath continued driving toward his destination. The call from the Firm requested his presence immediately.

Turning the car around would accomplish nothing but delay him in his task. Sam could handle herself…he hoped.

Traffic lights slowly stopped whizzing by his windows the closer Heath drove to downtown and the car and pedestrian traffic congesting the streets and sidewalks of Midnight Harbor's tourist strip. Weaving his sporty coupe between cars, Heath jockeyed positions to get ahead of the small pack of cars and out of the clumps of traffic. Driving allowed him the few moments for quiet reflection before the start to his daunting days. During this time, he approached his cases with a second look, allowing his mind to wander where it willed. But now, he let his mind wander back to Sam and what he had come to understand was a breakdown of their marriage. How did happy couples grow apart? What was the demarcation between couple and other? He never thought he might be one to experience the division himself. Ever since he first saw Sam in a shared entry level class, he'd been smitten.

The way Sam looked tonight left little room for thought or speech in Heath's mind which typically rattled with too many thoughts. He often found her at home wearing her new daily attire: his faded Charleston College hooded sweatshirt and black leggings, her chestnut hair pulled into a messy bun. He accepted she was hurting, her emotions causing a retreat from the woman she used to be, a woman always impeccably dressed and beyond charming.

Tonight was different. Heath glimpsed a sweep of mascara and lipstick, something she previously would never leave the house without. She made an effort which caused a feeling in Heath he wasn't expecting.

Desire. Intense, domineering and urgent rushed through him when he saw her sitting at the table in the restaurant. The candlelight flickering over her delicate nose and lush lips. He wanted to taste her so badly he was driven into a frenzy. The desire to take her home was overwhelming as he pictured spending the night slowly seducing her into their bed. He wasn't sure he would even make it that far.

Instead, Nathan called and he answered, ending any chance of reconnecting with Sam.

The evening lights of Midnight Harbor flew past his window as he turned on the radio to tune out his masochistic thoughts. The heavy bass pounded against the car speakers as a woman's voice sang in tandem to the beat. Heath felt the muscles loosen in his back, slowly releasing the coiled tension he held in his body, the music a salve. As he lost himself in the music, Heath recalled with fondness the dinners he cooked with Sam, their favorite music playing in the background while they danced with each other.

A smile broke across Heath's face. They'd spent their last cooking lessons together making chicken parmigiana. Sam had still been herself, not the ghost he interacted with lately. Her vibrancy an infectious spell, bouncing off her in waves, giving life to those around her. When was the last time they cooked together?

Heath couldn't recall the last time Sam cooked a meal. Her interest waned in most things except for sleep and reality television shows. Heath recognized her actions as a coping mechanism. A way to suffocate the heartache of the past six months and move beyond the grief. His heart ached too for what might have been. Only, Sam stayed stagnant and rarely left the house or interacted with anyone but immediate family and Josie.

A shrill ring interrupted his daydream, the harsh repeated tone replaced the music through Heath's audio system. Heath punched the accept button on the LED display with his index finger.

"Where the hell are you?" a male voice growled through the speaker. He recognized the rough voice belonging to Rex Brown, his boss, mentor and head of the law firm Heath was employed at.

A deep sigh echoed through the speaker. "Listen. I'm sorry for the gruff asshole I'm morphing into. I need you to hear this in person." A slight pause. "A phone call won't do it justice."

"I'll be there in a few minutes," Heath said before Rex disconnected the line. Heath's brow furrowed. The sophistication Heath associated with Rex was lost from his voice, replaced with a curt gruffness not normally found in the son of old Southern money. Older, experienced and dedicated to his practice, Rex expected the same devotion from his staff. Demanding everything from all involved from senior attorney to intern. The dedication Rex brought to the Firm was one of the reasons Heath sought out his practice as a law student searching for an internship.

Arriving at the Firm, Heath pulled into an empty parking spot next to a flashy red convertible. Located in the downtown part of Midnight Harbor, the Firm occupied a former dilapidated building Rex purchased and contracted a Charleston builder to restore to the original Georgian splendor of the brick building. Colorful flower beds hedged up against a cobblestone path, beckoning visitors to enter.

Wooden floors waxed to a high sheen covered the entire first floor where large windows filtered the natural light inside, providing a comforting light. The room was a study in colors reminiscent of the forest: vibrant, earthy tones were seen in the chairs and paintings on the wall.

A young woman sat behind the gray marble receptionist desk, her dark blonde hair twisted into a low bun, a pair of brightly hued glasses stuck in the vee of her purple dress.

She glanced up from the desk as Heath's footsteps announced his approach. "It's about time you get here. Rex is driving us all crazy. I was tempted to hand in my resignation letter." Maggie Hart, paralegal and firm manager, ran the office for Rex with an undisputed iron first. Though she may have resembled a college coed, she was an experienced taskmaster few dared cross.

Maggie pressed a button behind her desk to lock and alarm the front doors to the Firm.

Heath glanced toward the doors then back at Maggie then raised an eyebrow. "So, it appears Rex has the idea to kidnap us for the evening."

"I think he has something far worse planned for us all," Maggie said as Heath followed her past the reception desk toward the white French doors which led to the center of the Firm, where the offices and conference rooms were located. Maggie stopped before grabbing onto the handles of an antique serving cart overladen with food. She pushed on the cart, struggling to move it from its place near the French doors to the back.

"Here, let me help you." Heath took over control of the cart with a chuckle. "Though, I would've enjoyed watching you struggle." He looked down at the contents of the cart. "Exactly how long does he expect us to stay in here for?"

"Thank you. I didn't realize how much food I ordered until now." Maggie held open the French doors leading to the back offices of the Firm. "Rex said to make sure I had enough food for everyone."

Heath glanced down at the variety of food and beverages loaded on the cart. "Don't you think you should've brought the hard stuff?" Heath said as he passed by her through the doors.

"I'm afraid it's too late for that. Nathan and Rex came straight from client meetings." Maggie shook her head with a frown. "My best hope is to sober them up with some food so they can make intelligent decisions."

Maggie led the way through the hallway, past Heath's office and those of his colleagues until they reached a heavy wooden door which he pulled open, revealing a large office lined with bookshelves.

Rex paced a path behind a huge mahogany desk, still dressed in evening wear, his tie loose around his neck a dress jacket draped over his desk and shirt sleeves rolled up to reveal muscled forearms.

Heath's colleagues, Nathan Lee and Claudia Vasquez, were already in the room, the only person missing was Tyler Anderson, the resident technology whiz.

Nathan and Claudia sat at a behemoth antique table in the center of the room, dubbed the war table, since it was often the meeting place for heated discussions concerning strategy and other small dramas. Heath once thought he saw blood stains on the table. When he asked Maggie about the stain, she laughed and reassured him no blood had ever been drawn, by the current owner of the warrior table.

"Here arrives the knight in shining armor," Nathan announced as Heath took a seat at the table, his voice steady despite the glassy look in his brown eyes.

The newest member of the team, Claudia Vasquez, rolled her eyes then turned to face Heath, giving him a smile. "Hi, Heath," she handed him a large file, "glad to see you were able to make it." Her accent was more pronounced than usual.

"What I want to know is how Sam made it out of the restaurant without a single comment to the media gathered outside?" Nathan asked as he opened his manila folder.

Heath knitted his brows together as he accepted the file folder from Claudia. "Sam? How do you know about the journalists?"

"Your wife is all over social media," Claudia said, handing him her phone. "That is your wife Sam, correct?"

Heath accepted the phone in her outstretched hand with trepidation. His stomach rolled in waves as he recognized Sam's photograph on the WM3 news site from earlier this evening. He returned Claudia's phone to her, leaned back in his chair and rubbed a hand over his eyes. "I didn't think the

Robinson case would draw that much attention from local media. It was a simple case."

Maggie handed him her tablet, displaying the local Midnight Harbor gossip webpage. "Nothing is ever simple at the Firm," she said. Another picture of Sam appeared at the top of the gossip article, her face partially hidden by the clutch she carried. "Sam didn't say anything to the journalists about the Robinson case," Maggie said, her tone soft and reassuring.

Heath gave her a weak smile before skimming over the headline and article. Sam understood the importance of discretion. He trusted her with his life. It irked him the media thought they could levy their relationship by going after her for a hot sound bite to broadcast on the 10 o'clock news.

"Sam did a great job amidst the media frenzy from today's court ruling," Rex's deep voice boomed, cutting through the chatter of the team. "The media is one of the reasons why I called everyone to come in tonight."

He halted his pacing by his desk, instead his razor sharp focus on his team seated at the war table. Rex walked toward the front of the war table where a large screen was mounted on the wall behind him. "The first reason being, a longtime friend contacted me tonight asking if the Firm would represent him." Rex paused, an emotion skittering across his face that Heath thought looked like pain. He looked up, his deep blue eyes staring down each of them at the table. "He needs representation in what could be possible charges in the disappearance of a young woman."

Rex leaned his hands on the war table. "The second reason is I need everyone here in this room prepared to give everything they have to this case. For the possibility they and their loved ones will be followed and ambushed by the media. This case is precarious. The scrutiny we will face goes beyond the scope of Midnight Harbor and Charleston. This case could put the Firm on the radar of everyone in the state. We must give our best. There is no opportunity for failure in this."

His hard gaze fell on Heath. "I need you to take lead on this case, Heath. Do you think you can give me more than you have in the past? Do you believe you can clear our client's name?" Rex asked.

Time moved in slow motion as Heath allowed Rex's question to sink in. He exhaled, calming the skittering of his stomach. This was it. This was the opportunity he had worked for every day since his internship. He tempered his excitement at the opportunity to lead the case. "Yes," Heath answered, hoping his voice was even.

Maggie gave him a tight hug. Nathan was next with a fist bump. "Nice work." Claudia was last with a strong handshake. "Congratulations. You'll be a great lead on this case."

Heath thanked his colleagues in earnest. This was the culmination of his hard work since his early years as an intern for Rex. If the case was so important and he won, Heath could leverage his success for a senior counsel position. Rex may be even promote him to partner. There was no other choice, Heath had to prove his worth by successfully representing this client.

"Good. Then let's dig in," Rex said as he powered up the large screen behind him. "I'm warning you now, it's going to be a long night. You may no longer like each other by the end of the evening."

"I never liked Heath much to being with," Nathan said as he grabbed a bag of chips from the serving car then tossed them over his shoulder to Heath.

Claudia's hand reached out, snatching the chips in midair. She tore open the bag and popped a chip in her mouth. "Are you going to tell us who this friend is? Or are we supposed to magically create a defense from nothing?" she asked Rex.

Rex had his back toward them. Heath caught sight of the muscle twitch in Rex's shoulders, as if he concealed a great emotion. He turned around, his face set in firm lines. "My friend is well known for his real estate endeavors in Midnight Harbor and surrounding areas. I call him Nic but the rest of you may know him as Nicholas Davi."

All sound stopped. Around him, Health only heard breathing as the implications of the relationship between Rex and Nicholas Davi hung in the air. Heath looked around at his colleagues to see their stunned faces match his own surprise. Sobriety returned to Nathan in a matter of minutes. Claudia's usually dark complexion looked noticeable paler and Maggie…she had a small smile on her lips.

Heath cleared his throat, bringing everyone out of their personal reprieve, back to the present. "I want to be clear everyone heard you correctly. I thought I heard you say Nicholas Davi, as in the celebrity real estate mogul Nicholas Davi." Heath couldn't help hiding the grin that broke out on his face.

"You heard me correctly. I told you to be prepared to handle this case with increased scrutiny from the media. Once word gets out of the possible charges, the media is going to go into a frenzy running with the news," Rex said, once again leaning his hands on the table, his presence swallowing all the available space in the room. "He came to me early this evening with concerns. Last night, he received an anonymous phone call from a person claiming to have inside information in the disappearance of Bailee Talson. The person refused to reveal their identify but told Davi he is a prime suspect. How or why, I don't know but we need to find out to help him."

"The college coed reported missing?" Heath asked, quickly reviewing what he knew about her case. "What would Davi have to do with her disappearance? There's a gap in age and occupation between them. Their social status alone would keep the two apart. I fail to see how he could be connected to her disappearance."

"That's what we need to discover," Rex said, his posture

relaxing as he leaned away from the table. "I have my doubts as well. Nicholas made it clear to me he had nothing to do with her disappearance. He has an alibi who can make a statement on his behalf." Rex rolled his shoulders. "However, he found the caller and the tip to be a real enough threat to ask for help."

"I don't understand why someone would volunteer that information?" Heath said as he looked around the room at his colleagues. "Why wouldn't he just go to the police? Unless…" his voice trailed off, not wanting to wish the thought into fruition.

"Unless the caller intended to blackmail Davi with information the police may find…troubling," Maggie added from her seat across from Heath.

He nodded his head in agreement, his eyes locking onto Rex's. "I'm unsure of his net worth, but Davi is the one who spearheaded the revitalization of Charleston's restaurant district. He owns most of the buildings. His net worth has to be in the billions." The other man was first to look away as he walked back toward his desk, resuming the prior pacing.

Heath thought for a moment he saw an emotion pass over Rex's eyes before he turned. Pain? Anger? He wasn't sure what was eating at Rex but would have to make it a priority to find out. "Well, team, it appears we're going to be spending a lot of time together," Heath said, writing DAVI in bold letters across the tab of a manila folder.

———

FOR THE NEXT FEW HOURS, Heath guided the team through different scenarios and known acquaintances of Nicholas Davi and Bailee Talson. Tedious yet necessary, the work would be the foundation of their case, if it got that far. The goal was to eliminate the potential for any charges to be brought against Davi.

Rubbing his eyes, Heath watched Claudia stifle a yawn, smiling at him from behind her hand. He gave her a wink and closed his laptop with a soft thunk. "I'm done," he announced to the team. "Why don't we all go home for a few hours rest before our first daily stand up meeting tomorrow." Heath glanced at his watch and grimaced. He didn't realize how late, or early, in the morning it was. Sam was likely fast asleep, curled up around her favorite pillow. He had one task left to do. If he left now, he could make his call and snag a few hours of sleep himself before returning to the Firm tomorrow.

"I'll see you out," Rex said to Claudia, grabbing his keys and his suit jacket from the top of his desk. He turned from Claudia to face the team. "Nice progress tonight. Nic will appreciate our preliminary efforts. Now, like Heath said, let's go home and get some rest."

Heath was ashamed to admit the drive home was a blur, ending with him tip toeing into the house with a concentrated effort not to wake Sam. He damned the wooden floors when each step caused a creak. A blue light flickered through the bottom crack of the bedroom door and the muffled voices from inside the room were the only sounds in a quiet house.

He gently pushed open the door and entered the room. It was as he guessed, Sam fell asleep with the TV on again.

Chestnut hair pooled across a white silk pillow, Sam's breathing deep and even, her body huddled in downy blankets. He leaned down to gently press a kiss to her forehead, her brow furrowed as if in displeasure. Not even in sleep could she escape her darkness.

Heath gave her one last look, soaking in her softness, then grabbed his pillow and crept back out of the room, careful not to disturb her. Goose feather pillow in hand, he walked into the guest bedroom, where he frequently slept for the past few months, desperate for a few hours of sleep before beginning his endless grind all over again.

Exhaustion fluttered at his mind, but Heath pressed through the feeling.

Rubbing at the stubble on his face, Heath had one last task to complete, a call to Detective Hart, the lead detective on the Bailee Talson case. His finger punched in the familiar number and he waited. A conversation about Bailee Talson was the last thing he wanted to do but he needed to speak with the detective before the team proceeded any further with the case.

Heath needed details leading up to the young woman's disappearance. If it came to it, Heath would use the information to reconstruct Miss Talson's last steps and compare the details to that of Davi's statement to clear him from possible involvement in her disappearance. But only if the case reached that far.

Recalling the emotions Heath saw on Rex's face this evening, he delayed this call until he was alone. Heath waited through the rings, certain the detective would answer.

"Hello? Detective Hart."

"Detective Hart, it's Attorney Crenshaw from the Firm. I hope I'm not waking you with my late night call. I have questions concerning the Bailee Talson case. I believe you can answer them for me."

"Attorney Crenshaw, I'll give you five minutes of my time...what can I help you with?" A laugh from the other end of the line. "How is my favorite prick?"

Heath sighed, sinking onto the bed. "Tired, Theo. Aside from that, I need your help. I want to clarify some information we received on Bailee Talson. The case report I have here states you're the lead detective on the Talson case, correct?"

"Yes, that's correct. I received the missing person's report."

Heath opened the manila case folder and balanced the light weight of it on his knee, Bailee Talson's smile looked up at him from an old photograph. "I see here you mentioned Bailee Talson was reported missing by her roommate?"

"Yes, her roommate placed the call with our station. She was frantic. The roommate said Miss Talson never showed up at her parents' house or returned to their shared apartment in downtown."

"It's not unusual to have travel delays during spring break. Is the roommate certain Miss Talson isn't just ignoring her calls?"

"No, she was adamant Miss Talson never contacted her again after leaving the apartment."

"Why didn't her parents report her missing?"

"That's just it. Her parents were unaware of her visit. They weren't expecting her. Miss Talson told them she was going to be traveling to Miami for spring break," Theo said.

"Interesting. I wonder why she would keep information from her parents. Did the roommate say Miss Talson was going to surprise her parents with a visit?"

"No, she didn't mention anything of the sort when I spoke with her. She said Miss Talson left the night of her disappearance in a hurry after receiving a phone call. She told her roommate she decided to forgo her spring break visit to Miami so she could stay with her parents."

"Could you drop me the roommate's contact info?"

"Annie Delong. I'll text you her number."

"Thanks. Is there any other information you can provide me?" Heath asked.

"I can't think of anything that would be able to help you. Miss Talson was a young woman from a small town on the outskirts of Midnight Harbor. She attended Charleston College, lived with a friend and worked as a waitress. Nothing stands out as to why she would go missing."

"Miss Talson sounds like she was a good girl who was in the wrong place at the wrong time," Heath said sadly, throwing the folder on the nightstand.

"Yeah, I would agree. There's nothing else I could garner from my interviews with her parents and roommate that would suggest otherwise," Theo said his voice trailing off. "Well, except her roommate did mention Miss Talson was behaving out of the ordinary over the last two weeks, anxious and paranoid. The roommate figured the increased behavior was nervousness with the upcoming exams."

Heath pondered what the detective said about work. "Theo, which restaurant did Miss Talson work at?"

"Let me check for you." A shuffle of paper before Theo responded, "She was a waitress at Bar Nonne's downtown."

"Thank you, Theo. I may need to reach out to you in the future if I have any additional questions concerning the case."

"No problem. Let my baby sister know I'll stop into the Firm later this week. You know how Maggie is with unexpected visits."

Heath chuckled. "Will do. Take care, prick."

He disconnected the call with Detective Theo Hart, in contemplation of the information he gained. He felt a chill run though his body along with a nagging suspicion he couldn't wrap his head around. There was more to Bailee Talson's disappearance than they knew. And he intended to hunt it down.

Small town girls didn't vanish in Midnight Harbor.

Heath would need to dig deeper to discover how Davi was connected with the young woman and why he was so concerned with the anonymous caller. The first thing on his agenda tomorrow was to schedule a meeting with Davi. Heath was determined to assist Theo any way he could with finding Bailee Talson. Sam's little sister, Sadie, would be graduating high school in a few weeks. He couldn't help but think of Sadie in Miss Talson's place. What the young woman's parents and roommate were going through.

His personal involvement was beyond his responsibility

as a defense attorney, but if Davi was innocent, there was a suspect loose and posing a threat to Midnight Harbor.

Exhaustion finally overcame Heath as he rubbed his jaw. He grabbed the pill jar on the nightstand and quickly swallowed two pills. He fell back onto the bed, hopeful for a few hours sleep. As Heath drifted off, his thoughts were of Sam, and how he wanted to touch the softness of her curled hair at dinner. Sleep overcame him swiftly and all he could do was dream of a chestnut-haired woman running away from him. Though he kept pace with her, she was so close yet so far beyond his reach.

CHAPTER FOUR

SAM SAT on the cushioned bench of the bay window of her home, her mobile phone a heavy weight in her hand despite the small size. No matter how many times she dialed the same phone number, the young woman never answered. Sam closed her eyes, pressing her forehead against the window pane, the glass cool against her skin. Why did she even bother?

She chided herself for continued efforts to reach the young woman. Of the multitude of possibilities running though Sam's mind, she couldn't accept the obvious explanation. The young woman arrived safely at her parents' house, the kind gesture of a stranger she met a few days prior forgotten.

Ever since she dropped the young woman off at the train station and the nagging feeling that something was off wouldn't shake. Sam couldn't stop herself from continuing to call the number.

A shrill ring startled Sam from her thoughts. She glanced at her phone, recognizing an old photograph of her and Josie, laughing in an embrace, appeared on her screen.

Josie. Of course, it would be Josie.

Sam grimaced. She promised Josie a call after her the

dinner date with Heath. Sam's finger hovered over the red decline button, threatening to send the call to voicemail, like she had done often with her loved ones during the past few months. Her finger touched the green accept button and she mentally prepared herself for the onslaught of Josie's questions.

"Hello?" Sam answered. She straightened her legs on the bench and watched the school-age children outside take turns blowing bubbles and chasing the iridescent spheres before they floated away from the children's sticky hands. Sequels of laughter punctured the air each time the children were successful in their bubble popping contest.

"Hey, heifer!" Josie yelled into the phone. "I didn't expect you to answer. I thought for sure you were going to send me to voicemail like you love to do instead of talking to your best friend."

"If you don't stop yelling, I'll reconsider answering your calls from now on," Sam said, holding the phone away from her ear.

"Love you too. It's late afternoon, way past time for the sleeping princess to wake up. Didn't your prince give you a morning kiss?"

"Remind me again why I'm friends with you?"

"Good food and you know I'm the only one in Midnight Harbor who will tell how it really is. I'm sorry for using you as my punching bag. My AC stopped working in my car and I need to be in downtown Charleston for a photo shoot," Josie said her voice at a lower decibel. "This heat wave is ridiculous. It's not fun driving with the windows down on the highway. It feels like I'm stuck in a hurricane."

Sam snorted.

"Hey! I heard that, heifer!" Josie countered.

"I don't mean to laugh. How many times does this happen? When will you decide it's time to retire your car?" Josie's current car alternated between docile transport and finicky she-beast. It appeared the she-beast won the day and was intent on making mischief again.

"Why would I get rid of Sheila? She's loyal...most of the time.

Sam laughed. "Who is the photoshoot with?"

"Oh no, no, no. I don't think so. You're not sidetracking me that easily. A girl needs details."

"Details about what?"

"Don't play with me, Sam! How did your dinner date with Heath go? I'm as parched as the desert and the only thing that will quench my thirst is all the juicy details. Start spilling or we're trading cars for a day during the summer. I'm sure Sheila would love it," Josie said over the roar of wind.

"You'll be disappointed to learn nothing happened," Sam said carelessly

with conscious effort to keep the bitterness and hurt from her voice.

Josie *tsk*ed. "You didn't shave your legs, did you? I told you to shave before you went out. You probably scared him away with your hairy Wooly Mammoth legs."

"Oh, stop it," Sam said. "I did too shave my legs," she added softly. "He received a call from the Firm and left dinner early."

"Damn him and that stupid law stuff," Josie said before launching into another diatribe about websites and hackers and new employment opportunities for Heath.

Sam half listened when she noticed a figure appear across the street from where the children played. She squinted her eyes for a better look but found she couldn't focus. She rubbed her eyes and looked again. It was like she was only seeing a misty outline then nothing.

"I'm not asking him to quit. He wouldn't anyway, he loves his career," Sam responded automatically, her voice trailing off. Even when she strained her neck, she couldn't see the figure again or anything else out of the ordinary. As Sam turned away from the spot when the hair on her arms prickled and as goosebumps broke out over her skin. An uneasy feeling much like the other night came over her, quickening her pulse. She steadied her breath.

Not a panic attack. Please no.

"It's his job. He's damn good at it, too," Sam said through gritted teeth, her breaths measured while she slowly steadied her heartbeat. She could fight though this.

Ground yourself.

"I'm sorry. I know you love him, but Heath is just being a nitwit," Josie said, breaking through Sam's rising panic.

Sam continued listening with half her attention as Josie continued to talk about the different ways Sam could seduce her husband. Her pulse and breathing were steady and the anxious knot in her stomach slowly unraveled.

"That's it! You should hide out in his office and surprise him," Josie exclaimed.

"Next you're going to tell me to surprise him wearing nothing but a pair of stiletto heels." Her attention returned to the children playing when the figure appeared. She sucked in her breath. There was no misty outline this time.

"Yes, girl! Now you're thinking like a woman who wants her husband to throw her on his desk and have his way with her. How about—"

"Josie, I gotta go…pick up Heath's dry cleaning," Sam interrupted her friend before Josie went into details of her ill-advised yet tempting plan. "I'll call you back later." Sam disconnected the phone, letting the phone drop from her hand onto the bench.

She covered her with a hand mouth as disbelief washed over her and forced herself to continue her slow, measured breathing. Sam rushed out the front door. She didn't have dry cleaning to pick up. What she had was an urge to greet the blonde woman who stood across the street from her house. A young woman who resembled the pretty blonde woman she had been calling for the last two days.

Her bare feet slammed down along the sidewalk and driveway, gravel digging into the underside of her feet as she tried to reach the young woman before she disappeared. How did the young woman find her address? Sam ignored the pain as she ran across the street where the woman stood only seconds before. The blonde woman was nowhere to be found. Sam spun around in a circle in the middle of the street, looking for where the woman would have run to so quickly. How had she lost sight of her?

"Ouch," Sam yelped as something dug into the bottom of her foot. She glanced down and chided herself for being so engrossed in what she saw out her window, she didn't bother putting on her shoes. Sam looked up and down both sides of the street, shielding her eyes from the sunlight.

Tall palmetto trees grew like stoic guardians along the street, pushing through the grass and threatening to overtake the paved sidewalks. The giddy children playing moments before now stood still and stared at her.

Sam stumbled backward away from the children and walked toward the intersection bisecting her street, Briarwood Lane with Marigold Drive. A few cars passed by, the drivers briefly staring at her before moving along.

She glanced down at herself, noting the black leggings and holey Carolina Panther T-shirt she threw on this morning. Oh boy, did she ever look a sight. Conscious of her appearance, Sam crossed her arms over her stomach and paused. The young woman she thought she saw was nowhere to be found.

Sunlight slowly receded creating a gathering darkness as the afternoon lapsed into evening. Sam shook her head, taking her time walking back toward the house.

The logical conclusion being there never was a young woman outside her house. Her sleep had been miserable and infrequent, which may have caused her to be more scatterbrained. The figure was most likely a jogger or a friend visiting a neighbor and, in her confusion, Sam mistook the person for the young blonde woman. She understood those were logical thoughts, but her mind raced fitting the pieces into a tidy box of logical explanations for what she knew existed. She realized now, she needed to know what happened to the young woman in order to ease her mind.

Inside her house, Sam rushed through her kitchen, briefly stopping to grab her purse and keys and slip on a pair of sandals.

She remembered the young woman said her car broke down along the country road somewhere near the fork before the train station. There was only one way to find the young woman, she decided. Sam would retrace her footsteps from that night and see if the tow company had picked up the woman's car.

If not, maybe she would find some information in the car about where the young woman's parents lived. She drove off, the light fading to dark all around her as a new feeling settled into her bones. An emotion other than grief or anger touched her for the first time in months.

Determination.

SAM FLIPPED on her highbeam lights as she drove along the back road slowly, searching for skid marks where she swerved off the road a few nights ago. There were no other cars along the country road. No recent indication another vehicle had ever pulled over. No skid marks or overturned grass except the debris churned up by her car.

The grassy shoulder of the back-country road closed in around her when she saw the skid marks leading off the road into the dirt shoulder. A familiar unease rolled in her stomach. She parked her car but hesitated stepping outside. A feeling pricked at the back of her mind. This had to be the spot where she found the young woman a few nights prior. And there, that's the spot where she quickly swerved off the road to avoid hitting the sweatshirt the woman threw at her car.

This was it. The feeling intensified with that thought.

Inhaling deeply, Sam settled herself before stepping out of the car, her eagerness turning to uncertainty. The tall grass and overgrowth swayed gently, the slight breeze licked over her skin as she stood, enveloped on either side of the road. Sam rubbed at her arms and hoped there would be something left behind to help her discover the identity of the young woman. Paper from the woman's notebook, jewelry or a credit card, anything would be useful in tracking down where the woman traveled after Sam dropped her off.

She needed confirmation the young woman made it safely to her parents' house.

When walking proved futile, Sam crawled on her hands and knees, searching through the shorter pieces. The last vestige of sunlight glinted off on object along the roadside. Standing upright, Sam wiped her hands on her pants and picked it up, her fingers closing around the small weight of a thumb drive. Disappointment tugged at her consciousness when Sam found the exterior cracked and the insert scratched.

She kneeled, sitting back on her heels, and frowned at the battered drive, wondering if it dropped from the young woman's pocket. She shoved the thumb drive in her pocket, knowing even if she could access the files, it could be nothing related to the young woman. But it was all Sam had. Luckily, she knew someone who could help her.

Sam stood up from her crouched position, brushing the dirt from her hands onto her leggings. She wouldn't find anything of value here.

Before she walked back toward her car, she gave the

grassy field one last look. Her eyes caught the broken grass she must've missed before while she was busy looking on the ground.

The stalks were bent every which way like a large animal crawled through it, damaging the stalks and digging up dirt in the process. Against her better judgement, Sam walked toward the broken opening, her steps hesitant, ready for a tomcat or stray dog to rush out at her.

Soft ground squished beneath her sneakers, making a thick sound with each step until she reached the edge of the tall grass and stopped before entering the thicket. Broken, shoulder-height blades marked a path. Squinting her eyes, she could make out prints of some sort left behind in the soft ground.

She stepped carefully around the path, avoiding the prints in the dug up mud and entered deeper into the path. A chill nipped her neck then snaked down of the column of her spine as she walked further along the broken trail. Grass swished through her hands as she pushed away those in her path.

Time meant nothing as Sam walked. Above her day faded into an indigo night. All around her the sky darkened to the colors of midnight. She noticed the moonlight shining on a translucent mist gathered around her, beckoning her forward. The determination Sam felt earlier intensified as she stepped toward the mist. Then, an invisible string pulled her taut toward an unknown destination, deeper into the field, and with each step, the mist swirled around her ankles, urging her forward. And at that moment she knew the source of the invisible string was in this field.

Ahead, Sam stopped abruptly as a light colored object stuck out from the side of the path. She crept closer, the grip of unease now a familiar friend in this darkened place. Sam cleared her mind of negative thoughts before she moved any closer. She continued her creep toward the broken area ahead of her where the white object was only partially visible. All around her the grass lay broken against the earth, as if a struggle occurred but the aftermath allowed for easy navigation.

It was at this distance Sam realized two things: she was at the end of the path and the light colored object was a dirt-smeared sneaker. Sam knelt, her trembling hand reaching out as a single fingertip brushed the top of the sneaker. She yanked her hand back as a light flashed behind her eyes, momentarily blinding her. When she opened her eyes again, she sucked in shaky breath and covered her mouth.

The white sneaker sat turned over on its side and beside it, a mate still on the foot of the person lying prone on the ground. Sam felt tears prick at her eyes, her breathing quickened.

She squinted her eyes shut against the horror of what she saw next.

The mist that had followed her to this broken place parted, allowing the moonlight to shine onto her, lighting the area around her. The invisible string pulled on her and she carefully stepped around the white sneaker to see if what she thought was true. Her eyes followed the blue gray skin of a long leg to the cutoff shorts and dirty white T-shirt. Long, blonde hair covered the face of what Sam suspected was a woman.

Sam bent closer and against the instinct screaming from within to run, she brushed away the hair, her hand trembling as a finger touched cold skin. With the long hair smoothed away, Sam could make out the features of a familiar face. The young woman she picked up from this place only two days before stared back, her once vibrant eyes glassy and her lips a bluish grey.

"No, no, this can't be," Sam cried.

She fell back, landing in the crushed grass and soft earth. Using her hands and feet, Sam instinctively crawled backwards, her heels digging tunnels in the earth as hot tears trailed down her cheeks. Her heart raced and the only thing she could think of was to get as far away from the body as she could.

Sam spun around, tripping over her feet. Once steady, she ran with such speed back through the broken path, the blades from the grass stalks whipped at her, marking angry welts on her cheeks. Sam sobbed, relief flooding through her when she saw the entrance to the road ahead.

Breaking through the grass she fell to her knees and retched until the contents of her stomach emptied and only bile remained. She wiped at her mouth and stared back at the entrance of the field. Using the last bit of strength, she crawled to her car and with shaking hands grabbed her phone from the driver seat. She leaned her back against the tire of her car and dialed the number ingrained in her from when she was a four-year-old girl.

"Hello, this is Midnight Harbor 911, what is your emergency?" the woman answered.

"Hi, my name is Samantha Crenshaw. I need an officer at my location right away." Sam choked back a sob. "I just found a dead body."

SAM OCCUPIED herself during the wait by repeating the alphabet forwards then backwards as fast as she could. It was a game she played with her little sister to help her learn the alphabet and quickly became a contest to see who could say the alphabet the fastest without making a mistake. She began her sixth attempt when she heard the unmistakable sound of a siren in the distance. Sam stood, her legs still wobbly, watching a small red and blue flashing dot in the distance until the blacked-out vehicle pulled up beside her.

"Hey, are you okay?" a man asked, his voice gentle but firm. The detective climbed out of the undercover vehicle and walked over to where Sam stood by her car. Gratefulness washed over her as she recognized the voice of Theo Hart. She was no longer alone.

Sam wrapped her arms around herself to stop her shaking. She shook her head. "No, I'm not." Sam bit the inside of her lip to keep herself from bursting into tears.

Theo fetched a wool blanket from the inside of his vehicle and gingerly wrapped the blanket over her shoulders. "I called Heath. I told him what happened. He said he'll be here as soon as he can." Theo smiled at her.

Heath...how could she forget about him, to call him? Sam turned away from Theo, the unshed tears pooling in her eyes. "Hey," Theo said squeezing her shoulder. "It will only be a few minutes. Heath wouldn't leave you alone. Everything will be okay."

She heard the hesitation in his voice. His blue eyes squinted as if he thought of a question but then he turned toward the dug up dirt and broken grass and exhaled. "I'm going to have to ask you a few questions. Do you understand?"

Sam looked into his eyes and nodded. "Yes, I understand. I'll help out however I can."

Theo gently led her over to his vehicle, asking a series of questions until the coroner and backup officers arrived on the scene. As Sam recounted her steps, they worked the crime scene efficiently. Barricading the road from both directions and stationing officers at points along the road and field. No curious locals or reporters would be getting though.

When Theo finished questioning her, she waited inside his car and he stayed nearby until Sam heard tires crunching as they rolled over gravel. She looked up to see Heath's sleek sports car barreling down the road toward her. Despite the police presence, Heath skidded to a halt beside Theo's sedan.

"Sam, baby, are you okay?" Heath said, his voice cracking. He burst out of the driver side of the car and ran toward her.

He opened his arms and Sam fell into the strength of his warm embrace, his touch dissipating any remaining chill inside her. She broke down, allowing herself to cry the tears she fought earlier to contain. She cried on Heath's chest for herself and the woman she found until she tasted nothing but salt on her tongue.

"It will be okay, I promise," Heath said to her, his hand stroking her hair, his lips pressed to the top of her head. Sam turned her head to lay her cheek against his chest. She looked up through the grittiness of her swollen eyes to watch Theo disappear into the tall stalks of swaying grass where a young woman's life had been cut short in an act of violence.

CHAPTER FIVE

MORNING ARRIVED with a warmth so unlike the cold darkness of the night before. Sam squeezed her eyes shut and
stretched. Her hand ran along the length of an empty pillow,
the fabric cold. Heath was long gone.

She rubbed her face, the memories of the back road
flashing through her mind. A sadness sunk into her bones.
While not unusual for Heath to already be gone, Sam thought
after last night and the tenderness he showered on her, things
might have been different between them. She shoved a short
robe over her shoulders and padded to the guest bedroom.
The curtains were open, the room empty.

Disappointment flooded her and she returned to her
bedroom turning on the shower in the master bath to the
hottest temperature she could tolerate. Sam leaned her head
against the cold tile and cried while the hot water soothed her
aches and washed away the griminess of the back road.
Maybe if she showered enough, she could rid herself of the
images haunting her. She dried off, slathered on some lotion
and dressed herself in leggings and an old hooded sweatshirt,
her damp hair curling at the ends.

The faint aroma of coffee lingered, and she felt hunger

pains gnaw at her stomach in response. Sam ambled down-stairs to the kitchen in search of breakfast and a much needed cup of coffee.

A note next to the coffee maker caught her attention. She recognized the heavy scrawl as Heath's writing. She picked up the note and read:

I'm sorry, baby, I had to run into work this morning.

Call me if you need to talk.

P.S. I have some good news to share with you.

Love, H

Sam placed the note aside on the island beside a manila folder. Heath must have left it behind this morning, and she made a mental note to file it in his office later. She poured the now lukewarm coffee Heath made earlier that morning into her favorite coffee mug, an oversized cup Heath made for her on a pottery date during their first anniversary vacation.

"If I had a penny for every time that man said sorry to me, I would be a rich woman," Sam muttered to herself. What did she expect? That he would stay with her today? She dragged her feet to the pantry where she quickly ate a granola bar. She lacked the energy to cook herself a meal. Sam walked with her coffee into the living room where she plopped herself onto the sofa.

She sat there in complete silence.

No television, no radio, no cellphone.

No anger, no sadness, no fear.

Only numbness.

It's not everyday someone finds a corpse in the middle of a field. Bonus points if the corpse was a missing person you met a few days ago. Sam wasn't sure if she was in shock or denial from her gruesome discovery last night. Her body sunk lower into the sofa. She faintly realized she needed time to process the events.

Leaning back in the sofa, Sam closed her eyes. A knock at the front door interrupted her mental gymnastics. She ignored it. Hopefully, the person behind the door would take the hint and leave.

Knock, knock, knock.

The pounding continued, developing into a persistent pattern on her door. Sam moaned, dragging herself to the door and peeked through the peephole. A young woman with an angled haircut, the tips dyed lavender stood on the other side. "No thank you, I'm not interested," Sam said through the thick wood. Sam watched Josie stick out her tongue.

"Well, I guess I'll have to eat these donuts all by myself. Are you sure you don't want a taste of these?" Josie said in a sing song voice, holding up a box of donuts in one hand and a steaming cup of coffee in the other. A bow curled around the white bakery box and a gold embossed logo barely peaked under the ribbon from her favorite bakery. Sam's stomach growled in recognition.

"Okay, you win this time," Sam said. She unlocked the deadbolt and held open the door.

"What type of food blogger would I be if I didn't share the love with my best friend," Josie said entering the spacious foyer. She gave Sam a quick kiss on either cheek as she walked by.

Josie peered at Sam over the cat eye sunglasses perched on her nose. "You look like shit. You looked much better in those pics circulating the local media site from the other night."

"Thanks, heifer," Sam said using the nickname they used with each other when they first met in high school. Sam was the new kid, Josie the outcast. Somehow, they connected and a deep friendship had formed and blossomed over time. "I wasn't expecting to be greeted by the media when I left the restaurant."

Josie winked at her then flopped onto the sofa. "It's my sworn duty as best friend to tease. Plus, you look like you haven't slept in two weeks. What's going on?"

"I'm fine. Heath is working a lot of late nights lately. You know I hate being alone in this old house." Sam brushed off the comment and hoped her playful attempt fooled her friend.

Josie opened her mouth then closed it. A mighty task for an outspoken woman.

Sam sat across from the other woman on the loveseat.

"I heard a rumor down at the coffee shop," Josie leaned in, her voice pitched lower. "Do you remember the missing college girl? She worked at that restaurant you used to go to with the auxiliary club?"

Sam thought back to when the story about the waitress first broke. "Was she the young college coed from Charleston College? Hasn't she been missing for over a week?

"That's the girl. I saw her picture, cute girl. The rumor going around is the police have a person of interest. It sounded like there might be a news conference or arrest in the next day or two."

Thunder sounded in Sam's ears as she placed her cup on the coffee table in front of her, her vision blurred while her head spun and her hand shook. She closed her eyes and inhaled, forcing herself still. There was no way the missing coed and the young woman she found last night could be the same person.

"Do you have a picture. Of the missing coed?"

"Sure, here it is. Abby Jones is running a piece." Josie offered her phone.

Sam glanced at the picture of a pretty, young blonde on the phone. Coldness washed over her, her throat constricted.

"Hey, what's going on?" Josie walked around the low coffee table and kneeled in front of Sam, grasping her hands in her own. "You suddenly turned white as a ghost." Josie's eyes flashed concern and kindness.

Sam leaned into her friend as the sob broke from her lips. Tears streaked hot rivers down her cheeks while she tried to regain her composure and get out the words without stuttering. Josie wrapped her arms around Sam, giving her a comforting tight hug. Sam took strength offered from her friend and when her tears lessened, she slowly recounted the story of how she found the lifeless body of a young college coed the night before.

"SO WHERE IS HEATH? I can't believe that he just left you alone this morning after what you went through last night." The two women sat beside each other on the sofa. Sam, having cried throughout much of the recount, was amazed Josie understood what occurred.

"He's gone before I wake up. We don't have the same amount of time to spend together since he took on more responsibility at the Firm." Sam peered down at the top of her coffee. "The night of our dinner date he left early. He received an urgent call from Nathan about a new case. Since then we haven't spent more than a few minutes together." Sam shrugged her shoulders, feigning confidence in her words, and found Josie staring at her, an eyebrow raised.

"You're telling me Little Miss Housewife no longer cooks her dear husband his morning breakfast? And this all started before last night?"

Sam gave her a small smile, grateful for her attempts at lightening the mood. "I haven't felt like it lately." Sam wasn't ready to venture into this topic of conversation. She shared many details of her life with Josie, including what happened last night, but a broken marriage and grief she kept to herself. It was her battle, her loss, her failure to endure.

"No more shit, Sam. I haven't seen you for weeks prior to Kerri Reid's book signing and you want to play like you're all right? You push me away anytime I reach out. I wish you would confide in me like you did before. I thought I was your favorite heifer." Josie smiled and her eyes were glassy. "Or did Gia finally win you over?"

"Ugh, you had to bring her up." Sam stuck out her tongue. "Of course, you're my favorite. Now tell me more about what you have planned with Lulu's Cafe?" Sam asked to redirect Josie.

Josie broke into a huge smile, her eyes bright. "I'm working on a featured project with the bakery and coffee shop. If everything goes well, I might even have a chance of being published in the Midnight Harbor Ladies' Journal as a featured story," Josie exclaimed.

"That's wonderful," Sam said. "I'm sure the ladies of the auxiliary club will be utterly scandalized at the thought of an outcast writing for their journal."

Josie smiled slowly, her fuscia painted lips parted, revealing her teeth, and leaned back in the sofa. "You bet. Josie the outspoken, now the hottest foodie in Midnight Harbor. I wanted only to wrinkle those old biddies knickers, but the exposure? Priceless. Can you imagine how far reaching the audience is for the journal? Not just here but in Charleston too. I could easily increase the visits to my blog by a few hundred per month."

Josie opened the box of doughnuts. "We had so much food at the shoot this morning, I thought you would enjoy the left-overs." She picked up a French apple pie flavored donut. "Heaven in a box."

Feeling less morose, Sam offered her friend a sincere smile and reached for the cherry topped Boston Crème donut. "Thank you," Sam said, knowing Josie understood the depth of the words counted for more than just a donut and shoulder to cry on.

Sam took a small bite, the decadent chocolate paired rich against the creamy vanilla custard. Before she realized what happened, Sam had devoured the entire donut. Josie raised a sculpted eyebrow. "You going to lick your fingers, too?"

Sam laughed. The two friends spent the time catching up between mouthfuls of donut and sips of latte. When the doughnuts disappeared, leaving only crumbs behind, the women sat in silence. Sam fidgeted with her hoodie strings, the string twirling around her fingers.

"I'm glad to see you eat something," Josie said, breaking the silence between them. "If you kept losing weight, you might wither away to nothing and I'm not sure Heath is into the waif look."

Sam looked down at herself. Leggings, hoodie, comfy socks…she looked fine. "Really, I haven't lost that much weight. My appetite isn't what it used to be."

"Mhm," Josie murmured though pursed lips. "I see the dark circles under your eyes and feel your absence. I know there's more going on than what you want to tell me. I'll let you keep your secrets for now."

"I don't have any secrets. You've known me since high school, Josie. I wasn't expecting you. If I had, I would've dressed in nicer clothes."

"Sam, you just told me you discovered a dead body! I don't expect you to do anything but get help to cope with what you saw. Plus, I was talking about the past few months. What, you don't bother checking your phone anymore now that you've withdrawn from polite society?" Josie imitated one woman from the ladies auxiliary. She stretched out on the sofa, tucking a velvet pillow beneath her head.

Sam stared at her latte, worrying the laces of her hoodie between her fingers. She glanced up, meeting Josie's eyes. Love, concern and warmth filled her friend's green eyes. Josie had always been the person she could trust besides Heath, so why couldn't she confide in her friend now?

"The ladies at auxiliary mentioned you haven't been to a meeting in a few months."

"Josie, I'm fine. I promise. If something was wrong, you would be one of the first people I would tell. It's just a lot to take in with everything that happened. I'm probably going to have to meet with the police again. I'm not sure if I'm still in shock or just numb. I don't know what to feel."

"I don't think so," Josie scowled, "look at you, when did Samantha Crenshaw bum it in a dirty hoodie and leggings past ten a.m.? You're always so well put together. I don't think I have ever seen you get the mail without your mascara on."

"Heifer!" Sam said, throwing a pillow at Josie, forgetting last night's terror. "What's wrong with my clothes? This is my favorite college hoodie."

Josie snatched the pillow before it sailed over the top of sofa. "Oh, did I touch a nerve, Mrs. Crenshaw," Josie said before breaking into a fit of laughter.

"No, I'm just not feeling like it," Sam said. Really, she didn't look that badly. Even if she did, everyone was allowed to have bad days.

Josie rolled her eyes. "Yeah, okay. What does Heath think of your dirty hoodie? Does it get his motor humming?"

"Ugh!" Sam brushed off her comment with a wave of her hand. "It's fine, he thinks it's fine." She focused her attention back to her latte hoping Josie didn't hear the falter in her voice.

"I'm not buying it, Sam." Josie leaned forward, her elbows on her knees, lavender tipped hair falling around her heart-shaped face. Sam looked up to meet her friend's eyes. "When was the last time you and Heath got down and dirty?" Josie said, her eyebrows waggled at Sam.

Sam plugged her fingers in her ears. "La la la la," she sang, "I'm not listening." She walked into the kitchen to stop Josie from prying for more information Sam wasn't ready to admit to herself. Why did Josie have the ability to hone in on her innermost secrets?

Close on her heels, Josie doubled her efforts, chasing Sam

around the kitchen island, giggling between sexual euphemisms fit for a sixteen year old boys locker room.

"Josie, stop it." Sam held up both hands when Josie cornered her. Josie grabbed her hands and placed them at her side.

"Be real with me, Sam," Josie begged, placing her hands on Sam's shoulders, her gaze direct and unflinching. "When was the last time you and Heath had sex?"

Sam avoided Josie's eyes. "I'm not sure." And there it was, one of her secrets bared for Josie to judge. But this was her best friend. They shared this type of information in the past, yet this grain of truth was difficult for Sam to say. If she said it, it would be true, and she didn't want to face the consequences of her marriage falling to pieces.

"You should just tell me. I'll find a way to ferret out the information from you somehow," Josie said.

Sam placed her hands on her hips and fixed Josie a dirty look. "I'm not sure when the last time was."

"What was that? I think I heard you say you didn't remember?" Josie said. She stared at Sam aghast, her mouth gaping open as if she had grown two heads.

"That's about right." Sam felt her cheeks growing hot and definitely bright red.

"Good God, Sam!" Josie placed her hand over her heart and exaggerated a faint on top of the kitchen island.

Sam rolled her eyes. "It's not that bad. Most couples go through a dry patch." At least that was what she read in all those magazines in the doctor's office. "I told you he has been working late hours."

"Most couples also don't have the same sexcapades you and Heath have," Josie said. "Don't you understand, us celibate women live through your stories."

Sam snorted. "Since when are you celibate?" Her embarrassment wearing off, Sam relaxed with Josie's teasing. Even though her misfortune was the source of her enjoyment, this was the first time in months Sam felt something instead of a constant numbness. Despite last night and a failed dinner date, Sam felt close to how she used to feel...normal.

"Since all the good men left Midnight Harbor, that's when. Anyway, don't change the topic of conversation," Josie said. "Let's get back to you, Heath and the lack of intimacy." She tapped her finger on the kitchen island. "I need all the details."

"I told you, Heath has been working long hours. We don't have the same opportunity to see each other as we did a few months ago. His time has been taken up with the most recent cases," Sam said.

"Let me ask you a serious question. Have you tried to seduce him?" Josie's green eyes shifted up and down her length. "Wait never mind. What am I thinking? Not in those clothes."

"What's wrong with what I'm wearing?"

"What's wrong? Did you miss the whole prior conservation?"

"You don't have to be so mean," Sam said. Josie could be too blunt for own good.

"I'm sorry." Josie pulled her into a tight hug. "I'm just concerned about you. I know how much Heath means to you. This isn't like you two." Josie pointed to Sam's clothes. "This isn't you either."

"Sometimes I think he doesn't find me attractive anymore," Sam said. "Like he doesn't want to be around me." Her eyes burned with the threat of unshed tears. She sniffled as she stared at the ceiling, blinking back the tears.

"Oh, I doubt that," Josie said. "You just need to clean yourself up a bit." Josie grabbed Sam's hand to inspect her naked nails and ragged cuticles. "When was the last time you went shopping or had your nails done? The Sam I know always had fresh manicure."

Sam pulled her hand back. "It's been awhile."

"Well, it's time we changed that," Josie said. "Now march your little butt upstairs, put on something clean, and let's get you ready to seduce your husband." Josie pumped her arm in the air in victory over a hard-won battle. A victory over mismatched clothing and a married couple's dried-up sex life. Sam thudded up the stairs, grateful for Josie's interruption.

She allowed herself to play along with her friend's ridiculous plan. Maybe this was the way to feeling normal again. To feel again. To forget for a few hours she had discovered a dead woman on a backroad in quaint Midnight Harbor.

———

SAM SAT on the edge of a lake, the night dark and the water crystal clear. A reflection of the crescent moon glimmered on the surface of the water. A cool breeze brushed over her skin. She watched as an island emerged from the center of the lake. Though far away on land, Sam was certain she could swim to it if she tried.

She stole a quick glance around to see if anyone was near and when she was certain she was alone, she slipped off her dress, the fabric pooling around her feet, and stepped into the water.

Cold water lapped at her ankles as she stepped forward. Her movement broke the surface of the lake, creating a series of small waves flowing outward from her position. She relished the feeling of water against her bare skin.

When the water was waist deep and the ground gave way, she dove under and broke into a freestyle swim. Kicking her arms and legs in rhythm, Sam swam as fast as she could to the island in the middle of the lake, never tiring from the exertion.

Suddenly, a hand grasped her ankle, pulling her down. Sam resisted, kicking her opposite leg at the hand but she couldn't break free of the grip holding her underwater. She thrashed about using the strength in her arms and legs to pull herself free and toward the light above her. She saw the light fade and she struggled as the strength left her body. She sank, the coldness of the water saturating her mouth and throat.

Gasping, Sam sat up, covers tangled around her arms and legs in a firm hold. She realized it was another dream as she loosened the sheet from around her legs. Sweat dripped down the middle of her back despite the cool air blowing into her room from the open window. It was still dark outside, the moonlight casting a pale light in her room. Josie had left earlier after eating take out with her in front of the tv.

Noticing Heath's spot empty, she crept out of bed and using her phone as a flashlight, she checked the guest bedroom to discover the room empty as well. Heath never came home last night.

Sam was acclimated to his tedious, late hours but he always managed to come home, even if it was only for a few hours of sleep. She didn't know how to feel at the realization her husband never came home. Loneliness, anger, sadness? The usual emotions escaped her this time and she realized she didn't feel anything.

Sam returned to her bedroom and used a foul word to describe what she thought of these hybrid nightmares that left her uneasy when she awoke. The imagery and sounds felt so real. It had been a year if not longer since she had this particular haunting dream. Not since the unexpected passing of a colleague's mother. There was always an island in the middle of a lake which she wanted to explore. Only her efforts to swim there resulted in her struggling against an unseen force.

Sam wrapped herself tightly in the warm fuzzy blanket while the coldness clung to her skin. She felt like she was still submerged in the water, a nascent reminder of the dream. She settled back against her pillow and closed her eyes.

Restless, Sam cuddled the pillow desperate to sleep.

Despite her best efforts, sleep alluded her. The continued effort futile, she flipped on the television. An old movie played, and she watched the two lovers dance in black and white until the images lulled her into a place between wakefulness and sleep.

Before she nodded off, a movement caught her attention in the corner where an oversized armchair nestled against the wall, a white blanket thrown over the top of the chair. "Stupid blanket," Sam muttered, turning over in her bed.

A breeze caressed the nape of her neck and an uneasy feeling crept along Sam's spine. She stood up, disgusted, and walked over to the chair and froze mid-step.

The outline of a body, transparent but solid, sat in the chair. Sam gulped and found she couldn't move. "What the hell?" she whispered. Frozen in place she contemplated her next move. She could run or confront the ghostly blanket.

"It's another dream." Sam repeated the mantra to give her courage. She took a step forward with her arm outreached, the white blanket a mere hand's length beyond her grasp. Her hand closed around the soft fabric and pulled the blanket free, the length dropping around her feet.

The moonlight bathed the chair with an otherworldly eeriness, giving the shape better definition in the light. The outline wasn't a blanket or pillow but a person, its shape familiar. Sam recognized long, light-colored hair that shimmered in the moonlight.

Sam covered her mouth and she stepped backward until her legs hit the bed. She crawled back onto the bed, the blankets gripped tight in her hands.

The outline of the young woman she met a few days ago sat in the chair. Sam gasped aloud, the sound startling the transparent young woman from her peaceful position. She spun toward Sam, her face a ghostly white, empty black holes where her eyes should've been. The young woman lifted an arm toward Sam, the rose tattoo clear on her wrist as a finger slowly uncurled outward to point at her, in accusation or recognition, Sam knew naught.

Sam's eyes widened, watching the shape stand and float toward her, long hair blowing back in an ethereal breeze. A scream escaped from a lipless mouth and Sam repeated the scream when the apparition vanished, leaving her alone with a cold bead of sweat dripping a trail down her back.

Sam fell backward onto her bed and closed her eyes as exhaustion blanketed over her.

CHAPTER SIX

"WHAT DO you mean the Davi file is missing?" Heath's fingers pinched the bridge of his nose. He refused to allow his anger to show. Cool, calm, that's what he was. "We just reviewed the files a few hours ago before the daily stand up meeting with the team." This was just what he didn't need. Since Sam discovered the dead body off the side of the road, he'd been crashing in his office after spending countless hours working on the case. He hadn't seen her since the night of her gruesome discovery.

Tyler sighed, taking off his tortoiseshell framed glasses and rubbed his amber flecked brown eyes, a contrast against his light brown skin. He wore his black hair closely cropped unlike the long tapered fade from his security badge photo.

"It's just like I told you. I came into the office early to run additional analytics on the potential outliers for the case. The file I needed to utilize was gone." Tyler folded his lean frame in the chair across from Heath's desk. "The folder and its contents disappeared from the network."

Cool, calm. Heath repeated his mantra while taking a few deep breaths. It wasn't Tyler's fault and the other man didn't deserve his anger. Standing up, Health paced around the open area of the room behind Tyler, rubbing his jaw. "How does a file disappear without a trace?"

"I wish I could tell you." Tyler pivoted in the chair around and watched Heath pace. "I ran through a few different modifiers to my program to see if I could find the source. Nothing! I ran a recovery for an earlier version. Nothing!" Tyler leaned back in his chair with his hands clasped behind his neck. "It's as if the file never existed."

"Did you try the backup files?" Heath asked. "There has to be a backup available or another way to retrieve the files." There was no way the files could disappear. "This is bad." Heath covered his face with his hands. He was going to be in some deep shit unless he recovered those files.

"Heath, I told you I tried everything. Including our backup files. It's all gone." Tyler sighed, his face crumbling in defeat. "I managed to trace the IP address back to Kiawah Island. I couldn't find anything else of value."

"Hey, man, it's a start. Check into any persons or companies of interest that may harbor ill will toward Nicholas Davi based in Kiawah Island or the surrounding area," Heath said. He slapped Tyler on the shoulder. "Do you know how many times I pissed off Rex with mistakes? We'll recover the files. I have confidence in your ability."

"Thanks. Hey, do you have anything in the paper files I could use to recalculate the potential outliers?" Tyler asked, knowing Rex insisted on digital and paper files for this exact reason. "It's not as up to date as the digital files but, I could use it to recreate the analysis before the next meeting with Rex. And save both our asses."

Heath's face fell. The paper files. He was a damn fool.

"Don't tell me you forgot about the file?"

"Of course, not." Heath rummaged through the messy stacks of folders and piled papers on his desk. He frowned. He hated messy desks. When the hell did his office begin to look lije this? "I don't believe it. I thought I had it right here."

He checked his briefcase next. Nothing. Heath glanced at Tyler, his eyes wide. "Damn. I don't have the paper file. I must've left it at home." When was the last time he was home?

Tyler groaned, leaning on his legs and covering his face in his hands. "We're ruined!"

"Hey, we got his under control. I'm sure Maggie has another copy in central filing. She created the checkout system for the files in order to track who had which file," Heath said. "She'll let us borrow it."

Tyler looked up at Heath through his fingers. "You're on her list."

He snorted and placed a hand on the young man's shoulder. "We'll figure it out. I need you to keep running analytics to see if we can recover the file and determine who bypassed our security measures."

"Thanks. I can't believe someone hacked through my firewall!" Heath understood Tyler was concerned with more than the firewall, he had the feeling his pride hurt as well. Tyler was a tech whiz; he ran the analytics and network department for the Firm. Of course, he would take the loss personally. He would feel the same about one of his cases.

Heath froze. "Tyler, who else did you tell about the missing files?" he asked softy.

"Not a soul other than you. I wasn't about to tell Rex I lost the Davi files."

Tyler stood up to leave, "I'll let you be the one to have the talk with Rex, lead counsel. Don't worry I'll give you back up, buddy." Tyler slapped Heath's shoulder.

"Gee, thanks," Heath said. The last thing he wanted was to appear incompetent when his future with the Firm was at stake. If Maggie had the files, there would be no need to advise Rex of the mishap.

"Let's go check central filing for the information we need," Heath said as he walked toward the door with Tyler.

THEY FOUND Maggie in the library on the second floor of the Firm.

"Hey, Maggie. I hope you have a minute to help your favorite colleagues," Heath said.

Maggie eyed the men suspiciously. "My favorite changes daily. But I'll help. I'm getting bored up here with just interns to keep me company."

"I hope you copied the Davi file," Heath asked. "We need to borrow it to fact check something Tyler is working on."

"You're on my list Heath."

Heath gave her a smile and silently hoped it worked. "Please?"

"You're pathetic." Maggie rolled her eyes as she fought back a smile. "I completed the last updated before I left last night. Let me find them for you," Maggie said, Heath and Tyler following her to the central computer. Heath knew Maggie was proud of the archive she designed for the Firm. She could find anything amongst the multiple bookcases and file drawers.

"This is strange," Maggie said. "I know I signed in all the files from yesterday before I left." Heath watched her scroll through the screen. "I'm can't find the record for the Davi case."

Heath looked from Maggie to Tyler. "Whoever hacked into the system was also aware of the additional copy Maggie has on file."

"Who hacked into what?" Maggie's brows furrowed and she glanced between the two men.

"Tyler discovered the Davi file missing from the drive this morning. We hoped you had a copy of the file he could use to finish up the analytic portion of the research before we met with Davi," Heath said.

"We...need a copy of the documents," Tyler said giving Heath a dirty look.

Heath grinned in return then stopped. "I'll call Sam. If I left the file at home, I could swing by to pick it up before we meet with Rex this afternoon."

Heath's stomach knotted at the thought of Sam. He left her a note for her to give him a call if she needed anything. The night she found the body, he comforted her until she fell asleep, holding her while she cried.

He knew it hadn't been enough.

He hadn't been enough.

There were no missed calls, so he assumed she was asleep. She should know about his lead position on the Davi case. His intentions were true, but that was before the grisly discovery Sam found forced him to abandon his plans. Why did the thought of her make him feel guilty?

The universe must have heard his plea, because his phone buzzed with notification of a new text message. Heath checked and saw Sam's name.

"Tyler, I'll leave you and Maggie here to tie up any loose ends." Heath waved before leaving the library. He needed privacy with Sam. No one knew about her finding the body, yet. That wasn't what kept him from sharing the news with the team this morning.

His conscious gnawed at him. He would reveal the discovery soon. Right now, there was no need to involve other team members in the missing file beyond Tyler and Maggie. If the situation escalated, Heath would speak with Rex. It was his responsibility and he didn't want the information to make it back to Rex without it coming from him personally.

Heath ran down the stairs, taking two at a time and jumped over the last stair, landing with a pivot before he turned down the hallway leading to his office. He rounded the corner when he collided with a much shorter person.

"Ouch!" an unfamiliar voice cried out. Heath heard a thump and swish and watched as papers and folders fell to the floor. Loose papers were stuck between rainbow hued folders, scattered across the floor.

"I'm sorry. I assure you, I know better than to dash around the corner like a kid after the ice cream truck." Heath saw the woman's shocked face and gave the woman a lopsided smile, picking up some of the paperwork lost in the shuffle. "I was lost in my own thoughts and clearly not paying attention." He noticed a set of keys with large Greek letters embossed on a keychain. He grabbed the keys and handed the young woman the pile of papers and folders.

"It's, it's fine. I wasn't really looking where I was going either."

"I don't think I've met you before. My name is Heath Crenshaw." He extended his hand to the young woman.

She accepted his outstretched hand. "It's nice to meet you. My name is Amanda Millner. I'm one of the new interns." She shook his hand, her grip lax and hand damp. Heath studied the young woman in front of him. She looked to be about twenty years old and nervous. She tucked a long brown hair behind her ear and avoided his eyes. Between Maggie's orientation and a bristly Rex, Heath often wondered how the Firm retained any interns.

He smiled, remembering his excitement on his first day as an intern at the Firm. Most interns were nervous the first few weeks while they adjusted, but not him.

Heath stifled a groan and shook his head. "I forgot the spring semester interns began assignments this week." He should've been prepared for the new semester. Glancing at the folders, he turned toward his office. "It's nice to meet your acquaintance, Amanda. I'm sure I'll be seeing you around in the near future." Heath walked away, the missing file a nagging gnat he couldn't swat away.

"Excuse me, Attorney. Crenshaw? Do you know where I

can find Mr. Anderson?" Amanda called out after him. "Ms. Vasquez asked me to deliver these files to him."

"Tyler? I suggest the library. He may still be in there with Maggie," Heath said as he turned around. "Wait, I'll show you the way."

"That will be all right, Mr. Crenshaw," Amanda said, the folders clutched in her arms. "I'll find my way." She waved and turned toward the staircase.

Wishing the new intern the best, Heath dialed Sam's number while he walked quickly back to his office. He waited for what felt like a lifetime for her to answer.

"Hi," Sam answered, and a warmth washed over Heath at the sound of her familiar voice and wondered when was the last time he called her for their usual mid-day chats?

"How are you?" He hoped Sam could recover from what she found. She made great progress socializing again. He would help her through this.

"Okay. I mean, I'm okay. It's like I'm watching a movie only it's my life on screen. Josie stopped by for a visit. I've been watching the latest celebrity drama to try to keep my mind off of last night," Sam said softly.

"I'm sure the ladies are entertaining," Heath said. He immediately chastised himself for the stupid statement. He didn't know the best way to broach the Davi files without sounding like an ass and uninterested in her feelings. He cared about her, but he also needed to know if she had the files before his meeting with Rex.

"I saw the note you left," Sam said. "You mentioned you had something to tell me."

Heath dropped into his desk chair. What should have been happy news was marred by the lost files dark discovery. "It hardly seems like the appropriate time to tell you." Heath paused before continuing. "I have good news. Why don't I share it with you in person instead of over the phone?"

When Heath didn't hear anything from Sam, he checked his phone to make sure the call didn't disconnect. "Sam?"

"Oh, okay," Sam said a few seconds later. He swore it was almost as if she wasn't listening.

"I have favor to ask. Do you think you could see if I left something at the house this morning?"

"Yeah, I mean yes, of course. What is it?" Sam said.

"Would you be a love and check to see if I left a manila folder there?"

"You did. I found it on the kitchen island this morning," Sam said.

"Great! I'll be by later to check on you and pick it up," Heath said, his anxiety fading with the news. Although he swore he grabbed the file, Sam had saved him from a huge embarrassment. Disaster averted, he could send Tyler the file and attend the afternoon meeting without worrying Rex would discover the missing file. At least not yet.

"Would you like to have lunch when you stop in to pick up the files?" Sam said, her voice hesitant.

"Lunch is a wonderful way for me to make up for our lousy dinner the other night." Heath paused before saying goodbye, remembering her text from earlier. "I almost forgot, why did you call?"

"It was nothing important," Sam said.

"Are you sure? Because it doesn't sound like you're sure."

"Yes, I'll be fine. See you soon."

"All right babe, bye."

"Bye."

Heath disconnected the call and stared at his phone. Sam didn't sound like herself. He dropped the phone on his desk. He couldn't shake an uneasy feeling ever since Theo's phone call. He worried about her and what ate away at her conscious, causing her to withdraw from everyone. How could he broach the subject without upsetting her more?

What if he said the wrong thing? Would he cause her another panic attack.

Heath pushed the thought of Sam aside, needing to focus on the present. He leaned back in his desk chair with his arms behind his head. Today would be the turning point in his career, launching him into a senior counsel position. He would talk to Sam at lunch to set her up with a doctor to help her through any post-traumatic stress and Tyler would be able to upload the paper file before they met with Rex.

Everything was falling into place. The long hours and tedious work would pay off allowing him to reap the benefits of everything he promised himself he would achieve, everything he had worked for to bring him one step closer to his dream of becoming partner.

CHAPTER SEVEN

SAM PUSHED AWAY the ugly images of last night's dream. Only she wasn't convinced it was a dream. Logic told her it wasn't real or possible for people to see ghosts. She'd woken up from a recurring nightmare she had since she was a young girl. A ghost visited her last night. For what purpose she didn't know. And wasn't going to entertain the ghost or the nightmare.

She wasn't going back to that headspace to try and figure out her dream. Her real thoughts and memories of what she saw that night on the side of the road were enough. She didn't need to recall the horror again. She locked the intrusive thoughts away to focus on the present. She could tell Heath what she saw another time when the feeling wasn't so fresh.

Located on the first floor of their townhouse, Heath's office was nestled into the corner, decorative glass windows adorned the French doors leading into his office. Sam inhaled, letting the scent of Heath tickle her nose, stirring up long forgotten memories.

She'd spent a fortnight designing the perfect office space for him. The effort had been worth it. Masculine, sleek and completely Heath. A dark espresso stained desk with a cushioned chair sat along one wall, the bookshelf and file cabinet against the other wall. Heath's degrees hung on the wall beside a photograph of a young couple, fresh faced and green.

Sam touched the faces of the young couple in the picture. How time and life shaped them since that picture. She pressed her forehead to the wall, nostalgia washing over her, and allowed herself a few moments to be lost in memories, before life became so complicated. When life was simply the love shared between two people figuring out life.

Not that life had been unkind. They lived in a beautiful restored townhouse not far from the downtown area of Midnight Harbor, an upgrade from the shoe box-sized apartment they shared above a bar in Charleston while Heath finished law school and Sam worked for the college library.

A heaviness settled in her heart as Sam thought fondly of her old position. She'd been a research assistant at the college library before her hospitalization. After Sam returned home from the hospital, Heath worked with her administrators to ease Sam back into the position. Unable to handle the stress, Sam often hid between bookshelves, silently sobbing until her relief clocked in hours later. It quickly became clear to everyone involved Sam would not be able to handle the workload. Half a year had passed, yet Sam still felt pain at the loss.

Sam forced herself out of her painful reverie. She feared how often she spent lost in memories of the past.

The cream-colored folder Heath requested with the name DAVI written in thick, black ink on the tab sat on his desk. Her eyes widened, recognizing the name. She let out a whistle. No wonder Heath sounded tense on the phone this morning. He tried to cover his emotions with faux levity, but Sam knew him too well. Nicholas Davi was his new client. Sam's thoughts reeled at the possibilities of why he would need Heath's help.

Desperate to leave the room dominated by memories of happier times, Sam walked into the living room and tossed the file on the coffee table. She sat on the sofa and quickly typed a text message to Heath.

Heath's response was immediate. He would be home shortly.

The only thing left for Sam to do was to wait. She focused on the conversation she shared with Josie on the best way to entice Heath into coming home early from work. The perfect opportunity presented itself when Heath called to inquire about the file. Sam no longer needed a made-up excuse for him to come home.

Her preparations for the seduction of her husband were complete. Sam sat back in the sofa, prepared for his arrival. This wasn't about last night or long forgotten memories. This was about the present and reconnecting with her husband.

Time ticked by and Sam crossed her legs, her foot shaking, and stared at the file folder on the coffee table. It was a simple file folder, nothing of interest except for the name printed on the tab. Sam knew it would bring nothing but trouble, yet her hands still reached for the folder, the contents like a siren song edging her closer to her doom. She opened the file and began to read.

Sam jumped up at the sound of the garage door opening. She must've been so engrossed in reading, she didn't realize how much time had passed. Sam flipped the cover shut and sat up, straightening the creases in her dress as Heath walked in the door.

Her heart jumped at the sight of Heath standing in the doorway. A smile broke across his face when he saw her then his eyes darted to the file folder.

"Thanks for finding the file," he said, shutting the front door behind him. "You have no idea how much time you saved us from trying to reconstruct the contents."

Sam waved off his comment. "I noticed you left the folder

behind. I placed it in your office not thinking you may need it. You must have been in a rush," Sam said walking into the kitchen, Heath followed closely behind her.

"What is that amazing smell?" The aroma of their favorite dishes from a local Asian take-out restaurant permeated the air. "What's the special occasion?"

"No special occasion." Sam walked to the small dining table, spooning noodles onto white plates. "I'm happy you were able to come home to have lunch with me."

Heath stood at the head of table, his mouth open and eyes on Sam. She felt the heat of his gaze rove over her body from head to toe. "Is that the dress from Las Vegas?"

Sam smoothed the vibrant fabric over her hip, a coy smile on her lips. "I'm glad you remember. You were the one to buy it for me after all." Sam turned her back to him as she set the food back on the table and she peeked at him from over her shoulder. "I remember you said how much you like it."

She motioned for Heath. "Come, sit and eat. You can tell me what's so important about the file you needed to pick up." Heath stood still as a statue, his keys still in his hand, his brow furrowed as if he couldn't comprehend her request.

"Come on, before it gets cold."

Heath shifted on his feet then sat in the high back chair across from Sam. Picking up the pitcher of sweet tea to pour them a drink, Sam noticed Heath struggled with something within himself. No doubt related to the Davi case and what information he could share.

Heath took a deep breath, then spoke, his voice steady despite the crease lines beside his mouth. "The case is high profile. The client is Nicholas Davi, who you probably know of for his frequent galas in downtown Midnight Harbor. He is a philanthropist, real estate mogul and well-known playboy."

"Really?" Sam feigned surprise at Heath's admission. "Isn't he a hometown boy turned billionaire?"

Heath nodded, twirling the spicy red noodles around his

fork and taking a bite. "We anticipate the Davi case to bring an onslaught of media attention based on his notoriety in Midnight Harbor and surrounding cities, including Charleston and beyond. You know with your run-in with the media the other night, they can be relentless in their pursuit of a story."

His face softened at the mention of their dinner date. His brown eyes, the shade of caramel and so easy to become lost in, met hers across the table, the apology deep in those brown eyes. "I wasn't expecting the Robertson trial to garner such significant media attention, much less journalists watching us rather than the defendant."

Sam waved him off with a flick of her hand. "Thank you, for the apology. I'm grateful Abby Jones found me first, she's the kinder one of the bunch. I know what to say to keep the others away."

"Judging by the notoriety Davi brings to the Firm, I'm sure this won't be the last time the media seeks you out, either," Heath said. "The next time it may not be Abby."

Sam smiled. "You forget, you're not the only one who can charm around here. I was taught by the society ladies how to deflect and charm when needed. I'm not concerned." Heath raised an eyebrow in her direction but said nothing.

He had her so entranced with the Davi case and what she read, Sam forgot all about her seduction plan. She sipped her iced tea, the cool liquid quenching her thirst as she thought of her next move. Deciding brazen hussy was the way, she ran a hand down her neck toward the top of her dress. Heath's eyes followed her hand, watching as she played with the v neck opening near her décolletage.

The movement caught Heath's attention, his face flushed and he took a large drink of tea before clearing his throat. "Nicholas Davi also happens to be the longtime friend of Rex." Heath leaned toward her. "I think he feels a certain obligation to Davi. It could be a repayment of a debt, a barter or true intention. I'm not sure which."

Sam mulled over his words as she took a bite of noodles. "Why would Rex assign you to lead the case? Why not handle it himself?" Sam covered her mouth, her eyes wide. "I didn't mean—"

"No," Heath held up a hand, "I wondered myself. My best guess is Rex desires distance from the case, for one reason or another. He feels compelled but won't involve himself in the case other than provide support and overall management." Heath paused and caught her gaze. "The case...it's mine."

"Yet?" Sam searched his face. She could tell something didn't sit right with him. She leaned forward, closing the distance between them until she could reach out and touch his hand.

Heath set down his silverware. "Claudia is the Firm's senior counsel. She's new but has an impeccable track record handling high-profile cases. Why not ask her?" Heath shrugged his shoulders. "Rex only speaks highly of her."

Sam shook her head. How she wished she had the answer for Heath. All she could do was encourage him to seek his answers within himself. "Does it matter?" Sam asked. "If Claudia was lead counsel on the case, would it matter to you?" Her question two-fold as her eyes implored him to answer.

A long pause stretched between them until Heath answered, "Yes, it does matter to me."

His words were true. A truth he may have just recognized in himself. Heath looked down at his plate, emotions flashing over his face as he avoided her eyes. Sam had so many more questions for him about the Davi case...and them. Where did she stand?

Realizing the conversation quickly took a sobering path, Sam had moments before Heath lost himself in his thoughts and excused himself to return to work. Before he left her alone, again.

"What do you think of the spicy noodles?" she said picking up the plate. "Would you like another helping?"

"Everything has been wonderful," Heath said though his mind appeared to be elsewhere. Her time was almost up. She had to act fast.

"I have something special planned for dessert." Sam picked up a half-eaten plate in front of Heath. "Let me just...Oh no!"The plate slipped out of her hand, the contents of the spicy noodles spilled from the plate onto Heath's crisp yellow button up shirt. Red sauce and noodles splattered the front of his shirt while a single noodle clung to his collar. Heath held his arms out to his side as he glanced down at the dripping mess covering him. His eyes wide and mouth frozen open.

Sam's hand covered her mouth, hiding the smile quickening at the corners of her mouth. Heath looked utterly defeated sitting there. "Oh no, I'm so sorry," she said as she tried her best to reclaim her composure. Sam used Heath's napkin to pick up the stray noodle hanging from his shirt. She continued to pat the front of his shirt in an effort to fix the mess. Her cheeks flushed as her hands brushed against the hardness of his chest. She remembered the strength coursing through his body and how she relished the feel of it against hers. Boldness overtook her by bounds, her determination a steadfast twin.

"This will never do," Sam said. She placed her left hand on her hip and motioned to Heath with her right hand. "You're going to have to take off your shirt so I can clean you up."

"I need to get back to the office," Heath said.

"You can't go back looking like that." Sam motioned for him to hurry up. Heath looked down again before his fingers started to unfasten the buttons.

"Don't worry, I have something else you can quickly put on." She stepped closer to Heath while her hands reached for the front of his shirt. "Here, let me help you."

A brazenness she never felt before overtook her, holding her hostage as she found herself willing to do just about anything to keep Heath home with her. She slid her hands over the fabric of his shirt, ignoring the sauce coating her hands. Heath stared at her, his mouth parted slightly. He dropped his hands from his shirt as her hands deftly worked the buttons. Sam licked her lips and stared at his mouth as she stood above him. She knew the softness of his lips and the warmth of his body pressed against hers.

His lips were so close to hers. She only needed to move a bit to kiss him. She leaned down and closed her eyes, moving her head towards his, eager to close the space between them with a kiss.

"What!" Sam cried, the heel of her stiletto slide in the puddle of noodles at her feet. Instead of the soft warmth of Heath's lips, Sam fell backwards, watching the distance between them grow. His face looked panicked and a hand shot out toward her.

Oh no, she thought, this wasn't a part of the plan.

Sam hit the floor with a jolt, her dress up hiked over her hips up to her waist, butt and hands covered in spicy red sauce and noodles.

She heard a hoarse noise coming from in front of her. Sam glanced up to see Heath cover his mouth. His attempt failed. Heath snorted, then doubled over at his waist, the loud bark of laughter escaped from behind his hands.

Sam sat there on the kitchen floor, covered in sticky sauce, and couldn't decide if she wanted to cuss or cry. Her plan was an utter disaster. Instead of feeling sorry for herself, she opted for laughter with Heath at the spectacle they made. "If only the media saw us now, what pictures they could run of the

Crenshaws, indecent and covered in spicy red sauce," she said.

Heath offered her his hand. "Are you okay?" Sam nodded, the only thing hurt was her pride. "I'm sorry but that was the funniest thing I have seen in a long time."

"We look like two suspects in a murder mystery show," Sam said. Except the only thing dead was the once smoldering desire between them.

The failed seduction caused enough distraction to put Heath's mind back on the Davi case. "I have to get that folder back to the office. I'll grab something else to wear on my way out," Heath said as he helped her stand up. "I'll be home late. Don't feel obligated to wait up for me."

Sam stood, Heath's words reverberating through her body. The remnants of their lunch on the floor, the failed seduction heavy in the air. Any thought of seduction quickly vanished with her misstep and subsequent tumble. Heath waved to her on his way out. All that remained to keep her company from her dark thoughts was the promise of cleaning and laundry.

Not sure what hurt more, her pride or her butt, she stood at the kitchen counter for a few minutes after Heath left to take in what had transpired moments before. Her failed seduction attempt left a mess of noodles and sticky sauce on the floor. Somehow the noodles and sauce landed in a splatter on the kitchen island.

Groaning, Sam picked up a roll of paper towels and set her intentions on clearing away the mess on her kitchen floor. She figured if she scrubbed hard enough at the stains, she could remove her embarrassment as well. As she scrubbed, she thought about Davi and his involvement with the missing college coed. Did she really find the body of Bailee Talson? And if so, what did her creepy visions and dream have to do with it?

Sam felt as lost as she had before. Nothing made sense.

Not Heath's case or the missing coed and especially not the visions she experienced of the dead woman. The uneasiness gnawed at her from before.

She had to do something.

What if the visions were a cry for help? Sam couldn't let this go. Throwing out the remnants of lunch, Sam knew she had to do more than wait for Heath to come around. If he was going to distance himself from her, let him. She knew the visions she saw were related to the missing coed. In that moment she recognized the truth of what she needed didn't involve waiting around. Sam needed the truth about the young woman in her visions and how she could be connected to the missing coed.

CHAPTER EIGHT

HEATH ENTERED the Firm lobby after his lunch with Sam and walked straight for his office. Maggie sat with her phone cradled against her ear while motioning Heath with her free hands. He ignored her eager wave. Stifling the guilt for brushing her off, he continued toward his office.

All he could think of was Sam. Anything and everyone else could wait.

Inside the privacy of his office, Heath shut the door behind him, throwing the Davi file on his desk. His phone followed with a thud. He poured a finger width of bourbon in a glass and threw back his head, swallowing the amber-colored liquid in one gulp. A warmth flowed through him as he set the glass down, poured another finger width, intending to savor this glass, much like the replay of his impromptu lunch date with Sam running through his head. Try as he might, he couldn't shake the image of her from his mind.

What was she thinking with her lunch date? He imagined she'd be in bed, agonizing over the dead body she found. Not seducing him while wearing his favorite dress which showed off every tantalizing inch of her curves.

The lovely lunch and increased intimacy from her

surprised him, leaving him caught unaware and unsure. It was the first time in months Sam showed him any interest beyond the chaste good morning kiss. Her intentions had been clear. Heath wanted her desperately. His fingers tightened on the glass. No matter how strong his desire for her. He had a commitment to the Davi case. He couldn't, wouldn't waste this opportunity.

Instead, he laughed at her as she fell on the floor, both of them covered in spicy red sauce. As beautiful as Sam looked wearing the dress he bought on their last vacation, he couldn't stay with her. Not today. Soon he would make things right like it was before between them.

A vibration from the desk jolted Heath out of his thoughts. He checked his phone, finding a curt and colorful text message from Rex, demanding an update to the Davi case. Heath sent Tyler a text along with a quick photo of the Davi file. He swallowed the remains of his bourbon, squared his shoulders and prepared for the meeting with Rex.

Heath entered Rex's office and found Nathan, Claudia and Tyler around the war table. He had the unmistakable feeling like something had transpired while he was at home. His heart quickened in anticipation of what he was about to hear. He inhaled deeply through his nose. Slow, slower, until he reached his desired mental state. Until he was calm, cool.

Heath dared a covert glance at Tyler, catching his attention. He gave Heath a small nod in return. Satisfied, Heath took his seat at the head of the war room table, prepared to handle the next challenge in the Davi case.

Rex faced the window behind his desk, his back positioned toward the war table. Heath could sense the stiffness to Rex's posture, his attention focused on something beyond this room. Heath wondered again what had Rex preoccupied when his deep voice broke through the silence.

"The coroner notified me an hour ago. The police found a body in a field a few a miles from the train station. The deceased was a young woman identified as Bailee Talson." The silence in the room was palpable. Rex turned toward the team, his face weary yet determined. He didn't take the possible trial and conviction of a client lightly, especially a longtime friend. "A reliable source also informed me District Attorney Fabien is preparing a discovery concerning the arraignment of Nicholas Davi on charges related to the disappearance of Bailee Talson."

"How?" Nathan said, breaking the somber atmosphere as he voiced the team's joint concern over the bombshell Rex dropped. "The charges are farfetched at best. Doesn't Davi have an alibi for the evening Bailee Talson went missing?" Nathan glanced toward Heath.

"The only way the DA would pursue the charges is if she sensed a weakness in Davi's case or if she had dirt on him. She wants him paranoid." Heath said.

Claudia nodded. "She thinks he'll talk, spill his contacts. Maybe catch him up in illegal trading else in the process," she said.

Heath thought it over. "It's a possibility. Use Davi's influence, pressure the right people. Does he have affiliates with ties to something bigger than the current case?" Heath glanced around the room at his colleagues. Claudia looked at her hands clasped in her lap, her eyes avoiding his gaze. Nathan shrugged and Tyler shook his head. No one in the room voiced concerns.

"Let's reexamine everyone Nicholas Davi is involved with and bring Davi in for questioning along with his alibi." Heath thought he saw a shadow of strong emotion pass over Rex's face. There was a conversation he had delayed. What was it with this case that had Rex out of character. He seemed paranoid. What was Rex hiding about his friendship with Davi and the other secrets he kept. "How much time do we have?"

"Days."

The door behind them opened, interrupting him and the

meeting. Heath turned toward the intruder. All employees at the Firm understood a few explicit rules, one of them having just been broken. Do not disturb the team when the team is behind closed doors at the war table. All questions, concerns including death or dismemberment were directed to Maggie.

Heath recognized the intruder from his run-in earlier. The intern, Amanda, stumbled into the room. She had an embarrassed look on her face, her cheeks turning a brilliant shade of pink.

"I'm, I'm so sorry," she stammered. She backed out of the room into Maggie. Heath caught the stern expression Maggie directed toward him and mouthed, *Later*, as she escorted Amanda out of the room. He suppressed a shudder at the thought of what Maggie had in store for Amanda…and him.

The interruption allowed for a moment of reprieve. The air had cleared and was no longer thick with the unspoken tension of the team. Heath seized the opportunity, refocusing the team and proving his ability as a leader.

"Tyler," Heath said as he turned toward him, "bring up the interconnections between Nicholas Davi and his business associates. I need the team to visualize the connections between all individuals involved." Heath's shoulders tensed in anticipation, waiting in suspense to discover if Tyler recovered sufficient data to reconstruct the files. Or, discover if he was about to make a fool of himself in front of his mentor and team.

Tyler straightened up at the mention of his name. With a few clicks, the LED screen lit up, the flow chart he designed moments before displayed for the team. Heath let out his breath, deciding he owed Tyler a drink for his quick work.

"The DA could pressure Davi to gain access to any one of these individuals." Heath stood to move closer to the screen. Names and photographs flashed across the screen. Rex's face was the last of the connections to fill the screen. Heath examined the names and faces, trying to draw connections between which individuals the DA may want to use Davi to get to.

"There are so many," Claudia said in awe. "Men and women from all over the Charleston area. How can we accomplish this with only a few day's time?"

She was right. Heath needed a quick way to eliminate individuals outside the DA's scope.

"Tyler, bring up Bailee Talson's family, friends and known acquaintances in a split screen." The data was collected from the young woman's laptop after her disappearance and volunteered by Theo. A connection Heath would no longer have access to as a defense attorney. He would have to use his own resources and wait until the DA presented any reports, statements or evidence in a discovery to him.

"I can do better than that," Tyler said as his fingers clicked against the keyboard of his laptop. The screen split in half, one side for Davi, the other for Bailee Talson. Then, one by one, the faces and names between the two halves merged into one, until only a few photographs of individuals remained, a shared connection between Nicholas Davi and Bailee Talson. Heath grinned at Tyler.

"Our next step is to eliminate these connections," Heath said to the team as they viewed the remaining photographs. With Tyler's expertise, they eliminated all connections except for a handful they could question in a day or two.

"How is a college coed from a state school related to some of these businessmen?" Claudia asked.

"Maybe she babysat for the families," Nathan suggested. "It's not an unusual side hustle for a college coed. There are plenty of families between here and Charleston eager for a responsible sitter."

"It's a possibility," Heath said. "We'll eliminate each thread individually. We can't risk making a mistake. Heath caught the eye of Rex as the other man walked back toward the window, his hands in his pant pockets. Heath had the feeling Rex knew more than he was letting on. Heath shook away the thought and turned back to the team, awareness of his own secret shared with Sam lashing at his conscious. "Before we begin interviewing, there is pertinent information to the case I need to share."

THE TEAM HANDLED the news about Sam and her discovery of Bailee Talson's body as eloquently and with as much empathy as possible. Heath was grateful and almost sorry he made them work through the remainder of the afternoon to eliminate suspects. Rex excused himself early, saying he needed to prepare for a charity gala that evening. Heath excused the team not long after. It would do them no good being sleep deprived so early in the case.

The walk to his office was filled with shame and chastised thoughts for not checking in with Sam. She had been through hell with the discovery of the body. Heath wondered at the sudden change in her demeanor that afternoon. She'd kept to herself and rarely initiated conversation, let alone intimacy, in months. Heath missed the old Sam, her homecooked meals and the attention she would lavish on him. Had he lost his chance of bringing her back for good? He shook his head, refusing to believe Sam was lost to him. He glimpsed a brief spark of who she used to be during lunch.

His concern over his carelessness at lunch and fear he may have extinguished the small spark, his abrupt departure combined with her finding the body of Bailee Talson wracked guilt through him. Heath sighed, how could he be so careless? His behavior failed to reflect the person he was. Heath knew he was a better husband than what he had proven himself to be.

His decision made, Heath dialed Sam's number, needing

to hear her voice and more importantly, make amends for his actions today.

"You've reached Samantha Crenshaw, I'm not available to take your call. Please leave a message after the tone." Heath pressed the end call button, not bothering to leave a message. He'd send her a text to call him and call her again later.

Heath glanced up from his phone to find Maggie waiting for him. She leaned against the wall beside his office door, her lips pursed and arms crossed over her chest. She looked like an angry pixie. Heath smothered his laugh and slowed his stride, not wanting to anger this pixie.

He forced a smile and held his hands up in a faux surrender. "Maggie," Heath said, "you know I would never knowingly ignore you. I was in a rush so I could review the Davi case before meeting with Rex and the team."

Maggie silently stared him down, her eyes boring imaginary holes in Heath's head. With a sigh, she rolled her eyes and stepped aside so he could unlock his office door. Holding the door open for her to enter, Maggie walked into the office with Heath close behind. He reached for the light switch to flip on the light and a brightness flashed before the room went dark.

"Strange, I just changed the light bulb last week," Heath said. He shrugged and turned on the freestanding lamp in the corner as well as his desk lamp, the soft light filled the room, chasing out the darkness.

"Listen, I get right now is a bad time with everyone working overtime on the Davi case but…" Maggie paused and sat in the armchair near his desk. "You're the only one I trust to handle this issue. I wanted to talk with you before Rex's meeting."

"Seeing you caught me unaware, I suppose I could grant you my undivided attention. What's going on?" Heath asked as he glanced at his phone. No missed calls or texts from Sam.

Maggie inhaled deeply then released her held breath

slowly before easing herself out of the chair. She stood and paced around the small room, Heath watching her nervous movements. "I'm not sure how to say this without coming across the wrong way, so I'm just going to say it."

"Maggie, when have you been anything but brutally honest with me?" Heath raised his eyebrows, waiting to see if she took his bait. She didn't even have the audacity to look shocked at his admission, or give him a dirty look. Rather her razor focus was turned inward at the nagging issue she couldn't say.

"I don't like the new intern, Amanda," Maggie blurted out. She spun around in a circle, placing her hands over her heart. "There I said it. I feel so much better." Maggie sagged back into the armchair, the weight of her thoughts no longer an anchor pulling her down.

Heath wasn't surprised by her admission, though Maggie seemed to be. She managed the Firm with a strong hand and was well liked with staff and clients, except the interns. Maggie held the interns to a high standard and most respected her. Even so, each semester she found one intern who was the Firm antagonist in her mind.

Heath shrugged at her admission, as if to cast it aside with other petty dramas. "It's not unusual for you to find someone you don't get on with from the new class of interns." Heath leaned against the front of his desk. "Has it even been a week since the beginning of their assignment?"

Maggie gave Heath a sheepish look then darted her eyes and when she finally spoke her voice was soft. "Well, not exactly, but can you believe she barged into Rex's office! During a meeting at the war table! Only I'm allowed to do that!" Maggie threw her hands up in the air. "She waltzed right in as if she had some big news. I saw her. She didn't even hesitate to knock. She just brazenly turned the doorknob like she had a right to be in the room with the team."

Heath rubbed at the stubble on his jaw and leveled his

eyes at Maggie. She was pissed. He knew from past experience this incident would blow over in a week. Maggie and Amanda would be quick friends before the end of the semester, all cheek kisses and hugs on her last day. "While I will admit Amanda's...tactics weren't the most diplomatic way to impress Rex, it's not the first time this happened with an intern. Do you remember Anthony?" It wasn't unusual for interns to be a bit green, they were interns after all. They were here to learn.

Maggie rolled her eyes and crossed her arms over her chest then glanced at Heath. "Anthony wasn't trying to barge in during a war room session concerning one of our most high-profile clients."

"True," Heath said. "Make a deal with me. Give Amanda another week or so to assimilate with our work culture here." Heath sat beside Maggie. "If you still feel the same way then we can meet next week. I'll decide if I need to speak with her or worst case, broach the topic with Rex, okay?"

Maggie harrumphed, then a smile peaked through her disgruntled face. "Fine, but I'm holding you to this."

Heath laughed. "I know you will."

"Theo told me you reached out to him about the Bailee Talson case," Maggie said, changing the subject. She wrapped her arms around herself. "It's not normal for a young woman to go missing from around here. Midnight Harbor is a safe town. I know the tourists can cause trouble but...and poor Sam to see that!"

Maggie and Theo were born in Midnight Harbor, had lived here their entire lives. If Heath felt unsettled then Maggie must be shocked. And as a single woman, she was likely concerned for her safety.

"You have the best detective in the county as your brother. He'll find Bailee's killer and make sure you're safe," Heath reassured her. "Take the same precautions you normally do."

"You're right. I can't help feel sad for her and what her

parents must be going through," Maggie's voice quivered. She cleared her throat then stood and walked to the door, turning toward Heath before she left. "Go home, Heath. You have someone waiting for you. Someone who needs you."

"I will. Promise. I have a few things to do before I leave." Heath glanced at his phone again, knowing it would only be a few minutes to write his wrap up and secure his office.

"That's the third time you checked your phone since we sat down to talk. There is nothing you can do that can't wait for tomorrow."

Heath looked back to her and smiled. "Bye, Maggie."

"Have a good night, Heath." She left the door open as she exited. Heath sat at his desk and leaned back in his chair, staring at the open door. Maggie sensed something amiss between him and Sam. If Maggie noticed, he wondered who else did.

Heath needed to rekindle his relationship with Sam. He wondered when his life had diverted from the path he first envisioned many years before. He felt torn between Sam and his commitment to the Firm and his clients.

Understanding washed over him. Heath needed to clear Davi's name and help Theo and the police department find the true culprit responsible for the disappearance of Bailee Talson, then he could focus on mending the broken pieces in his marriage. He wasn't sure he could withstand not receiving new updates from Theo on the status of the Bailee Talson investigation. He would have to mount his own investigation.

Heath rubbed his jaw, thinking of the balance he needed for both this case and his strained marriage. Sacrifices would need to be made because Heath refused to fail. He had to make it work, otherwise the last time he saw Sam could be when she walked out of his life for good.

CHAPTER NINE

HAVING DECIDED to take matters into her own hands after Heath left, Sam set out to discover what she could about Bailee Talson. Well, that's what her intent was. Only now she cradled a half empty pint of cookies and cream ice cream on her lap, a spoon balanced in her hand as the replay of DA Fabian's news conference aired, announcing the body of Bailee Talson had been discovered.

The body she discovered.

The body of a young woman who went missing over a week ago. Sam couldn't wrap her head around the notion that the body she found was of the missing coed. She spoke with the woman! Drove her in her car! How could it be possible if the woman was missing…or worse, dead?

Like much of Midnight Harbor, Sam wondered how the young woman ended up dead in the field in a tourist town nearly free from violent crime. Sure, petty crime existed but kidnapping and murder? Not in Midnight Harbor.

She thought of Bailee and the blueish pallor of her skin, of the terror she experienced when she stumbled upon the young woman. Since that night, Sam suspected more than an accident occurred. There were too many details which were more than coincidence and her thoughts leading her to these conclusions were more. It was a feeling, an instinct she felt within her. Maybe it was that knowledge that helped her fight through the horrors of what she experienced. Sam recounted her conversation with Bailee for the hundredth time. She was heading for her parents' house, and Sam saw her exit the car and walk to the train station ticket booth. How did the young woman end up back on that country road, not far from where Sam initially picked her up?

Thinking of Bailee wouldn't be such a problem if what Sam observed since then had not shook her belief system so much that she was forced to question what was real. The visions she observed of the ghostly young woman were real, she knew it with all of her being. Not delusions or paranoia. But, why were the visions happening to her and what significance did they have?

She couldn't shake the feeling Bailee Talson and the visions were connected. If Sam could help find Bailee's killer, she was convinced her visions would cease as well.

She needed more information than what she had available if she wanted to assist in finding Bailee's killer. She owed it to the young woman.

Sam dropped the spoon in the ice cream pint and rested the container on the coffee table. She picked up her tablet and perused the internet, searching through new articles from all over the state about Bailee when the chime of the doorbell rang. She groaned. Josie would not let her rest with the Kerri Reid invitation. Sam didn't want to meet with anyone, especially if she would be forced to make small talk about party planning. There was so much more going on that needed her focus and time.

Sam answered the door. Theo Hart stood on the other side.

"Good afternoon, Sam."

"Hi, Theo. How may I help you?"

"I'm sorry to bother you." Theo managed to give her a sheepish smile, his police badge hung around his neck on a chain. "Do you mind if I come in?"

Sam's stomach hit her toes, rolling over the entire way down. *No, not now, not me.* If she wasn't holding on to the doorframe, she was certain her knees would've buckled.

"Um, certainly, uh please, come in," Sam said. She held open the door for Theo to enter. This was the last thing Sam was expecting.

"If you would like, you can have a seat in the living room." Sam grabbed the ice cream pint off the coffee table as she walked past, turning off the television. "I'll fix us something to drink," Sam called as she scuttled into the kitchen. She quickly pulled down two glasses and arranged them on a serving platter with the pitcher of iced tea. She dumped a few cookies on the platter for good measure. The tray rattled but try as she might, she couldn't stop her hands from shaking.

Deep within her heart, Sam knew it had only been a matter of time before Theo or another detective wanted to speak with her about finding Bailee's body. She didn't do anything wrong. So why was she suddenly so nervous?

"I'm sorry to keep you waiting." Sam set the tray on the coffee table and poured them both a tall glass of tea. Theo graciously accepted the glass from her.

"Thank you. I apologize I didn't call before I came over." Theo looked slightly disheveled. Sam watched him run a hand through his wavy blond hair, the same color as Maggie's.

"It's okay," Sam said. "You must be busy right now with everything that is going on in town. I hope I can help you."

Theo sighed. "You have no idea." Theo turned his green eyes on her. "Well maybe you do. I've been working on what information I can find about the body you found." Theo placed his glass on the table and turned toward Sam, his forearms resting on his knees. "I expect the last few days have been trying for you. I don't want to bring up the experience unnecessarily. I'm here because I need to know how it was you came about finding Bailee Talson in that field?" His face serious, he asked, "What were you doing out there alone, Sam?"

Sam felt the color drain from her face. She focused on the drink in her hand, afraid to meet Theo's eyes. How much she could divulge to Theo without sounding like she needed to be admitted to the psych ward. Who tells police officers they picked up hitchhiking ghosts? Not her.

Theo waited silently for her answer.

There was no way she could lie to this man. Theo was a member of the police force and brother to her friend and husband's colleague, Maggie. A lie, even if for her protection, would betray her relationship with his family and discredit her integrity. However, she didn't have to tell him all the details. She doubted he would believe her anyway if she told him she saw Bailee's ghost.

He would likely convince Heath she was experiencing PTSD and needed a doctor who would prescribe her more medications to numb her into oblivion. Once, that's what she'd wanted. Now though, there was no way she would allow herself to be a passenger in her life. She wanted to, no *needed* to help Bailee.

Sam looked up at him, her brown eyes connected with his. "I hope I can help you. I was traveling the back roads home from town when I noticed tire tracks veered off the road. I stopped to check when the next thing I knew I was following tracks into the field."

Theo pulled out a notepad from his back pocket. "What time was it when you stopped?"

SAM SPENT another two hours answering queries Theo had concerning the disappearance and murder of Bailee Talson. He paced around the room and asked her a variety of the same questions, each worded differently. She knew it was to be thorough but it felt more like he hoped to could catch her in a lie.

By the end of it all, Sam was exhausted. She saw Theo out with a promise she would call him if she remembered anything else from that night.

All she wanted to do was take a few minutes to rest and research a few more news articles so she could begin her own investigation. She felt nervous and uneasy, never knowing when she would have another panic attack or have another vision. Sam noticed her panic attacks had a pattern, occurring frequently before she experienced a vision.

Sam pondered the possibilities when her phone rang. She looked at the caller ID, the phone number unrecognized. She debated whether or not she should answer the phone, finally deciding it was better to just answer the call. What if it was Heath calling from another phone?

"Hello?"

"Hi, is this Sam Crenshaw?" the feminine voice asked.

"Yes, it is. May I ask who is calling?"

"Sam, darling, this is Kerri Reid. We met the other night at my book signing."

Sam stood up from her seat on the sofa in surprise. "Oh, Kerri, I wasn't expecting to hear from you. What can I help you with?"

"You mentioned you know a lot of history about Midnight Harbor. I'm interested in a small town like this to use as the setting for my next project. I hoped you could meet with me this evening to discuss more about the history of Midnight Harbor and any points of interest I could use as inspiration? I know it's last minute but I don't have much time here before I leave to go back on tour. My stop in Midnight Harbor has been a marvelous inspiration for a photo series."

"That would be great," Sam said, grimacing at her eagerness. Who was she? Wasn't Josie the one fawning over Kerri? The last thing she wanted to do was meet with Kerri after the interrogation she went through. Despite her experience, or maybe it was the polite upbringing instilled in her and further experience as a society wife, Sam couldn't brush off the woman on the other end of the phone. Heath would be working anyway. It's not like he would be home to have dinner with her. She wasn't sure she was ready to face him after today's lunch fiasco.

"Wonderful! Any suggestions on where we could meet?"

Sam quickly gave Kerri the directions to one of her favorite local cafés downtown. The location would be a great backdrop for Kerri to see the touristy parts of Midnight Harbor. Sam ended the call with Kerri to quickly prep herself for their meeting. Her phone call to Josie could wait until later.

They met at Café Luna's, a quaint café located not far from the main shopping district and one of Sam's favorite hidden secrets. She noticed Kerri dressed effortlessly in a soft yellow belted jumpsuit with an oversized straw brimmed hat. Tortoiseshell sunglasses sat on the bridge of her pert nose. If Kerri was trying not to garner attention, she was doing a poor job. She looked every bit the glamorous star as she lounged, waiting for Sam.

"This is such a darling place. I'm so glad you could meet me," Kerri said as she extended her hands to Sam in greeting. Sam gently took the other woman's hands in hers. Kerri gave her a friendly squeeze.

"I'm glad to hear you like it. I've been coming here since I attended Charleston College," Sam said, taking the seat across from Kerri.

"Wonderful! What else can you tell me about Midnight Harbor? Any local legends or famous villagers I can use as an inspiration for my story? I want it to be as realistic as possible."

Sam smiled at Kerri's enthusiasm. She loved to share the history of her town. "Midnight Harbor is what you would expect from any seaside town on the outskirts of a major port city. Our history is intertwined with the sea and rumors say we have a few local legends who lend a mysterious, magical atmosphere."

"Oh, how lovely. I can just picture the women patiently waiting on shore for their husbands to return from their deep sea adventures," Kerri said, a dreamy look on her face, her hands fluttering in the air.

Sam smiled at the other woman's pageantry. "The city was founded in 1670 around the same time as Charleston. The founder came from a large family of cattle farmers. The family later moved the operations to Kiawah Island. Pirates invaded Kiawah Island once they heard of the wealthy residents."

She paused for dramatic effect, finding her past audiences loved this next part and delighted Kerri seemed to as well. "Legend has it the pirate captain fell in love with the youngest daughter of a local wealthy family. The father disapproved of the man and vowed to run him off the land. Now, the youngest daughter was headstrong and refused to obey her father's demands. She ran away with her captain, evading her family the entire way. The eloped while on the run and their descendants founded Midnight Harbor. The city grew as more people sought a life away from the major city in Charleston."

"How romantic," Kerri exclaimed as she placed her hands over her heart. "Sam, I think you just gave me an idea for my next project. The Pirate and the Princess!"

"You're welcome. I love reading and have a passion for history, especially of Midnight Harbor and her secrets."

Sam felt Kerri's gray eyes focus on her, as if she could lay her heart bare and Sam shifted in her seat, uncomfortable with the fierce scrutiny from Kerri. She had a feeling like Kerri knew exactly what transpired this morning with Theo. Would it feel like this all day, like a bullseye marked Sam's forehead, telling all to look at the person who found Bailee's body?

As if Kerri could hone in on that bullseye, she brought up the current topic around town.

"It's such a shame about the young woman they found on the side of the road." Kerri *tsk*ed. She pulled out a little pot from her purse and spooned some of the substance into her cup of tea. Sam watched as she swirled the liquid around with a teaspoon. Kerri seemed to notice Sam's insightful gaze on her. "Manuka Honey, I'm quite spoiled when it comes to how I like my tea," Kerri said with a slight smile. She placed the honey pot back in her purse. "I can only use a certain brand from Australia. I carry a small jar with me no matter where I go."

Sam offered Kerri a smile, afraid the rising panic she forced down would cause the other woman to notice something unusual. "Horrible things like what transpired recently don't usually happen in Midnight Harbor," Sam said to bring the topic of conversation back around to Kerri's question. "Naturally we have our petty crime and disturbances. Anything worse than that is usually due to people from the surrounding areas passing through town or a college kid getting rowdy. Theo Hart is helping with the investigation and he is the best Midnight Harbor has to offer."

"I wouldn't think that would be the way in Midnight Harbor. Life feels idyllic here. Simple. As I mentioned earlier, this would be the perfect spot for my next project."

"I'm glad I was able to help you," Sam said.

"I would love to be able to reach out to you with any additional questions," Kerri said. She picked up her phone. "I would pay you of course," Kerri continued. "I know, you could serve as my official consultant. I would even give you credit in the acknowledgments. What do you think, is that something that would interest you?"

Was Kerri Reid offering her a job? Sam couldn't believe it. She didn't know what to say. "Yes, that would be wonderful," Sam said as she practically stumbled over the words. She couldn't believe she accepted a job. Was she ready for this new step?

"Great! Lilliana will be in touch to set up our next meeting. It was a pleasure meeting with you again. I'm happy to have someone with your knowledge on my team," Kerri said, extending her hand.

Sam shook the woman's hand. "Thank you for the opportunity."

Kerri smiled and waved before turning to embrace the wake of women having gathered outside the café. Sam watched Kerri laugh and sign autographs. Sam smiled to herself then began to laugh. She couldn't believe her luck, within the span of a day she became a potential murder suspect and employed by a B-List actress. Her smile faltered as she thought about Heath. How was she going to break the news to him?

As Sam prepared to leave, she thought back to Bailee. Although Theo didn't say it outright, Sam knew she was a person of interest in the murder of Bailee Talson. What happened that night she saw Bailee was not her fault. But she had to be strong if she wanted to help find Bailee's killer. Sam knew exactly what she needed to do to get her answer.

SAM PARKED in the spot closest to the ticket counter at the Midnight Harbor Train Station. It wasn't a busy metro like some of the major cities nearby. The main source of travel were the local college students, tourists and locals wanting to travel into surrounding cities. It was enough to keep the local station busy. The brick building had a small waiting area near the ticket booth.

Sam approached the ticket booth, debating how to politely broach the subject of Bailee's disappearance. Luckily, Sam found the two attendants huddled around a small television in the ticketing booth, the local news station playing.

"Excuse me?" Sam said to catch their attention.

"Yes, I'm so sorry, miss." The attendant fluttered her hands and met Sam at the ticket window. "How may I help you, dear?" The attendant appeared to be in her fifties, salt and pepper streaks in her hair with laugh lines around her eyes. Sam felt a kindness surrounding this woman almost like she could spill her secrets to her over tea.

"My…friend traveled through here and lost her…uh." Sam stumbled over what she could pass off as a sentimental object when an image of a watch appeared in her mind. "A watch. A gold watch with tiny diamonds around the clock face. It's very sentimental. I hoped you could look in your lost and found for it?" Sam said. She wasn't sure how she suddenly thought of the watch but she hoped her excuse was sufficient. She was never very good at lying on the spot and it was the best she could think of at the moment. She rubbed her forehead as a pain shifted behind her eyes, a sign of a pending migraine.

"We do keep a lost and found for travelers but I don't recall seeing a gold watch turned in recently." The attendant flipped open a calendar. "About how long ago was she here?"

"Oh, it was only a few nights ago," Sam said with a wave of her hand, the pain in her head subsiding.

"Let me check for you." The attendant walked away into

the back room. Sam guessed the train company kept the lost items in the back. A few minutes later the attendant returned, her head shaking and hands empty.

"Sorry, dear. I couldn't find a watch in the lost and found area. Are you sure she lost it here?"

Sam frowned unable to hide her displeasure. She turned away then, she had an idea. "Do you know who worked the ticket booth a few nights ago? Maybe I could ask them if anyone turned something in?"

"Robin here," the attendant motioned her head toward the other employee, "was the one working the last few nights." She turned back to Sam and whispered, "You have to forgive her. Robin helped that poor dead woman purchase a ticket."

Sam's eyes widened at the information. "You mean Bailee Talson? When did you last see her?" Sam's words came out in a rush of breath.

The young woman, Robin, turned to Sam, her eyes rimmed in red. "I don't exactly remember the time. It was over a week ago. She was alone and purchased a one-way ticket for Charleston. I know it was her because I remember looking at her state ID." The young woman sniffed then wiped her nose with a tissue. "I saw her sit over there under the portico to wait for the train to arrive. Another woman arrived and sat near her. People buy tickets online all the time. I thought nothing of it. Next time I looked over the two women were gone. I assumed they both boarded the train."

Sam swallowed. Over a week ago? She forced the next words out. "Did you catch the other woman's name or what she looked like?"

Another sniff as the attendant rubbed her nose. "It's like I told that detective. I didn't get a good look at her. I think she had blonde or brown hair, I'm not sure. I remembered she had her hair tied up in a scarf and wore a red hip length jacket. She looked well put together. I didn't think anything of it. The two women talked for a time before I had to start my countdown of the daily sales. By the time I looked around again, both women were gone. I'm sorry I'm not much help."

Sam nodded as she took in the information. "It's not your fault." Her heart hurt for this woman who clearly was upset with the news of Bailee's death. Sam grabbed Robin's hand and squeezed. "You did nothing wrong. Thank you for your help with my friend's watch." She hoped her words gave some sort of comfort.

Sam turned to leave but before she left one thing tugged at her mind. She turned around. "You said Bailee used a state ID to purchase her ticket? Don't you mean she used her driver's license?"

"No, it was a state ID, I'm certain. She said that's why she needed to take the train; she didn't drive," Robin explained.

Thanking the women again for their help, Sam declined to leave her number in the event the watch showed up. She didn't need Theo finding out she had been at the train station after their talk.

Sam walked back to her car with a pit in her stomach. The dead woman she found was Bailee Talson, a woman missing for over a week. Which meant what? That Sam picked up a ghost on the side of the road? She scoffed at the idea. No, the woman she picked up had to be someone different. But she knew that was wrong. The women looked identical.

Pushing aside the crazy notion of ghosts, Sam decided she would approach the problem as if she picked up a real woman that night. Why would Bailee lie about driving? She mentioned her car had broken down when Sam picked her up. The ticket attendant swore Bailee only had a state ID and not a driver's license. What could be the cause of the lie? Was she embarrassed about being found on the side of the road? And who was the woman the attendant saw Bailee speaking with?

Sam got in her car and drove away hoping she would be able to let the questions that clouded her mind go. Instead, the longer she drove, the more the answers to the questions haunted her.

It wasn't until Sam slowed down near the yellow-and-black-taped site did she realize what she was doing. Sam looked around to find herself on the same back country road she first met Bailee Talson. Why did everything come back to Bailee and this road? It was almost as if the same force from that night called to her, a magnet pulling her in this direction. She couldn't explain it if she tried and wasn't sure she wanted the answer.

The young woman was unknown to her before that evening she found Bailee on the side of the road. Sure, she felt guilt for what happened to the woman. But, who wouldn't? How was Sam to know after she dropped her off that something horrible would happen? Or was it something horrible happened before Sam picked her up? The only fact she could understand was the death of the woman wasn't her fault. Yet, the guilty feeling remained.

Sam slowed her car around the mile marker she thought she first saw Bailee. She pulled over to the side of road to sit while she cleared her mind in order to better remember the events of the night. Bailee mentioned she had car trouble when Sam picked her up.

Sam put on her four-way blinkers and climbed out of the car to check the side of the road for any signs of disturbance. There was still enough light outside she didn't need to worry about a flashlight. She quickly saw ahead the spot where she pulled off the side of the road to pick up Bailee. The tire marks she made in the grass when she screeched to a stop had dug up some of the tufts of grass that remained on the roadside.

Bailee mentioned she had car trouble about a half mile up the road. As Sam thought back to that night, she remembered leaving dinner with Heath. She was upset he left early for work. Despite her distracted state, she never recalled driving past another car on this road, let alone seeing one parked on the side of the road. She was too concerned with Bailee and too spooked from almost hitting her that she must have ignored the car...or the lack of a car.

She strode along the side of the road toward the direction she thought Bailee would have experienced car problems based on her response. Sam didn't see anything unusual from her last time here. She felt like she was being pulled around in a never-ending circle. She felt responsible for Bailee's disappearance but knew she did nothing wrong. Yet, here was that internal and external tug of war over her emotions. She felt compelled yet had no idea why or reason to believe she had any power to help Bailee. Why was she being singled out with these feelings?

Sam trudged back toward her car, determined to avoid this road at all costs in the future. Every time she drove by, she would think of Bailee and her inability to be of any help. She had to let it go.

She had made progress on getting back to her old life. Soon, she would talk to Betty about rejoining the auxiliary club, even if it wasn't as chairwoman. This experience provoked Sam to get back to her normal routines and life. If she allowed herself to spend too much time thinking about Bailee, she was afraid she wouldn't be able to stop.

She wasn't capable of investigating a murder. She was a fool to think she could ever do anything to help the woman.

Sam turned on the engine and pulled out on the road. She rolled down the windows, the warm breeze blowing through her hair. She reached the intersection near the train station, when her eyes were drawn to a figure standing in the middle of the waiting area.

A young blonde-haired woman stood off to the center of the outdoor waiting area wearing cut off shorts and plain white shirt. Sam did a double take. *Bailee Talson*? Sam shut her eyes and shook her head as if the movement would clear her vision. She opened her eyes to see the figure still there.

The warm breeze turned ice cold as the warmth faded and goosebumps rose all over her arms as the temperature suddenly dipped from warm to freezing cold. The music playing screeched to a stop, the sound like nails on a chalkboard. Sam held her foot on the brake and covered her ears with her hands. The screech turned into a piercing noise.

Her ears rang and she didn't know what to do. She silently wished the noise away.

Silence. The noise stopped.

Sam opened her eyes and saw the radio station tuner on her LED screen scrolling through a series of stations before settling on station 120.0.

A scratching noise played.

"Help me," a voice whispered through the speakers. "Help me."

Sam uncovered her ears and recognized the voice as feminine, muffled as if the person was speaking under water. The person sounded far away and despite that, Sam heard the plea and knew exactly who the voice belonged to. Sam shut her eyes and covered her mouth with her hand, willing herself not to scream or get sick. She reached her hand out, desperate to turn off the speaker and silence the haunting voice. Her hand a finger's width away, the radio went silent and the temperature rose, a warm breeze circulated once more through her car windows. Sam gasped, realizing she held her breath the entire time. She opened her eyes to look at the train station again.

The figure was gone.

She blinked and forced herself to drive the rest of the way home with the radio off and her body trembling. This was the third time she saw Bailee Talson in a vision. The young woman was dead yet Sam still saw her standing in the center of the waiting area of the train station.

She heard the young woman pleading for help.

Sam was afraid something was seriously wrong with her. That or someone was playing a sick trick on her. She knew for certain she had to get to the bottom of it before she lost her mind.

CHAPTER TEN

SAM SAT in her parked car outside the restaurant, contemplating whether she should continue with what she was about to do. The images of Bailee laying cold, abandoned in the grass field forced its way into her mind. As best she could, Sam kept the worst feelings and images at bay. She wouldn't let this go until she discovered what happened to Bailee. But she knew she was in over her head.

She shook her head. What was she thinking? She wasn't an attorney or law enforcement, she had no specialized education or training. Despite those odds, a compulsion pushed her to help the dead woman. What did she posses?

Intuition.

That part of her she always held back or aside. That part of her, who Sam was afraid of. She could it do. With her commendable knowledge of Midnight Harbor and the people living here.

In her town.

The notion a young woman was killed in her town? Midnight Harbor. No, she couldn't let it go. Not with Sadie ready to graduate.

Buzzing with an energy she had missed these past few

months Sam made up her mind. A part of her broke inside when she saw the body of the young woman laying the grass and was rebuilt into something else. Was it the bitter realization her life was cut short? That she would never feel the love of a friend or her parents again? Sam still had those opportunities before her that were stolen from the other woman. She didn't want to squander any more time. Sam doubted she could be the perfect imitation of a society wife she was before, but she no longer had to be the scared and lonely woman she was yesterday.

With her new realization about her life, Sam did something she just faked for the past few months. She showered, brushed her hair, did her makeup and took time to pick an outfit that was something other than leggings and a hoodie.

Sam contemplated calling Josie to go shopping, or the ladies' auxiliary to see when the next meeting was being held. Deep within herself, she knew the energy that compelled her to break out of her depression was meant for a purpose far more important than shopping or gossip. For the first time in months she felt like she mattered, that she could contribute to something with a purpose greater than the next dinner party.

She thought of Heath and how much she missed him. He always knew what to say to her. Recently though, thoughts of him were a painful mix of loss and desire, so she placed those away too.

Sam stared at the picture of Bailee saved on her tablet, downloaded from the Davi files she copied from Heath's laptop while he slept. Sam silently thanked Heath for his meticulous record keeping. Everything she needed to be up to date on the Bailee Talson case was on his laptop including the recent photograph of the young woman.

She read Heath's files the day of her failed seduction attempt but never realized who Bailee was at the time. If she did, she would've asked Heath more.

Memories from the past skittered across her mind as she

remembered the restaurant from when she frequented along with the ladies from the auxiliary club. The restaurant used to be a frequent meeting spot for the woman and other organizations to brunch and gossip while brainstorming the next fundraiser.

Unsure if the women still brunched here on occasion, Sam filed that thought away too. It didn't matter if she ran into someone she knew, she was here for Bailee, not a silly fundraiser for additional rose bushes outside the town square.

Sam smiled. How silly she was back then. She wanted to be the epitome of perfection — the perfect host, perfect employee, perfect wife, hopefully perfect mother.

The last thought gave her pause but she refused to fall prey to the monster of despair. She needed to fight to stay out of its grasp of numbness, otherwise she would lose herself to its endless pit of darkness. She focused on the restaurant, grounding herself in the present and her new reality.

The restaurant hadn't changed much in appearance despite the new ownership. The white brick exterior remained the same with a quaint black door and trim. The patio overflowed with greenery and flowers, which beckoned her like an old lover, the sweet smell of blossoms filling the air.

A young hostess greeted Sam at the entrance and seated her at a table on the patio. She sat at the bistro table near the waist high black iron fence, a small topiary disguised her from the view from the street. She admired the effort the owners put into retaining the charm she remembered.

"Hey, sugar, it's been ages since I last saw you!"

Sam turned to a voice coming from behind her and broke into a smile. Willa, her favorite waitress and cook, walked toward her, the woman's arms out in the expectance of a hug. Sam returned the woman's friendly hug. As a smile overcame her face, she felt a weight lift off her chest. If anyone knew anything about the missing woman it would be Willa, a woman well-loved for her cooking as she was for her friendliness and keeper of the town's secrets which she bartered with ruthlessness.

"Hi, Willa, it's been a while, hasn't it?"

"You look like you've lost weight." Willa clucked, giving Sam a once over with her big brown eyes. Willa's hair was an intricate twist of braids tied up with a gingham scarf, a coordinated match to the bright blue dress she wore over her well-endowed figure, the colors complimenting her dark complexion and mile wide smile.

"I see you decided to forgo the black and white dress code? Always the rebel, Willa?"

The other woman waved a hand. "Life is boring without color. Now enough about me, what is your handsome husband going to do with you wasting away? Most men I know like a thick woman."

Sam couldn't stop the flush of her face even though she smiled. "Willa!" Sam said, playfully smacking Willa's arm. "Believe me, I don't need the education."

"Honestly, how long have you two been married, five years? You should know how men work. Don't mind me, I'm just telling it how it is," Willa said. "How about we get back to how you've been."

"Great, I'm doing well. I was in the area and thought I would stop by for a coffee before I head back home. I hope you still make those delicious chocolate croissants?" Sam asked.

"You bet, suga. Henry tried to make them but he's not nearly as good at it as I am. I had to take over the task again. Husbands, am I right?" Willa clucked her tongue. "You sit right here while I go get you a latte and croissant," Willa said as she sauntered back toward the restaurant, her wide hips swaying gently as she walked.

Sam waited a few minutes before Willa returned with her

food. She bit into the chocolate filled croissant, her eyes rolling up in ecstasy. The buttery flakes were perfectly matched with the rich sweetness of the chocolate. She missed this place, missed being with people and she definitely missed life's simple luxuries.

Willa sat down across from Sam. "Believe me, you wouldn't look like that if Henry made them."

Sam smiled and wiped her fingers on her napkin, welcoming the conversation and hoping for an opening to ask the questions she really wanted.

"How have things been here at the restaurant since I was last here? Do the ladies' auxiliary still meet here?"

"Oh it's been just swell." Willa rolled her eyes with exaggeration. "The new owners ain't half bad. It's the management that sucks. Well, Mr. Davi is fine," Willa emphasized the word *fine*. "But Mr. Costa, that boy is something else."

Sam almost spit out the latte she sipped at Willa's frankness. "Who is Mr. Costa and what's so bad about him?" Sam questioned.

"The general manager. He's always playing favorites with the staff." Willa leaned toward Sam to whisper. "He has a thing for some of the waitresses. He tries to keep it hush hush but he can't hide it from me."

Sam's eyes widened at the admission. "Does Mr. Costa have a thing for a particular staff member?" Sam said, latching on to the lead Willa extended. "Perhaps a young woman who hasn't been to work in a few weeks?" Sam raised an eyebrow at Willa.

Willa gave Sam a nod. "Something like that. I think it was a mutual flirtation at first. She was using her advantage to pick up extra shifts before the other staff were notified of an opening." Willa straightened up and cleared away Sam's plate then said quietly, "Then something happened to cause Bailee to back off."

Sam leaned forward, her curiosity taking over, "What happened?"

"Some of the other girls heard her asking Mr. Davi for help one night. They thought it was about Mr. Costa. He had become aggressive in his pursuit of her."

"How long ago was that?" Sam said.

"Maybe a week or so before she disappeared," Willa said, handing Sam the check.

"One of the witnesses say they saw Bailee meeting with a man?" Sam questioned. "Do you know who that could be?"

"Those ditties wouldn't know their own fathers from their cousin," Willa continued. "Of course I know who it is...that handsome devil of a man your husband works for, Rex Brown."

Sam's mouth fell open and Willa leaned over, her hand gently pushing up on Sam's chin, closing her mouth. Grateful she was already sitting, Sam felt like the world just crumbled beneath her feet.

"Are you sure, Willa?" Sam whispered. "This can't be right. Rex? Here?"

"Of course I'm sure. He's the only man I know who comes around here with that sexy car of his. Every other man with money has an oversized SUV or obnoxious coupe. But a man who drives an antique Ferrari," Willa closed her eyes and smiled, "1967 Ferrari 275 GTB, red," she opened her eyes, "You know takes care of what is his," Willa said with a wink.

Sam pondered what Willa shared while she paid for lunch. What was Rex Brown doing with Bailee Talson? More importantly, how was she going to break it to her husband his boss and mentor was directly involved in the disappearance and death of a young woman?

STILL IN SHOCK about the revelation of Rex, Sam wandered aimlessly toward Main Street where small boutiques with windowed store fronts stood on either side of the road. How often had she walked along this road admiring the shops with Josie or Heath?

Sam stopped to find herself in front of one of the designer baby boutiques. She stared in the window at the small knitted hats, warm onesies and assortment of baby items. A longing deep inside her ached at the sight of the pink frilly dresses.

She caught a reflection of herself in the window. Willa was right, she had lost weight. Her cheekbones jutted out and dark circles were prominent beneath her eyes and she knew from the loose fit of her clothes, she'd failed to care for herself for a long time.

Her focus returned to the dresses and she stared at herself for a few seconds, caught up in the daydreams of what could have been. Sam felt the familiar tendrils of melancholy beginning to wrap their way into her again, threatening to take her hostage.

She pushed back against the intrusive thoughts and the rising panic she felt and, in that moment, caught a small movement in the reflection of the glass, behind her. Before she could focus, the movement disappeared. Sam stood still, feigning interest at the shop window, while waiting for the movement to appear again in the reflection of the glass.

"May I help you, ma'am?" the clerk asked, stepping outside the boutique to greet Sam.

Broken from her concentration, Sam backed away. "No, thank you. I was just looking for a friend."

Her concentration broken, Sam turned around, her eyes drawn to the direction of the movement. A few cars were parked across the street, a lady walked her dog while a couple passed by. Further along down the street shoppers mingled around the entrances of the many storefronts.

Nothing appeared unusual or out of place for a sunny, spring afternoon.

She should've taken the opportunity to walk away. Curiosity won the best of her intentions and she started toward the area where she thought she saw the movement, her strides a slow, deliberate pace down the cobblestone sidewalk.

A few storefronts down from the baby boutique, Sam lingered outside the window of a book shop. In the reflection of the window, her eyes darted to the area over her right shoulder and she could scarcely discern what appeared to be a person hiding behind a parked car across the street.

Sam watched through the reflection as the person held up an object and pointed it toward her.

"NO!"

Panic hit Sam with such force she ducked, cowering near the ground. When nothing happened and her fear passed, she stood, realizing the object pointed at her was a camera, not a gun. Her panic quickly turned to irritation laced with anger and a simmering rage.

If she allowed the person to continue to take her picture, she gave them the impression it was okay. It was an invasion of her privacy. Further, she didn't want anyone to see where she was or for Heath to find out she was anywhere near the restaurant, least he think she was involved in his case. Which she was but he would know she had been snooping in his laptop and files. There was no way Heath was going to find out of her subterfuge.

Sam quickly spun around. "Hey, you!"

The person turned heel, running toward the intersection straight ahead. Adrenaline kicked in and raced through her veins, clouding her judgement. Her other senses jumped into high gear and before she realized her actions, she followed the figure.

Sam bolted down the cobblestone street like she was back

in her high school 100-meter dash. Her feet thumped on the cobblestone road as she danced between tourists and flowerpots. The person reached the intersection and was just about to cross when a car pulled up to the stop sign, cutting off the walkway ahead.

A few feet away, the person turned, suddenly snapping her picture. Sam stalked toward the individual she recognized as the man who had been with Abby Jones and the other reporters the night she was ambushed by the media outside the restaurant.

"What do you think you're doing?" Sam said, her voice catching the attention of other shoppers around them. "Have you been following me?"

In a moment of weakness or even anger, she wouldn't remember, Sam shrugged off her tote bag into her hands and swung it in a wide arc, the forceful brunt of her bag flying at the man. He grunted at the impact, the bag striking him in the side. Stumbling against the force of Sam's swing, he lost his footing on the cobblestone sidewalk. He held out his hands as he began to fall and his camera flew out of his outstretched hands.

A loud crash sounded as the camera hit the sidewalk. Sam shuddered at the sound, grimacing to discover shoppers and tourists staring at her. Backing away she turned and walked back toward her car.

"Hey! Hey, you broke my camera!" the man yelled as she walked away.

"Then find someone to fix it!"

Sam took a few deep breaths to steady herself. She couldn't believe she confronted the man let alone assaulted him with her purse. Oh, Heath would not like the spectacle she just caused.

Hands trembled in her handbag, finding the car keys at the bottom of her tote. She unlocked her car, started the engine and pulled out of her parking spot with just a quick glance back at the scene she left behind.

Her heart raced and her hands still trembled as her knuckles turned white on the steering wheel. She needed to put as much distance between herself and the man as she could. What was happening to her? She never would've attacked the man as she did before. She didn't understand what had taken over her.

Sam wanted to forget the whole afternoon but she knew she had been hiding from things for too long. Her withdrawal from her life had consequences which impacted herself and everyone around her. For some reason, fate or coincidence, she was connected to Bailee. She could no longer hide away while this woman reached out to her from beyond the grave, her life stolen from her. Sam felt responsible. The only way was to help Bailee and hope her actions prompted forgiveness.

Another thought flitted through her mind. To help Bailee was to hurt someone she loved dearly. Sam understood what she had to do but feared she lacked the strength to break her husband's heart. Despite her feelings, she knew she had to reach out to Heath with what she had discovered about Rex Brown's involvement, and she needed to do it soon.

CHAPTER ELEVEN

FAILED AGAIN, huh prick?

Heath's best intentions of surprising Sam at home failed. Arriving home, he found her sleeping on the sofa, her tablet alongside her, a notebook lying on the floor. He roused her just enough so she could safely clamor up the stairs to their bedroom. How he wished she would wake up, and he was tempted to rouse her. When she sighed silently, he thought better of it and let her fall back asleep.

While Sam slept nearby, Heath spent most of the night awake, twisting and turning in the guest bed or pacing around the house, thinking of all the possibilities of the Davi case. The feeling Davi was being used as a political pawn was ever present in his mind, only Heath failed to have proof to his claim.

He needed more information if he was going to be successful. And he would need to go back gathering that information unconventially.

The next morning shattered any expectations Heath had of the Davi case being a slam dunk. He stood outside of the Firm when his phone rang. He answered, recognizing the number of the Midnight Harbor police department.

"Hello, this is Attorney Crenshaw."

"Heath, it's Theo. I saw your message about the Bailee Talson case. You know I'm not able to speak with you concerning details."

"Yeah, that's how this dance goes, right?" Heath said, the air heavy with the knowledge both men knew but couldn't share. Heath had a feeling a discovery and charges were eminent from DA Fabian's office.

"Listen, this line isn't recorded…off the record, Bailee's autopsy is scheduled for today along with toxicology reports," Theo said, his voice gruff. "I asked for the lab to expedite but there was some sort of attack last night in Charleston. The lab is bombarded with all sorts of requests."

"Off the record, thanks, Theo. There's something off with Bailee's death. I have a bad feeling about it."

"You're not the only one feeling that way. I'm piecing together the victim's last day before she disappeared." Theo paused then sighed. "Heath, I spoke with Sam about the case."

"Yes, of course. I wouldn't expect anything less." Heath ran a hand over his face, his heart tightened in his chest at the mention of Sam's name. "How did she take it?"

"She handled the questioning well. I don't have any reason to suspect her…the questions were just standard protocol."

Feeling a small relief, Heath pushed forward, hoping for something he could use. "Is there anything else you can tell me?"

"Bailee had a small rose tattoo on the inside of her wrist. And, you can expect the DA to be running a large media campaign with this story. It's an election year."

"Thanks, Theo. Midnight Harbor is about to be all shook up."

"I'll notify you if I have any additional information I can share."

Heath disconnected the call. Thanks to Theo, he confirmed what Rex told him yesterday, and the DA was eager to press charges.

Never one to wait for what he wanted, Heath employed charm and ambition to propel him this far. Davi had to be brought in for questioning immediately and it was well past time for Tyler to utilize his skill to ferret out additional information on who Bailee Talson was. Once they understood the victim and Davi, they could build the case. And possibly discover more about why Davi was being blackmailed.

Satisfied with his plan, Heath walked through the Firm doors, straight to Maggie's desk. He leaned down, folded his arms on her desk and gave her a rakish smile.

She peeked up from her typing. "You're looking at me with the devil's grin, Heath Crenshaw. That look means trouble." Her manicured nails beat a rhythmic click-clack over the keys. "I'm busy."

"Too busy to haul a billionaire in for a statement with his legal team?" Heath raised his eyebrows.

"And miss the opportunity to see Rex ruffled? Never." Maggie reached for her wireless headset, ready to do what she did best.

"Good. I need a meeting with Davi immediately and I don't care who sees him entering the Firm."

Heath pulled out his phone and punched in Tyler's number. "Send me a text when he's available to meet. In the meantime, I'm taking Tyler out to do some investigating of our own."

HEATH AND TYLER drove through downtown Midnight Harbor, past the towering palmetto trees and quaint cobblestone sidewalks, determination lashing at their heels to discover the last connection between Nicholas Davi and

Bailee Talson. They interviewed previous acquaintances to no avail. If Davi and Ms. Talson had a history together, albeit even professional one, no one was letting loose lips fly. Heath felt time slip by him with each dead end. They worked through the pieces of interviews, backtracking for information they missed.

"There has to be something we're overlooking," Heath said. He maneuvered into one of the last parking spaces on the street. Parking spots were sparse near this area of downtown Midnight Harbor. The shopping district buzzed with tourists and locals meeting for lunch and shopping.

"Theo mentioned Bailee Talson worked as a waitress at the restaurant over there," Tyler said, pointing with his whole arm from the passenger's seat, across Heath's face to the restaurant.

"Really? You think you could remove your arm from my face so I can get a better look?" Heath said. He pushed Tyler's arm down.

Tyler withdrew his arm and shrugged. "You know, us computer geeks don't have social skills."

Heath snorted. "Nice excuse but you're still coming in with me. You may not think it but we depend upon you for more than just your tech skills."

"Thanks man, you're making me blush."

"Let's find out if any of Bailee's coworkers are willing to talk," Heath said. He grabbed his phone and climbed out of the car. "Now, I'm letting you out of the tech room. Watch the employees for any unusual behavior, or hesitation in speech. And remember, please try to control yourself once we get inside and just…play along."

Tyler gave Heath a dirty look. "Really, man. I may prefer technology over sociology but I think I know how to act in public. Has anyone every told you, you're a prick."

"All the time," Heath said slipping his sunglasses into his shirt pocket. "Why do you think Rex hired me?"

Tyler stayed close beside him as they walked across the street to Bar Nonne, a restaurant popular with businessman and the ladies' auxiliary clubs. Heath rarely diner here. Sam, however, attended auxiliary club. The remaining clientele were tourists driving into town for lunch as they meandered down the coast. Occasionally, the bigshots, like Davi and his ilk, would travel from Charleston for a dinner meeting.

The men reached the entrance of the whitewashed three-story brick building. The restaurant's black painted doors were propped open, overflowing box planters spilled fragrant blooms from each window. Oversized planters lined up in a row decorated the sidewalk, the lush green succulents and flirty flowers spilling onto the concrete patio in a fairy tale cascade. A black iron fence ran along the al fresco seating area, covered in greenery from nearby ivy.

A young woman, her hair pulled back in a sleek bun and her uniform a crisp white button shirt and black pencil skirt, prepped the area for guests. She didn't look familiar but Midnight Harbor attracted all sorts.

"Excuse me, miss," Heath said, easing into a swagger, his steps deliberate and practiced as he walked toward the woman. She glanced up from her task. "I'm sorry, gentle-men," she held up a hand to stop them, "you need to check in with the hostess before you can be seated."

"No problem. Which way to the hostess?" Heath said as he flashed a kilowatt smile at the waitress.

She ignored his smile, her eyes moving beside him. A smile played at the corner of her mouth and she moved closer to Tyler. She pointed them toward the entrance near the black wooden doors with a slight smile. "Over there. You'll find Natalie inside." She resumed setting each table. "Have a nice lunch," she said, with a hair toss in Tyler's direction.

"Thank you," Heath said.

After this case was over, Heath and Nathan would need to get Tyler out of the office more frequently to work on those social skills. The waitress clearly gave Tyler *the look* while he stared at her blankly in return.

The open French doors of the restaurant allowed a light breeze to flow through the lobby. Large overhead fans circled above, pushing the air throughout to create a constant, soft breeze that followed Heath and Tyler. He noticed another attractive young woman stood behind a podium, a small headset in her ear and a name tag with Natalie written on it pinned to her white shirt.

"Good afternoon, gentleman," Natalie said practiced politeness. "Would you like a table for two on the patio?" Her hand motioned behind them to the patio they just left.

"Perhaps a seat at the bar would be best," Heath suggested. "We don't plan to be long."

"Absolutely." Natalie whispered something into the headset. "If you both would please follow me this way."

Natalie led them into the center of the restaurant, passing other waitresses and hostesses as they passed. The arrived at a lacquered wooden bar where a young female bartender floated around chatting with the two men seated at the bar and making cocktails or pouring beer. The two men were unfamiliar and likely in their early fifties, wearing dark suits and styled hair, martinis sat in front of them on the counter. "Gentlemen," Heath nodded a hello and sat on a stool a few spaces from the businessmen.

Heath turned to Tyler seated next to him at the bar. "Do you notice anything unusual about this restaurant?"

"At first glance? Nothing. But now I'm wondering why I only see female employees." Tyler said casually looking around. "And they happen to all be young and attractive."

"Exactly, young, attractive females. My wife used to hold some of her ladies' auxiliary meetings here." Heath drummed his fingers on the bar top, looking at the female staff throughout the restaurant. "Not one male employee in sight. I don't remember her mentioning the employees were all female."

The bartender walked over to the men. "What can I get for you, gentlemen? Jack and Coke?" the woman suggested. She placed a basket of salted pretzels and dry roasted peanuts in front of them.

"How did you guess I was going to order a Jack and Coke?" Heath smiled, popping a peanut in his mouth.

The bartender smiled in return. "You got it."

"How long have you worked here?" Heath asked, hoping his tone sounded carefree enough to open the door for conversation. The bartender filled two glasses with ice.

"For a few months," she said with a shrug. "Long enough to know who will come in and what they'll order."

"Do you remember a young woman who worked here as a waitress? She was thin with blonde hair, she had a small rose tattoo on the underside of her right wrist." Heath leaned in toward the bartender and jerked his thumb toward Tyler. "This one here was hoping to get her number." Heath slapped Tyler on the back, jolting him forward. "He chickened out at the last minute before he could ask her for it. We were driving by when he gained enough courage to drop in to see if she was working."

"I'm not sure if I know who you mean." The bartender paused then placed the drinks on coasters before them. She gasped. "Oh wait, you must mean Bailee?" she asked Tyler who sat, sipping his drink through the tiny cocktail straw.

Heath kicked Tyler's foot under the bar counter. "Uh, yeah, that's her," Tyler squeaked out.

"Didn't you see the news?" the bartender said. She bit her lip and looked over their shoulders before she said, "She went missing over a week ago. The police found her dead." Heath and Tyler traded glances, each feigning surprise.

"Sorry, man," Heath said to Tyler who had a crestfallen

look on his face. He turned back to the bartender. "How horrible. Does anyone know what happened to her?"

The bartender grabbed a bar cloth and began wiping down the counter in steady strokes. Heath noticed her bite the side of her lip again and he remained silent to draw her out. After a few moments of silence, the bartender spoke in a hushed voice. "There's some rumors."

She stopped wiping the counter and looked at Heath. "The situation Bailee had herself caught up in was strange. She always worked extra shifts, said she needed the money to help pay for school and rent," the bartender said. "A few weeks ago, she starts calling out a lot. I overheard her ask the boss if he could cut some of her shifts." The bartender started wiping the counter again in a slow circular motion. "She told me later that night she met someone."

Heath sipped his drink and leaned in to whisper. "This guy she met, was he helping her out, like a sugar daddy or something?"

The bartender whispered back, "I figured it was a guy she just didn't want to bother getting out of bed with." The bartender gave Tyler an apologetic look. "Some of the other girls here saw Bailee getting into an expensive car with a dark-haired man." Heath kicked Tyler's stool. He straightened and gave the bartender his saddest eyes before swallowing the remainder of his drink.

The bartender mixed another drink and slid it in front of Tyler. "On the house."

"Did any of the other girls mention what this man looked like? Any noticeable tattoos or piercings?" Heath said as he picked the bartender for more information.

The young woman crossed her arms over her chest and leaned against the back counter of the bar. She shook her head. "I don't remember anything that stood out."

Recognition flashed across her face, she stood straight, her eyes wide. "Oh!" She leaned closer toward Heath and Tyler, her voice barely a whisper. "Well, I didn't see it but the girls said about two weeks ago a guy came in here looking for her. Not just any guy but Nicholas Davi. The other girls said he told them he had an appointment to meet with Bailee. I would've loved to work that night. When I asked again, they all said he had a real money look about him. But, you didn't hear that from me," she said, her eyes catching the unfamiliar couple who just sat down to join the four men at the bar. "Excuse me," the bartender said as she left to take the drink orders of the new couple.

Uncomfortable with the increased attention, Heath stood to leave. He didn't want it to appear like he was doing anything more than gossiping. He tapped his finger on the bar to get Tyler's attention. He jerked his thumb over his shoulder toward the exit. Heath threw a few bills on the bar counter before walking away.

Halfway out the restaurant, Heath noticed Tyler wasn't behind him. He looked back to see Tyler sipping the remainder of his second drink through the tiny cocktail straw. Heath walked back over to grab Tyler by the shoulder, interrupting the slurping noises from the straw. "C'mon, man. We can drown your sorrows somewhere else," Heath said. Tyler stood up from the bar and followed closely behind Heath as they exited the restaurant.

Heath waited until they were back in the privacy of his car before he felt comfortable to talk. Tyler wasted little time. He turned toward Heath. "What do you think happened?"

"I'm not sure," Heath said softly, his eyes on the black doors of Bar Nonne, "but we may have found our missing connection."

THE DRIVE back to the Firm was precipitated by a heavy silence. The realization their client, Nicholas Davi, lied about his involvement with Bailee Talson at the forefront of Heath's mind.

Heath slammed his fist on the steering wheel, Tyler jumped at the sudden sound. "What's up, man? The steering wheel never hurt you."

He sighed, thinking of what he could say without coming across as a pretentious ass. "I can't shake this feeling I have. I made my career as a defense attorney," he began. "My responsibility has always been to provide people with a responsible defense so they are cleared of charges or receive a fair sentence. I always wanted to help those who don't have the means to help themselves, not to defend crooks and people with enough money to buy their way out of trouble."

He had a sick feeling in his stomach that Davi wasn't the only one being used.

"I wouldn't be so angry with yourself about not knowing more information about Davi. How were we supposed to know he withheld information? We didn't even question him yet. This case is moving so fast. You did the right thing by seeking out answers from Bailee's coworkers. We're on the right track now," Tyler said, slapping Heath on the shoulder.

"Thanks, I appreciate you sticking with me through this, even though this isn't your typical routine."

"I kind of like it," Tyler said. "Well, except for the part where our client lied to us." Tyler rolled down his window and stuck his hand out, his fingers playing through the wind. "You're not the police. You're just an attorney trying to help his client. You need to refocus. Don't allow the new discovery to eat away at you. It's not worth the cost." His voice trailed off as his gaze turned from Heath back to the window.

Tyler's words resonated with Heath, his companionship a familiar soul in the hardships of life and stories that make us who we are. Heath took the task upon himself to learn more about the case and his client's involvement. This is how cases were built, by doing the research and discovering connections between clues to build a defense. He was angry at himself for devoting so much time to this case, as well as Rex for risking the Firm's reputation on helping out an old buddy. He couldn't tell that to Tyler and place the other man's future with the Firm at risk.

Heath thought of the person he could lean on for support...Sam. He thought of all the time he spent away from her, drowning in deadlines, interviews and reports. Who was he kidding? She hadn't wanted him around anyway. Any attempts to comfort her were rebuffed. What else could he do but immerse himself in work? At least it was something he was good at and the heavy workload made it so he hardly had time to think about the pain and grief taking root in his heart since she had returned, broken and defeated, from the hospital.

Why did it feel like everything was falling apart, just as he thought he had everything together?

Back at the office, Tyler returned to the lab, determined to complete his search for who he referred to as the Demented Davi hacker, and cull through any loose ends with the rebuilt files.

Heath parted ways from Tyler and found himself wandering the hallways of the Firm, analyzing every piece of the case together, with no place in particular to go. When he stopped, he recognized the wooden door as Rex's office door and wondered again why he thought Rex was involved. What was worth hiding from the team?

Confrontation was not on his agenda nor something he desired, but Heath needed answers more than he needed a false sense of illusion if he wanted to continue with the Davi case. There were only two men who could provide Heath with the answers he needed and one of them he could easily reach behind the office door.

Straightening his back, Heath slipped into a different mindset, replacing his easygoing demeanor with the cold calculation the prosecutors feared in the courtroom. He steeled himself, prepared to knock on the door when a voice boomed from inside the room.

"Come in!" Rex called out.

Heath entered, and slowed, surprised to see Claudia seated in one of the leather armchairs near the antique desk. Heath often wondered if Claudia ever lost control of her emotions, she was the epitome of cool and collected, even during the most tiring times.

He was about to find out.

The perfectly coiled attorney was gone. The woman before him was no calmer or cooler than the blaze of the sun. Claudia's eyes fiercely bore holes into the person seated across from her. Red cheeked, her hands tightly gripped the arms of the chair despite the cold expression she wore on her face. Heath had a growing suspicion he interrupted a heated conversation between the two.

He noticed Rex's necktie loose, playing a pen through his fingers. Passive and bored to Claudia's inferno. whatever she told was the most tedious thing he ever heard.

"Listen, I'm sorry if I interrupted something," Heath said. He held up his hands in front of his chest in apology. "However, I made progress with the Davi case and I think it's something we need to discuss."

"Claudia, we'll revisit his later," Rex said, his tone indicating a clear dismissal. Heath glanced again at Claudia, the angry red blotches receding from her face, replaced by her usual cool smile. To her credit, she kept her tongue and nodded her head slightly in Rex's direction. "We'll discuss this another time." She stood, leaving behind indentations on the arm of the chair where her fingers had gripped. "Have a good evening, gentleman," she said as she slammed the door behind her with a force that told her feelings had not yet subsided despite the forced smile.

Rex walked toward the wet bar located between the two

massive bookshelves. Bottles of varying heights and shapes lined the shelf with crystal decanters, each a different hue of amber. Heath watched Rex, his mind going back to the other bar and drink he had a mere hour ago, and the information he gleaned from that fateful drink.

"I didn't have the chance to tell you earlier, it's a shame to hear about Sam finding the young woman in the way she did. I hope she is okay?"

Heath focused his attention back to the present, keeping his cool. "She is…well, given the circumstance. She is well aware of the unsavory aspects of my job. I foolishly hoped I could shield her from most of it."

Rex poured at drink from an ornate crystal decanter. "You're not here for my sympathies. I suppose this is the moment you want to question my motives in retaining Nicholas Davi as a client?" He poured another glass and handed it to Heath, the honey-colored liquid sloshing against the glass.

"How did you guess?" Heath said, the anger he kept controlled threatening to unleash. He steeled himself, this was his boss, mentor and a man he respected. Only Heath felt the respect he had for Rex slowly unfurl like a wound-up ribbon.

"You've come a long way from the days when you used to let your emotion control in the courtroom. I can hardly tell how angry you are with me," Rex teased.

"What do you mean by that?" Heath said his brow furrowed. "Of course I know how to control myself."

"What I mean is you haven't been yourself the past few months," Rex said. He swirled the bourbon in his glass and sipped. Rex leveled his ice blue gaze on Heath, the corners of his eyes crinkled from the smirk on his face. "Don't get me wrong, you've done a great job on the cases you've handled. Hence, one of the reasons why I assigned you to the Davi case."

"I'm in complete control and never been better. Everything is fine," Heath brushed off the comment and focused on the last part of Rex's comment. "What did you mean by one of the reasons you assigned me to lead the Davi case?"

Rex motioned to the arrangement of chairs near the bar and took a seat. "Yes, the other reason being I know you have an...unorthodox way of handling cases."

Heath followed and sat near Rex, staring at the bourbon before taking a sip. His mouth warmed with the taste of smooth wood and smoke.

"It's something I admire. Your concern for justice and serving your clients and all those other lovely things we admire in the legal system," Rex said. He placed his glass on the low coffee table and rubbed his neck. He leaned on his knees, holding his hands out in front of them. "But, you also know innocents can pay a price. You know the consequences and the dark side that isn't glorified by the media."

"Why the Davi case? Why not one of the other cases presented to the Firm?" Heath questioned. There was something here Rex wasn't saying, deliberately keeping Heath from discovering.

Rex settled back into the sofa and sighed, pulling at his neck tie. "Nicholas Davi is an old family friend. I need someone who cares about justice no matter the class or wealth of the person. Someone who can look past the prestige to the person underneath."

"I'm not sure that I am that person," Heath said as he stood up. Rex tuned to look at him pace around the room. "I care deeply about justice, that's why I became a defense attorney." Heath stopped so he faced Rex. "But I can never represent someone who is guilty."

"Who said Davi is guilty?" Rex demanded. Not waiting for Heath to answer, he pressed on. "You have a duty to represent your client, to help them understand the consequences to their actions and to resolve the case either by fair sentencing or my favorite, winning. Guilt is a luxury we don't have nor do we ask. You know better than that."

Heath peered at Rex, trying to see this man as the mentor he admired. What did he mean they couldn't afford to feel guilty? Wasn't that what kept them human?

"I understand my duty. Tyler and I went to interview some of Bailee Talson's coworkers today as part of my duty to the Davi case. The information we discovered suggests Nicholas Davi may have been personally involved with Bailee Talson." Heath stared down into his drink and glanced up at Rex, his voice soft. "He may have lied to you and you dare speak to me of guilt?"

"You did exactly what a good defense attorney does, look for information where you can find it, relentless in your search. Now you need to build the case. I expect nothing less from you. Interviewing your client, their alibi and potential motive for the crime should be at the top of your list." Rex paused. "And you're just now bringing in Davi for questioning? Don't ever take anyone's word at face value, especially a notorious businessman."

"Nothing in my record indicates Davi admitted to being involved with the dead woman," Heath said. "How can I build a case if my client isn't forthcoming with details of the case?"

"Davi is more afraid of the media circus his indictment could cause and the fallout he and his business partners would experience. Believe me, he is not worried about guilt. He came to me prior to Bailee Talson's disappearance seeking counsel."

Rex was still being evasive.

"What aren't you telling me about the case? I can't continue to represent Davi if I'm not privy to all the details. What type of person would I be if I let a guilty man walk free? To watch Sam, Maggie and Claudia walk around Midnight Harbor while a deviant like Davi is free? Who could be next?"

"What type of attorney would you be if you let an innocent man be imprisoned because you failed to do anything but take things at face value?" Rex countered. "There are things about the case I can't tell you." Rex held up a hand, his face implored Heath to listen. "It's not what you think. Claudia and I are...working on a speculative case with high-profile suspects. This isn't something I would normally look into but she insisted. She has great sense, much like you."

"Then why can't I be involved if the details are pertinent to my case?" Heath said. He reminded himself to stay calm despite the information Rex admitted to withholding from him.

"Claudia is the right person for the case, just as you're the right person to handle the Davi case. Her soft skills are what I need handling this rumor. With her experience, she'll have more than enough proof for our...investigation. If I thought the details of her case were of impact to Davi's, I would've brought you onboard."

Heath watched Rex pour himself another glass of bourbon. "What do you suggest I do? I'm not Theo," he asked Rex, the heat in his voice gone. He understood Rex was involved in more than the Davi case, it was part of running the Firm. Health found he desperately wished for guidance from his mentor.

"I suggest you go home to your wife and spend some time with her." Rex walked over to his desk and placed his drink on the coaster, giving Heath a knowing look. "Second, why don't you work with Tyler to discover what other information you can find out about this meeting between Davi and Bailee Talson? With the knowledge, the meeting is likely not for what you expected."

Heath placed his empty glass on the bar. "Thanks for the drink...and for the talk. I made assumptions about Davi without even speaking with him. I wasn't working at my best."

"We've all been there, Heath. As I said earlier, you haven't been yourself. You need to take some time to rediscover who that person is."

"I'm working on it," Heath said, his half smile fading.

"Why don't you put forth as much effort in yourself and relationship as you do your cases. If you did, then I wouldn't have to be the second person intervening," Rex said as he seated himself behind his desk. "If you excuse me, I need to finish this before Claudia has my head on a spike. Dulled as age has made me, I rather like my head and prefer it stay intact."

Heath felt the harsh words for what they were, the truth. He realized he needed to double down his efforts to repair his relationship with Sam. He had taken a step in the right direction with the Davi case. Soon, the case would be over and he could focus on rebuilding his marriage. He just needed to see the case through to the end and hope Sam was still there afterward.

CHAPTER TWELVE

ANOTHER MORNING CAME with more of the same, Heath missing from the space next to her, nor any indication when he would return. His absence hurt the more she thought of how far they'd grown apart. But she was thankful for the momentary reprieve from the task she knew was to be soon upon her. Heath's absence gave her an opportunity to delay the information she had to deliver and discover if Rex really was involved in Bailee's disappearance.

Sam mulled over what she learned from Willa. Could Rex really be involved in the disappearance and murder of Bailee Talson? How was she going to approach this new turn without bringing more suspicion upon herself?

She thought over the timeline of events, having accepted the new revelation that Bailee never stepped foot in her car the night Sam picked her up. In her eagerness to help, did Sam mistake a sign or clue that would've told her Bailee was a…ghost? Snorting to herself at the ridiculousness of it all, Sam couldn't help but wonder how she would proceed with her only information being a ghostly hitchhiker and a rumor Rex and Bailee met before her death.

Recalling the disaster of yesterday's confrontation with

the photographer, Sam winced at her actions then thought of how she felt in the moments after. Scared but also proud she stood up for herself when faced with a confrontation she would've previously avoided. Her actions prompted by a self-assured woman she didn't know was inside her.

Confidence. That was a new feeling. It felt...strange yet comforting. She was capable of more than being arm candy or another society wife or widow.

That's it! Sam jumped out of bed, stumbling into her closest clothes. Rex was always attending charity events, grand openings and galas. His family was one of the oldest and wealthiest in the state of South Carolina. Surely if a random photographer followed her because of her association with her husband's clients, then there would be even more evidence of Rex's whereabouts in the days leading up to the disappearance of Bailee.

And she knew exactly who she could talk to who had her hand on the pulse of news in Midnight Harbor.

SAM WALKED into the sterile lobby of local news channel WMZ3 with high a bounce in her step. Confidence bloomed within her and she hopes she wanted to quickly squash any involvement of Rex's with Bailee. Uniform white walls with generic furniture decorated the lobby. Neutral and straight-forward, she thought, no room for embellishments when trying to get the latest story.

She approached the middle-aged receptionist with one of her practiced smiles. "Hi, I was wondering if Abby Jones was available? I need to speak with her."

The receptionist peered at her from over the top of her bifocals, the guardian of the journalists and producers who brought Midnight Harbor the latest news. Sam met her look with an even sweeter smile, a deterrent to the grumpy gaze.

Lips puckered the receptionist picked up the phone and dialed without taking her eyes off of Sam. "Name?" she barked out in a throaty rasp.

"Samantha Crenshaw."

"Hmph." She turned her back toward Sam and whispered into the phone. Sam strained to hear but couldn't make out what was said. As the receptionist spun around in her chair to face her, Sam quickly smiled.

"Ms. Jones will be down shortly, Mrs. Crenshaw. Please have a seat."

Relieved she was found worthy, Sam sat on the nearest armchair and waited. It wasn't long before Sam looked up to the see the hallway door open and Abby step into the lobby. Wearing a navy blue dress and nude heels with a laptop in one arm, Abby's auburn curls bounced as she walked up and offered a hand.

"Hi, Sam. Cathy surprised me when she said you were here to talk."

Sam accepted the offered handshake and quickly thought over how much she wanted to share with Abby. Just enough to sound believable without drawing any attention. Not that it wasn't already too late for that.

Falling back to her default smile, Sam wrapped her arms around herself. "Yes, could help me with a few questions for the next issue of the auxiliary club's newsletter." She hadn't lost her touch. "I have a few questions if you don't mind. It won't take long."

"Sure, come on." Abby walked back to the hallway, holding the door open. Sam thought she saw Abby and Catherine the receptionist share a brief look out of the corner of her eye.

Yeah, here I am. Midnight Harbor's favorite recluse. She shrugged off the pity party. She wasn't going to allow a look to bring her down. Not when she needed answers.

Once in the privacy of the room, Sam shouldered her

purse onto the table. Abby sat down and opened her hands. "What can I help you with?"

Okay, this was her moment. Forcing herself to be courageous, Sam sat in the chair opposite Abby. "Look, there's no use in hiding it. I'm sure you know I was the one to find the dead woman." Sam saw recognition in Abby's eyes. She nodded her head for Sam to continue. "We've known each other a long time. I hope I can trust your discretion with what I'm about to tell you."

"Of course. That must have been terrible for you." Abby sounded soothing, encouraging Sam to open up.

"I'm here not to talk about my experience but to ask if you know of any recent galas or events within the last few weeks. A high-profile event."

Abby leaned back in the chair and chewed on the inside of her lip. "There's been a few events recently. Kerri Reid's in town with her book signing and a larger party dedicated to the release of her new book. Rumor has it she's looking for a location for hush hush project collaboration. Is there a reason why you want to know?"

Shrugging off her question, Sam distracted Abby without outright lying. "I've been out of the loop for so long, I'm not up with the latest gossip or news. I was curious what old friends have been doing in my absence."

Understanding shown across Abby's face. "Is there anyone or any event you want specifics about?"

Sam thought back to the night of her dinner with Heath, when he was called away from her. Her brow furrowed in anger at the intrusion. "Any event Rex Brown has attended."

"Let's see." Abby opened up her laptop and began typing. It wasn't long until she turned the laptop around to face Sam. "Rex attended two events within the last two weeks. The charity gala a few days ago and a recognition dinner with Nicholas Davi." The monitor showed a small article with details on the two events along with pictures. Sam looked up from the monitor to meet Abby's eyes. Curiosity was there along with suspicion. "Is there a reason why you want to know where Rex has been?"

"No, no reason." Thinking of the photographer, Sam stumbled over her next question. "The photographers...do they normally follow people around?"

Abby waved her hand as if to brush off the question. "You know how it is. They're always looking for the next scoop to sell to one of the papers or news outlets. Has one of them been bothering you. The other night...at the restaurant. I'm sorry, it's just work."

"I know. I never realized how intrusive it can be. Before..." Sam trailed off, not wanting to share that before she lost herself, she wanted the attention. She wanted to be seen on the arm of her husband in the gossip blogs and society papers. Not now. "Do you happen to know if Rex was seen anywhere. I mean, were there any photos of him?"

"Hmm...only these few at the events I mentioned. Oh and this one with the new attorney for his office."

Sam peered at the picture of Rex and Claudia sitting in his car outside Bar Nonne...the same restaurant Bailee worked at as a waitress. Willa was right. The photo wasn't proof, but it was enough to support her hunch all was not right with Rex Brown. "Thank you. That's all the questions I had."

Abby snapped her laptop shut and motioned to the door. "I'll walk you out." Sam followed and stopped short when Abby turned around to face her. The other woman leaned in to whisper. "If there's anything you ever need to tell me, you have my word I'll keep quiet. Some reporters just look for the latest frenzy but I hope you know I want the truth."

Taken back by Abby's words, Sam mumbled, "Thank you. I better get going."

Away from WMZ3 and Abby's suspicious gaze, Sam found herself wondering again if she had the heart to tell her husband what she learned. She needed proof of exactly what

Rex had been doing the last two weeks especially at Bar Nonne.

Sam quickly typed a text message to Heath, her stomach rolling at the implications her lunch request meant. Could she tell him about her visions of Bailee? About seeing a dead woman? Sam sighed. No, better not. It was her burden for now. Until the time came when she knew she had to tell him what was going on before it was too late.

CHAPTER THIRTEEN

"HEATH...HEATH, did you hear anything I just said?" Tyler asked.

"Uh-huh," Heath managed. He sat at his desk, daydreaming of how beautiful Sam looked in the sundress the other afternoon. Despite his best attempts to arrive home early to surprise Sam, he found himself working long past the time he should've been home. Another night lost, another dinner he had to make up to her.

"Earth to Heath, Davi will be arriving in thirty minutes."

A sudden pain in the middle of his forehead, startled his attention into focus. He dropped his legs from off his desk and sat up. Tyler sat across from him in one of the leather armchairs.

"You were daydreaming. It must've been good because I was wondering if you would ever come back," Tyler said.

"Did you just hit me?" Heath accused, rubbing at a tender spot on his forehead.

"Bro, it was a flick, not a hit."

"You didn't flick me, it was definitely a hit," Heath said exasperated. He slouched in his chair, rubbing his hand along his stubbled jaw. "What's this about Davi?"

"His arrival time for the interview is thirty minutes. No, make it twenty-eight minutes." Tyler held up his wrist, tapping the clock face.

"Good to go?" Heath asked.

"I did the best I could." Tyler took off his glasses, cleaning the lenses with the edge of his shirt. "You didn't give me much time. Be grateful I work well under pressure. fast."

"That's why I am grateful to have you on our side." Heath's smile faded. "Davi, huh. We need to learn his intentions or motive. to be honest with us. Let's run though some questions while we wait for Maggie's call."

With a few clicks and taps, Tyler accessed the familiar software program he used previously in the war room.

Faces and names once again flashed past Heath. He drummed his fingers on the desk eager for the discovery of an emerging pattern. He gestured to the monitor. "We eliminated these individuals though interviews." Davi's defense was almost complete given what information they had, except one last piece.

"It's all here. Everything we need for Davi's interview," Tyler said as he plugged in a few more algorithms into the program from his laptop.

"Good. If Davi doesn't divulge additional details about his relationship with Bailee Talson then I'll increase the pressure," Heath said as he continued to review the data on the white monitor.

A silence grew between the men until Tyler broke the tension.

"What did Rex say about you bringing in Davi for a statement?" Tyler said.

Heath recalled the conversation with Rex, of the high expectations placed on him by his mentor and himself, of the reassurance Rex game him. "I think he would appreciate the effort we put into understanding our client and building the case. I hope our faith in our client isn't our downfall," Heath murmured as they anxiously waited for the arrival of Nicholas Davi.

———

TRUE TO HIS persona curated by his staff and sensationalized by the media, Nicholas Davi arrived at the Firm with a flurry of activity amidst heightened scrutiny. Heath watched the spectacle from his office before greeting Davi in a windowless conference room, far from prying eyes and lenses.

News vans from Charleston and as far as Savannah, ascended upon the Firm, desperate to capture any images of Davi entering the Firm. Gossip magazines, businessmen and brunching ladies would be talking about his appearance for days. Abby Jones had a tough day ahead of her. But, if anyone could push shoulders with these city reporters, it would be Midnight Harbor's Abby.

Despite the rumormongering, no discovery had been presented to Heath or charges filed against Davi. Yet, a person closed to him must've tipped off the media to Nicholas Davi's meeting. Within ten minutes of Davi's arrival, Heath heard Maggie tell the unlucky few members of the media to get lost while they had the opportunity.

Not even Maggie could shoo away the media storm Davi created with his arrival. The media caught scent of something big and were hot on the chase.

Heath entered the conference room to find Nicholas Davi and Rex waiting for him. A lovely dark haired woman sat beside Davi and Heath recognized her almost immediately. He was a bit taken by surprise to find himself in the room with the woman and Rex. He thought the interview would be between himself and Davi with Tyler providing any needed research or technical support. Evidently, Rex had taken Maggie's poking to heart and decided to join the conversation. Tyler followed behind Heath and closed the door.

Heath sat at the small, intimate sitting area. A series of oversized chairs along with a loveseat were arranged in a semi-circle at the center of the room, a large coffee table positioned in the middle. A serene blue and gray with touches of gold mixed throughout the room, evoking a calmness Heath doubted would ease the tension building.

Rex and Davi sat side by side, talking quietly to one another. Rex glanced up at Heath and Tyler's entrance. Davi's intense gray eyes narrowed on Heath.

"Nicholas Davi, business associate... and an old family friend," Rex said clapping a hand on Davi's shoulder. Heath shook Davi's hand, not surprised to find the other man's grip strong but not overpowering. There was no struggle for dominance. Davi was self assured of the power he held in his position. Heath took it as the first positive sign that this interview could go better than he had hoped.

Styled black hair and neatly trimmed beard, Davi was Heath's height and not much older than him, despite having built a real estate business while Heath wore braces. His well-tailored navy suit and lavender tie, the colors complementing his gray eyes and fawn complexion. Damn, the man even wore freshly shined dress shoes. Heath took Davi's measure, admitting to himself he admired the man. Davi looked the part of self-made billionaire. His appearance polished to near perfection. Too polished. No wonder he was Charleston's most eligible bachelor. And, Heath suspected, he knew how to play people right into his palm.

"Nic, this is Heath Crenshaw, the attorney I mentioned. I assigned him lead on your case in my place. I've mentored Heath since he was an intern and he is one of my best. He's capable of handling your case with the utmost care and discretion," Rex said his hand resting on Davi's shoulder. "We'll make sure this annoyance doesn't come to any more than a week long rumor."

Rex gestured to the woman still seated on the sofa.

"Heath, this is Kerri Reid. She's a longtime friend of Nic's and…was with him the night in question. She'll be able to corroborate Nic's alibi."

Kerri extended her hand to Heath, a white band of skin evident against her tanned wrist, a large smoky topaz ring glinting under the lights, the color matching her silk dress and high heels. "It's my pleasure to be of assistance to a friend in need."

Heath took her hand in a firm shake, not returning her flirtatious red lipped smile. "Mr. Davi, Ms. Reid, it's nice to meet you both. I wish it was on better terms."

Rex continued after the greeting. "The gentleman next to Heath is Tyler, resident research assistant and IT whiz. He is the heartbeat of our technology department at the Firm. You can trust he will ensure everything said within this room remains confidential."

Davi extended his handed to Tyler in greeting. "It's a pleasure to make your acquaintance, Tyler."

"Shall we." Rex motioned to the seating area. "Thank you, Nic, for cleaning up availability on your calendar for this talk. We have a few minutes before Nic's next appointment. Maggie stocked the coffee table with food and beverages before their arrival. Heath grabbed two waters from the table and handed one to Tyler. Better to keep their minds clear than to cloud it with alcohol, no matter the temptation given how this meeting could go.

Heath took a deep breath and sank into the carefree demeanor he decided would best suit this interview…for now. He could easily change strategy during the interview, tactfully playing the long game in order to get the information he wanted. He was certain Davi knew the game well, how else would the man have come into such success at a young age? Though this wasn't a time for games. Heath needed information before they could proceed with the case. He hoped Davi was appreciative of the direct approach.

"Mr. Davi, I had the opportunity to review the information Rex disclosed in relation to the disappearance of Bailee Talson. He also expressed your concern for the possibility of criminal charges being brought against you by DA Fabian," Heath said, then motioned to Tyler. "Tyler, would you kindly bring up the information on Mr. Davi's case for us."

The white screen on the wall in front of them lit up pictures of Nicholas Davi and Bailee Talson along with all of the known connections and associations between the two.

"The team and I have gone to great lengths to review the possible connections between you and Miss Talson." Heath stood up from his chair and walked toward the screen. "However, we were blinded by the assumption a billionaire businessman and college coed would never met in ordinary circumstances. We were looking for another person to be the connection between you. It was oversight on our part to ignore the possibility you could have a personal relationship with Bailee Talson without need of another's involvement."

The faces and names on the screen slowly disappeared until only Davi and Bailee remained. "You're known around here as the hometown boy who made it big as a real estate mogul. Tyler discovered you recently created a partnership to buy out a local restaurant in an effort to diversify."Heath faced Davi, his hands open. "Of course individuals of different socio-economic classes could meet in a situation allowing for the intermingling of social classes, such as a newly acquired restaurant."

Nicholas Davi watched Heath, his face a perfect mask, careful not to betray emotion from the man behind it. Tyler displayed the statement taken from the bartender at Bar Nonne's.

Heath looked again at Davi, this time the man's eyebrow raised in acknowledgement. "I see you met Becca," Davi said, his tone inflicting boredom and arrogance in equal measures.

"I'm sure you have plenty of questions related to my involvement in the restaurant as well as with Bailee Talson."

Tyler choked back a laugh. Heath shot him a dirty look, then returned Davi's arrogance with a charming smile. "Mr. Davi, I'm on your side, but I need honesty from you. I will be unable to defend you in this case without it," Heath said, his eyes meeting Davi's and holding the other man's gaze.

Davi sighed as he reached for an empty glass on the table and the crystal decanter. He poured a finger of the spirit then leaned back in his chair, his eyes on Heath as he swirled the liquid. "Would it surprise you to learn Ms. Talson's not my type, given my status as an unrepentant playboy?" Heath caught the glance he gave Kerri. Davi sipped his drink before he continued. "I like my women with a bit more bite."

A soft knock at the door broke the heavy atmosphere. Maggie appeared with the copies of files Heath had requested. "Thanks, Maggie," Heath said to her as she handed them off. Maggie gave Davi a stern look before she left. "These are the files of your known business partners. We scoured them to find nothing relating your associates to Bailee Talson. The only person we can find who had a connection with Miss Talson...is you."

"I have an alibi who places me in another place, with them, at the time of Bailee Talson's disappearance," Davi countered, smiling at Kerri.

"Nicholas was my date to a dinner party for the celebration of my new book," Kerri said. "We left together to attend a private party." Her eyes met Davi's as a slight smile spread across her face.

This was new information to Heath. He tried to temper his frustration with Davi's less than forthcoming nature. "Ms. Reid, I appreciate your statement and, Mr. Davi, I understand you have an alibi. I never said you were the one to abduct her," Heath said, unclenching his jaw. Davi was intentionally testing him. He never rankled like this. He needed to remain composed.

"Listen, Nic," Rex intervened, noticing the increasing tension in the room, "Heath is trying his best to help you. We understand the night of Miss Talson's disappearance you were with Ms. Reid. What we need to know is why you wanted to speak with Bailee Talson prior to the evening of her disappearance. If the DA questions it, we need to be prepared."

Heath pushed away any disgruntled feelings and sat near Davi. He changed his tactics. "Mr. Davi, a young woman is dead, cut down before her prime. Her parents had to confirm her identify at the morgue. I need your cooperation to help her parents find justice." Heath owed it to her to remain calm and help find the person responsible for her death.

"Tell me about your involvement with Bailee Talson. I know you're an owner in the restaurant where Miss Talson worked as a waitress. From all accounts she was a hard worker trying to save as much money as she could to pay for college. Then all of a sudden her work ethic changed. She asked for her hours to be cut, she stopped coming in for her scheduled shifts..." Heath allowed his voice to trail off before picking up again. "Then you show up at the restaurant looking for her. That sounds to me, you at least knew of Ms. Talson."

Davi glared at Heath, his gray eyes penetrating, before his face softened. "Yes, I'm a part owner of the restaurant, though I have little oversight aside from finances. An associate was interested in the property. He offered the previous owner a large sum of money to buy them out. He sought me out as a partner once he found he needed help. I found it to be a sound investment in an already popular restaurant."

"Is there a reason why there are only women employed in the front of the house?" Heath asked.

"It was just a business decision to bring in a different

type of client. My business partner wanted to draw in a specific crowd. I had no objections. Having attractive women employ the front of the house isn't unusual to attract old, rich men, Mr. Crenshaw. I have men employed in the back of the house if it concerns you. I'm an equal opportunity employer."

"Was Bailee Talson one of the attractive women hired by you to work as a server?"

"Not by me personally, she was hired on by the general manager of the restaurant," Davi said.

"Can you confirm you did not know of or have a prior relationship with Bailee Talson before she was hired by the general manager?" Heath said.

Davi ran a finger around the lip of his glass. "Yes, I only made her acquittance once I took part ownership of the restaurant."

Davi stared at his glass then met Heath's eyes. "I apologize if I came off the wrong way. I'm angry the DA is using my position as her opportunity to climb the political ladder. Have you heard the news? DA Fabien is preparing a committee to determine if she should run for mayor."

Heath was taken back. This was the first he heard of it. "No, I was unaware of her aspirations. What better way to get publicity than by solving Miss Talson's murder and nailing one of the area's most influential businessman for the crime."

Davi nodded in agreement. "Yes, then you see my concerns. You want the truth? A few weeks ago, Ms. Talson sought me out when I stopped by while on tour of the restaurant. She introduced herself and requested to meet with me. Normally, I would brush her off to one of my assistants but something stuck with me. She appeared...distraught. I couldn't deny her request for a meeting, even if I couldn't help her."

"Sounds like she was involved with someone unsavory and the relationship took a turn. She wanted out and was hoping you would be able to help her to that end," Heath said as he stood to pace around the perimeter of the seating area.

Davi shrugged his shoulders. "I suppose. I'm not sure why she would seek me out for help with a boyfriend." Davi took another sip from his glass. "I was supposed to meet her the night I visited the restaurant, when Becca told you I had dropped in requesting to meet with her. She wasn't working. I waited for an hour then left. She never showed or contacted me again. I thought at the time she changed her mind and decided she didn't need my help after all."

"Do you remember how close that was to when Bailee Talson went missing?" Rex asked his friend.

"Absolutely. I keep record of all my appointments." Davi scrolled through his phone for a few minutes. "Ah, here it is. I was supposed to meet with her on April 21st."

"Bailee Talson was reported missing four days later," Tyler said.

"Something caused her to change her mind to meet with you, maybe it was something she thought she could handle on her own," Heath pondered aloud.

"A possibility. Beyond her initial request for a meeting, I promise you I had no involvement with Bailee Talson. That's the reason why I sought out Rex to begin with."

"I understand. I appreciate you coming in to speak with us. I have a better understanding of the timeline and gained additional knowledge to allow my team to better build the case in your defense," Heath said.

"If it comes to that," Rex said in a reassuring tone to Davi. "I'm afraid our time's up," Rex said to Heath and Tyler. "Nic and I have an event to attend in Charleston." Rex turned back to Davi. "I'll have Maggie see you out the back entrance. Hopefully we can avoid any additional media."

Heath extended his hand to Davi and Kerri. "I had the pleasure of meeting your wife, Samantha," Kerri said as she held on to Heath's hand. "She's such a lovely woman." A soft knock on the door and Maggie appeared. "I'm sure I'll be seeing more of you in the future, Heath," Kerri said before leaving with Davi and Rex, followed by Maggie.

Heath and Tyler were left alone.

They exchanged glances. "Why does it feel like we're back to the beginning. All we know is Bailee Talson reached out to Davi then flaked on him. It could be anything," Tyler said throwing up his hands. "Kerri Reid said they were at a dinner party together the night of Bailee's disappearance and left for a private party after."

"Something just isn't right. I have this feeling someone is lying. We need to take a closer look at Kerri Reid and her relationship with Davi," Heath said.

He walked over to the screen on the wall, staring at Bailee Talson's picture. "I have a hunch it would involve the restaurant. Why else would Bailee seek out one of the partners when she has no other involvement with him to begin with? Why not her parents or roommate?"

"Do we need to go back to the restaurant to question the staff to find out why?" Tyler asked.

Heath glanced at the message on his phone. Sam wanted to meet? For lunch? Taken back by her request Heath quickly replied before answering Tyler's question. "Yeah, we do. Let's discuss it tomorrow. I doubt anything with the Davi case will happen tonight, anyway," Heath said. "Anything the DA has on Davi is circumstantial and easily dismissible. I doubt she even has a chance at presenting a discovery."

CHAPTER FOURTEEN

HEATH SAW her seated at the bar before he entered the restaurant. His heart skipped as his eyes wandered over the length of her curves.

She was stunning. Even more so than ever before.

Chestnut hair braided to the side, the length hung over her shoulder. A pair of white jean cutoffs with wedge heels and a blue seersucker shirt tied in a knot over her waist completed her outfit. Her long legs crossed at the knee, a big straw bag sat on the seat next to her.

Something primal within him roared "mine," an instinct buried beneath millennia of evolution. He broke into a grin as he strode toward his wife, missing her smell and warmth. This was his moment to make up for the past. No excuses or interruptions would keep him from her.

Heath embraced her from behind, planting a kiss on the top of her head. Sam jumped, her movement followed by a whiff of sweet vanilla from her hair. The smell a reminder of his favorite vanilla frosted lemon cake she always baked for him on his birthday.

Pleasure hummed along his body at her concentrated effort to return to her former self, but was still surprised she wanted to meet for lunch. Unexpected, but a welcome distraction from the Davi case. They still hadn't talked since the disastrous lunch the other day. Maybe now they could find some time to work on rebuilding their relationship.

Sam turned to him, her cheeks flushed. He returned her gaze with a lazy grin. She brought out the terrible flirt in him. Heath took her hand in his. "Is this seat taken, lovely lady? Or are you waiting for your hunky husband?" he teased, pleasure racing through him as the flush on her cheeks crept down her neck.

She returned his smile and he thought the look on her face could brighten the entire room.

"You've kept me waiting, Mr. Crenshaw." Her smile turned into a playful pout.

Heath gently touched her chin, lifting her face so her eyes met his. He took a deep breath. Confidence, a simmering fire missing for the past few months, had finally returned to her eyes.

"Want to skip lunch and go back home?" Heath let go of her face and trailed two fingers down the length of her neck, watching the movement as she swallowed, then followed the dip in her collarbone toward her shoulder. He tightened his hold, his eyes lowering, suggesting she knew exactly what he wanted to do. Damn the talking, they could talk after.

Sam laughed, the sound a soothing caress over his soul. Oh, how long it had been since he made her laugh. "I would do anything to hear you laugh like that again."

"Stop, everyone is looking at us."

"We can leave. Go somewhere private," he whispered, his face close to hers. On cue, Sam's stomach growled. She laughed again. "Or not," he said tugging on her braid. "Let's make a deal. I'll feed you first, then take advantage of you." He winked.

"Are you all talk, Mr. Crenshaw, or can you back up your swagger?" Sam smiled and playfully hit him with the menu.

He leaned in and kissed her on the cheek. "I missed you," he whispered.

"I missed you too," Sam replied, leaning her forehead against his.

"Let's eat...unless you want to pick up where you left off the other day?" He pulled away and propped up the menu and peeped over the edge at her.

The color on her cheeks returned. "Shhh!" Sam playfully hit him again. "Other people can hear you."

He watched her drink the last dregs from her wineglass. "How was work?" she asked. Heath noticed a tremble in her voice that wasn't there during their playful interlude.

Heath pursed his lips then sighed. "Davi is less forthcoming with his information than most clients. He's also arrogant as all hell, unwilling to bend even though he knows his ass is on the line." Heath stopped talking as the bartender placed a beer in front of him and refilled Sam's wine glass.

Once the bartender was out of earshot, he continued. "Rex had to reason with Davi before he finally opened up to me. Even then I had the feeling he was withholding information from me."

Heath noticed Sam appeared distracted despite her question. She played with the knotted tie of her shirt, twirling the blue fabric around her fingers.

He placed his hand on hers, soothing the hand trembling beneath his. "Hey, is everything okay? You seem on edge tonight." He removed his hand to rub her back in a gentle pattern. "I want to forget the case for tonight and just spend the time with you. No distractions."

Sam cleared her throat and looked at him. His stomach knotted at the emotions moving over her face. He knew that look all too well...she was going to tell him something he didn't want to hear.

"Out with it, Sam. I can't have whatever it is you need to

tell me eating away at you," Heath said firmly. "Tell me so we can move on and enjoy the rest of our evening together."

Sam dropped her eyes, her fingers knotted in the hem of her shirt. "I've been thinking about the dead woman and...I went to the restaurant she worked at to talk to some old friends."

"What! Baby, what's gotten into you?" He glanced around as the other guests looked their way. He leaned in, keeping his voice quiet. "You don't have the training to become involved in a case, especially one involving criminal charges! How did you know about the restaurant?" Heath was taken back by her admission.

"Please, hear me out. It sounds worse than it is." She paused then met his eyes. "I was so angry at you for working so much lately, the day you had me get the file folder out of your office, well, I looked at it." Sam took a deep breath before she continued. "I couldn't help myself. I needed to know what was so important to keep you away from me."

Heath fell back in his seat, shocked at her admission. Sam was dependable, intelligent and understood the importance of integrity and the relationship he had with his clients. She always respected boundaries. He felt like she sucker punched him.

"What...I don't understand. Why?" Heath searched her face for an answer. "Why would you think it was okay to go through my case files without my permission?"

"I told you, something just came over me, like a compulsion after... I needed to know what was keeping you away from me." Sam tripped over her words. "Or if there was someone else."

"Are you accusing me of having an affair? Is this what this whole thing is about? You don't trust me to come home to my wife?"

Sam placed a hand on his arm. He recoiled, brushing off her touch as he struggled to maintain his composure when his heart ached at her accusation. "No. Please, I don't want to do this right now. Can we just finish dinner and go home?" Sam said. "People are listening and I feel more comfortable talking at home. I should've waited until then to tell you."

Heath placed his elbows on the bar counter and stared ahead at the multitude of bottles lining the bar shelf. Sam had been going through one hell of a time lately, with finding Bailee's body and the fallout after her hospitalization and departure from her job. He damned well knew he wasn't winning an award for best husband, but she never would've done this before. Sam respected his work.

"Sam, you know how much you mean to me. But I can't have you do this right now. This case is so important." Heath stood up from the bar stool feeling suddenly claustrophobic. He needed to clear his head.

Sam placed her hand on his. "Please don't go."

The look in her eyes broke his heart. He accepted her invitation today for lunch as an attempt to reconnect. Here he was, ready to run back to his work the moment emotions became too heavy for him. Like a coward.

Heath sat back down. "Sam, you can't do this." He took her hand in his.

"I didn't intend any harm," she said as she pulled her hand from his grasp. "I thought I could help."

"I appreciate your concern but I need you to understand this case is teetering on the edge. There are so many things in play, I'm just trying to sort them all out with the team."

"Okay, okay, I understand. I'll keep myself from getting involved but I still want to know what is going on with the case. Nicholas Davi is one of the most influential businessmen in the area and...I was the one who found Bailee." Her voice faltered on the young woman's name.

"Exactly why I need this case handled with care." His mind wandered back to the missing files and security breach. Damn him, if he didn't make enough mistakes on his own.

Now Sam had further instilled herself into the case despite being a person of interest herself.

Their conversation was interrupted by the return of the bartender to take their orders. The interruption allowed Heath a chance for reflection. He needed to relax and enjoy his time with Sam. There would be plenty of late nights ahead of him and time enough to talk about the case. He didn't want this time marred by worry or regret.

Heath turned to Sam to say something when he saw her worrying her lip. He closed his eyes. Damnit.

"Spill it, Sam."

She turned to meet his eyes. "There's more," she said, looking around. "This really isn't the right place to tell you."

"Now you have to tell me." Heath held up his hands. "No, don't tell me, you were caught snooping around where you shouldn't be?" It was unlike Sam to do something like that but at this point he wouldn't put it past her.

"No, why would I do that," Sam said accusingly.

Her face softened. "Heath, I learned something about your case that will be difficult to hear." She continued, "I would rather tell you at home, not here with people around."

He sighed, needing to trust Sam to fix what was broken in her. If it involved helping him, he couldn't fault her loyalty. "I can take anything you can tell me as long as it doesn't involve us." He placed his arm around her chair, bringing them in closer to each other. "Tell me."

She took a deep breath and exhaled slowly, holding his gaze. "While at the restaurant I spoke with a waitress I know from when I used to frequent there with the ladies' auxiliary club."

Heath groaned. *Here we go, ladies gossip*, he thought as he reached for his beer, a small smile twitching his lips.

Sam leaned in to his ear. "She told me Bailee Talson was seen getting in a car with a dark-haired man."

Heath smiled. Sam was so desperate to help him, he didn't

have the heart to tell her he already knew this from his conversation with the bartender. He had to stop her curiosity before she got hurt or further implicated herself in the case.

"It's nothing I don't already know. I found out about the car when I interviewed the staff at the restaurant."

"It wasn't a town car. Did they tell you who it was?"

"No, they implied it was Nicholas Davi. Bailee sought him out for a private meeting."

"I'm not talking about Nicholas Davi or a town car," Sam said.

"Then who was it?" Heath indulged her.

"Rex Brown in his vintage red Ferrari."

Time slowed around Heath as a roaring filled his ears. Heath saw Sam's lips moving as if she was talking to him but he couldn't make out what she said. The buzzing sound in his head intensified, his pulsed pounded and his eyes were glued to Sam's panicked face.

No, not here.

He forced his breathing to slow, calming his pulse until time returned to normal speed.

"Heath, Heath, are you okay?" Sam shook his arm, her voice clear and face distraught.

"Yes, yes I'm...fine," he managed, his mouth dry. "Are you sure your source is reliable?" He took a deep drink from his beer, the amber liquid spilled onto his hand.

"I've known her for a few years. She's the resident gossip and knows who you are and Rex from our conversations. What you both look like, too."

Heath continued his steady breathing until he felt composed again. The entire base upon which he built his career had been wiped out from beneath his feet. What remained was a cracked foundation built on fallacy. Why didn't Rex say anything when they met in private? And if Rex was innocent, what had Sam stumbled into, believing Rex could murder a young woman?

"Are you sure you're okay?" Sam asked him, a hand on his arm, her touch comforting but not enough.

"I think I need some air." Heath jerked his thumb toward the bartender. "How about you have him box up our lunch to go. I'll meet you out front."

"I knew it wasn't the best place to tell you!" Tears swelled in her eyes. Heath kissed her hand. "I'll be okay, I just need some time to gather my thoughts."

He walked outside and inhaled, drawing the sultry air deep into his lungs. The buzzing sound in his ears subsided at last. He climbed into his car and drove upfront to wait outside for Sam. Heath needed time to process what she shared with him.

When she appeared, he rolled down the window. "I'll meet you back home. I need more time to think about what you said." Sam's face softened at his words, the wetness of unshed tears in her eyes.

"See you at home."

Heath pulled away, her reflection in his rearview mirror fading. He drove the rest of the rest of the day, winding along the roads beyond Midnight Harbor, needing to forget all about Nicholas Davi and the duplicity of his mentor and boss, Rex Brown. Most of all, he needed to manage his feelings about a woman who was turning out to be someone he barely knew.

HEATH WAS CORRECT. Nothing important happened that evening. It wasn't until the early morning news broke out over all the media outlets in Midnight Harbor and surrounding Charleston.

The sound of his phone buzzing woke him from a deep sleep.

Heath climbed out of bed, pulled on his jeans from last

night and grabbed his phone, making his way into the kitchen. He flipped on the television to catch the early news as he brewed a pot of coffee.

"Nicholas Davi was brought in for questioning this morning in the disappearance and murder of Bailee Talson," the news anchor said as the image changed over to a video of Nicholas Davi leaving the courthouse with Rex beside him. "He was released on his own free will with attorney Rex Brown. Stay tuned for additional updates on the murder of Bailee Talson and Nicholas Davi's involvement."

The words of the news anchor echoed off the walls of the house. Heath faltered, bracing his hands on the side of the granite countertop. "Damnit!" He growled at the television.

Heath glanced down at his phone, the notifications displayed a multitude of missed calls and text messages.

"Shit!"

He made haste for the bedroom for a shirt. He spared a glance at Sam still asleep. The talk they needed to have would wait. Heath was already late and needed to get to the office. The video coverage played over again and again in his head. He had questions which demanded answers. Heath was going to get those answers, no matter what the cost.

CHAPTER FIFTEEN

SAM'S HAND patted the side of Heath's bed, finding the bedsheets cold and empty. Disappointed to feel the emptiness. She had grown accustomed to Heath's absence in bed but thought he would've come to her last night. Why did she think anything different would happen when he left her after her confession?

Rubbing her temples at the throbbing of an impending headache, she pushed away the depressing thoughts and opened her eyes to the truth — she was strong enough to make her own decisions and confront Heath. She refused the victim role to her constant wallowing in emotions concerning their relationship. It was time for her to look within herself to see what she needed to do in order to become who she wanted to be.

Despite her self-realization, she understood deep inside her, their relationship wouldn't be fixed with a talk and smile. What broke between them left sharp, jagged pieces unable to be rebuilt into their previous marriage. Those pieces fit differently now than during the early years of their courtship and marriage. Was it worth saving? Rebuilding? Yes, there was no hesitation in her decision. Sam would fight and mend those sharp edges into a love better than before.

She could do this. She was capable of more than she thought.

Anchoring herself to those thoughts, Sam reluctantly dragged herself from under the warm covers, mentally running through her agenda for the day. The first item, a hot shower followed by coffee, then she could settle into how to best approach Heath and find out more of Rex's involvement. She ignored the phone on her bed. Too many days she had stayed in bed, watching TV, trying to forget and numb her pain.

Life needed to be lived, what use was it withering away when women like Bailee would never have the chance to experience life again? The thought of Bailee and her untimely death propelled Sam to face her own hardships instead of hiding away from the world.

The person she loved most was back at work, buried in a case with personal implications that could hurt everything Heath worked for. While Sam was prepared to face her own demons, she understood Heath needed her support in the confrontation of his. She played the perfect wife for many years, would it cost her so much to pretend a bit longer in his time of need?

Sam's phone rang as she spritzed the last of her curls in place. She picked up the phone to see the caller ID read "Josie."

"Hey Josie, how's it going?" Sam answered, walking into the bathroom. She reached for her mascara brush when the shrill tone of Josie's voice stopped her hand.

"How's it going? Sam, did you see the news today?" Josie wheezed. She barely managed to speak between deep breaths.

"I just woke up. I didn't bother checking the news."

"Girl, turn on your television right now!" Josie hissed.

"What's going on. You sound hysterical."

"You will be too once you see the news!"

Sam sighed. Was this another one of Josie's upsets over a celebrity breakup? Sam shook her head, grabbing the remote from her nightstand. She sat on the edge of the bed and flicked on the television, the channel set to the local news.

"Oh no." Sam dropped the phone and covered her mouth with her hand. Her eyes widened, taking in every second of the video replay as she watched Rex Brown hold up a hand to the reporters while simultaneously guiding Nicholas Davi toward a dark town car.

Sam picked up the phone, Josie rambling and unaware Sam had dropped it. "Josie, I gotta go. I'll call you later." Sam disconnected the call as Josie made a promise to check on her soon.

She sat motionless yet only a few minutes had passed. Eyes transfixed on the same images of Davi being played over and over. Her finger hovered over the off button when the video loop changed. A tall, dark blond man climbed out of a car. The camera followed his clipped pace from car to a building.

Heath.

Abby Jones shouted questions at Heath amid the chorus of other reporters. Her stomach knotted, remembering her own experiences with Abby and the photographer, how the man had followed her, hidden behind cars and trees. Would the media dare come here? To their home?

Anger, hot and blinding red, overcame her before she steadied herself.

Where did that come from? Then realized her anger was not for herself but Heath.

Davi taken in for questioning, Rex's duplicity. Heath was likely at his breaking point. She felt an overwhelming need to protect him. Funny, since she always thought she was the one needing protection.

The Firm. She would go to Heath at the Firm. It would also give her an opportunity to pursue Rex's whereabouts using his own resources. What better than to take the battle to the beast in his own lair?

Sam grabbed an oversized bag from the closet and threw clothes in it for her and Heath and grabbed her jacket and tablet, throwing both in the bag. They could crash at her parents' house or a hotel until the worst of the case blew over and the media lost interest. Sam bit back a laugh, there wasn't a chance this would blow over quickly.

In the kitchen she grabbed a water bottle and protein bar in place of her coffee. There was no need for caffeine as adrenaline kicked through her grogginess. Sam quickly loaded the weekender bag in the backseat of her car and donned her oversized sunglasses and mentally thanked Heath for the tinted windows on her car. She pressed the remote for the automatic garage door and waited for what felt like an eternity.

The early morning light spilled out from beneath the door and Sam reversed out of the garage. Once clear of the door, she pressed the button and waited until the door closed with a thud.

With the house secure, Sam reversed into the street, her intention clear — move or be moved.

Sam drove toward downtown, knowing for certain she couldn't keep her promise to Heath. There was no way she could to stay out of the case.

SHE PARKED her car down the street and walked toward the Firm's back entrance, watching the crowd gathered outside the Firm fight for dominance over the front entrance.

The keypad beeped as she punched in the numbers 0815, Heath's birthday, remembering the first time Heath gave her the code back when he was just an intern, sneaking her in for a clandestine lunch.

"Please work," she whispered, praying the key code still worked. She was in no mood to otherwise push her way through the reporters and gossip hounds.

Lights flickered from red to green and a mechanism clicked, unlocking the door. Sam gingerly pushed open the door to discover herself in the midst of a mad flurry of activity. Interns rushed up and down the hall, speaking in hushed voices. Phones rang from all over the first floor.

Sam hailed the first employee she saw. "Excuse me, do you know where Heath, I mean Attorney Crenshaw is?"

"Attorney Crenshaw is with Attorney Brown," the young man said his eyes widened. "I wouldn't go anywhere near that office if I were you. Maggie warned everyone away from the second wing."

Sam smiled at the young man, likely an intern. "Thank you, if you see Attorney Crenshaw in the meantime, please let him know his wife is here waiting for him."

The intern nodded before running down the hallway.

There was no way she was going to interrupt Heath and Rex and she certainly wasn't that stupid to attempt it. With Heath unavailable, she decided to see who she could find to gather more information on Rex.

Sam spotted Tyler standing behind a grouping of computer screens.

"Hi, Tyler," she said, walking into the room.

Tyler peeked at her from behind the two massive screens. "Hey, Sam," he said, his voice cheery. "I haven't seen you around here for a long time."

He walked out from behind the desk and grabbed her in a tight hug. "You look good," Sam said leaning back to look him over. Tyler was one of the most welcoming of Heath's colleagues, always eager to speak with Sam at the Firm dinners or events they attended in the community.

"I guess this is our worst case scenario come true, huh?" Sam said, a slight frown on her face, a desperate attempt to find levity in the situation.

"That's putting it mildly. Heath had a suspicion the DA would act quickly if she had a smidge of evidence. We never imagined the case would come to this."

"How long have Heath and Rex been behind closed doors?"

"About an hour now. Heath wasted no time seeking Rex out." Tyler walked back to his desk to resume his task, his eyes back on the twin computer screens. "Rex was livid. Said he had been trying to get ahold of Heath all night."

Sam forced her face into a neutral half smile though her stomach rolled from the information. She wasn't about to let Tyler find out what she discovered about Rex. "Heath hoped the case would blow over. I thought Davi had an alibi."

Tyler peeked at her from around the screens, an eyebrow raised. "Aalibi, eh?"

Sam stuttered, "Oh, I mean, that, that's what Heath let slip during dinner." It was a poor attempt to cover up her misstep.

"Mhmm," Tyler said.

"What?"

"Don't forget I've worked with Heath for a few years. You've always shown an interest in his cases, some more than others."

"What is that supposed to mean?"

"It means if you ever wanted to help him with a case, now is the time." Tyler glanced at Sam. He must have seen the surprised look on her face. "Don't look so taken back. You know as well as I do Heath is in something deep. Rex wanted to have the case dismissed. It looks like it's too late for that now. Plus, you have personal involvement beyond your relationship to Heath." Tyler paused before he continued, his voice softer. "You're the one who found Bailee Talson. It was horrible what you saw but if you remember something, now's the time to tell Theo."

The phone on Tyler's desk beeped. "Looks like I've been deemed the next sacrifice. I'll let Heath know you stopped by if I see him." Tyler walked toward her and pointed to the door. "I'll walk you out."

He stopped before they parted ways. "Seriously, consider what I said. We're in some deep shit."

Mulling over Tyler's suggestion as she watched him walk away, she wondered if that's what she had been looking for all along? A sense of purpose? Bailee's death gave her a sense of purpose she missed. Didn't she tell herself she was coming here to support Heath? Now she was here, it seemed an insurmountable task to take on. She couldn't just jump into his case. But she could work in parallel with him.

How could a depressed former librarian who had visions of dead women help? That's it! Maybe she could call on Bailee's ghost on her own accord. Bailee appeared to Sam in visions but what if a way existed in which Sam could bring Bailee to her?

She decided it was worth a shot. Until Heath returned, she would have nothing else to do while she waited. She might as well recount her visions for similarities and take advantage of the Firm's resources while she was here.

At Heath's office, she turned the doorknob, discovering his office locked. As she dug around at the bottom of her purse for her key, she noticed faint scratches around the keyhole. She shrugged, thinking nothing unusual for a frequently used door and unlocked the door and entered Heath's office.

Using Heath's desk as her own, Sam emptied the contents of the hastily packed overnight bag on the desk, shifting though the clothing to separate her tablet and newspaper clippings. She made quick work of the reading stored on her tablet. An hour passed with nothing coming of her research other than a stiff neck and the sense she was crazy. How does one call upon the dead? A séance? Did she need holy water? Candles?

Sam stretched out her arms above her head and leaned back in Heath's seat. Her shoulders were tight and her eyes ached from hovering over the tablet. What she needed was Heath to talk in earnest with about the case and Rex. It was the remaining lead they had to explore other than her visions.

Spinning around in the chair, her eyes landed on a broken silver thumb drive on the desk. Sam picked up the drive and remembered she found it before stumbling upon Bailee's body. It must've fallen out of her jacket pocket when she dumped the packed bag onto Heath's desk.

The doorknob turned and Sam closed her hand around the thumb drive and straightened her back. Heath walked into the room followed closely by Tyler.

"Sam? What are you doing here?" Heath said. He looked rumpled, his hair disheveled and stubble shadowed his jaw, he wore the same clothes from last night.

"I told you I would let him know you were here waiting for him," Tyler said from behind Heath. "I'll let you two love-birds finish here. I have some things I need to go over with one of the interns."

"Tyler, wait!" He turned back toward Sam. She met him at the office door. "Here, it's beat up but do you think you could recover the contents from it," she said, offering him the thumb drive. "I thought about what you said, and this might be useful."

"I'm always up for a challenge. I'll let you know what I discover."

Sam dropped the thumb drive in Tyler's outstretched hand. "Thanks, I owe you one."

"Don't worry, I won't forget." Sam watched Tyler leave then turned her attention to Heath, waiting for the tirade she could feel brewing.

Instead, Heath closed the office door and looked at her, his face crestfallen. "What the hell am I going to do?"

Her heart ached for him. Going to him, she wrapped her arms around his waist, wanting to ease his hurt and the disappointment that hung heavy in the air. "You'll figure out what to do. You always do. That's what makes you the best." She hadn't seen him look this way since she was hospitalized.

"I'm glad to hear you have so much faith in me," he said sarcastically.

"I have faith in you because I know you're capable of great things. Don't you remember the work you've done in the past? The clients you helped to get you to this point?" Sam tilted her head back and looked into his eyes. "You can't let this side track your progress."

Heath sighed, tightening his arms around her so her head rested on his chest. "I came here as soon as I heard about Davi. I met with Rex. Do you think I asked him about what you told me? About why he was seen picking up Bailee Talson from the restaurant? No. I didn't."

"You need to wait for the appropriate time. If you asked now, it would've further inflamed him," Sam said. He believed her. That's all she needed to know he trusted her. The pieces of their marriage were not completely broken.

"You're right. We don't even know Rex's reason for being there. For all we know your source could have the wrong person."

"She's not wrong. I already told you I believe her," Sam said firmly.

"I don't think there will ever be a good time if he is responsible for her disappearance," Heath said his voice muffled by her hair. He ran his hand down her back, sending a shiver along her spine to where his hand stopped at her hip.

"No," Sam said softly, "there won't but...I have an idea."

"No, absolutely not. You're not helping me, Sam. I already told you."

Sam pushed away from the embrace. "What do you expect me to do? Go back home while you sit in here and berate yourself over something beyond your control?"

"Yes," he said, turning his back to her. Once again he distanced himself from her. When the emotion became difficult, he withdrew.

Sam followed him as he walked to pour himself a drink. "Too bad, it's not happening. I've spent too much time sitting in our house, wallowing in emotions and grief. I can't do it anymore. I won't do it anymore." She walked toward him until he was forced to face her. "Do you know interviewing Willa was the most thrilling thing I have done in months? You're not going to tell me no or what I get to do when I finally get a chance at feeling more alive than I've felt in six months." Sam's chest heaved, her hands curled at her sides in response to the strong emotions she felt racing throughout her body. She would fight him for what she wanted.

"I'm not controlling you. You have no experience and could put yourself at risk. I can't allow you to hurt yourself." Heath swallowed the rest of his drink and shrugged. "You can find some other way to help. Maybe ask the ladies' auxiliary to start a fundraiser."

"No," Sam said, her voice steady and strong, "No. I decide and I chose to stay." Sam reached out her hands to take his, pulling them closer together. "You need me."

Heath said nothing. Instead he closed the distance between them and grabbed her face in his hands, tracing a thumb over her bottom lip. He bent his head, his lips a space apart from her own. "Do I?"

"Yes" she whispered, staring back at him. His hand wrapped around the back of her head and he kissed her, his lips a comfort as much as a declaration of need. Heath's other hand pushed on the small of her back, bringing her against the length of him as he deepened the kiss. Despite the ugliness around them, Sam savored his touch and the thrill it sent racing through her. She enjoyed the moment with her husband, having spent too many days and nights apart from him to come this far. She refused to allow Heath to back away from her again. She clung to him, threading her fingers through his hair.

Heath lifted his face from hers, their breathing heavy, and rubbed his nose against hers. "All right, since you made your intentions clear and I have no further arguments, where should we begin?" He pointed to his desk. "I've scoured over my files and have yet to find anything leading me to believe Davi wasn't involved. Yet, Kerri Reid vouches as his alibi for the night of the murder. She can put him with her during the timeframe Bailee was murdered. Now we have Rex possibly involved from your source." Heath slumped into the armchair. "You can share your idea because I'm tapped out."

Sam paced in front of him, knowing full well her visions of Bailee drove her and yet not wanting to share with Heath. Her eyes closed, she visualized their next step without sharing her secret. "We need to know more about Bailee Talson and what made her tick. I gave Tyler a thumb drive I found that night."

"You mean, you forgot to hand over evidence to the police department?"

"I forgot until now when I was digging through the bag I brought. I don't even know if it's Bailee's. What we do know is she worked at the restaurant, was a hard worker paying her way through college," Sam said.

Heath stood pacing around the room with her at parallel intervals. Sam continued, "She was also being hit on by the manager and sought out Davi as well as Rex at separate times. For what?"

"We have to assume Davi and Rex were not aware of each other's interaction with her. If they were aware, they would have said something to me during my interview with Davi," Heath said. "They likely would've told each other."

"We need to find out," Sam said.

"Then it's decided. We'll return to the restaurant to talk with your friend Willa," Heath said as he advanced toward the door. "We probably want to have a chat with the manger as well if he was making advances toward Bailee and find her roommate. Then, I drop you off and contact Theo with what we discovered. This is too deep for me, moving into police territory we have no business in."

Sam stood still. She wouldn't budge on her decision. "We go to Theo together. Final."

"Fine. Are you coming or just going to stand there looking cute?"

Sam raced toward him, ready to assist her husband and maybe find her purpose along the way.

CHAPTER SIXTEEN

HE'D LOST HIS MIND. Why else would he agree to help from Sam with the Davi case? He peeked at her out of the corner of his eye, unnerved by her quiet companionship. He wished now, like he had in the past, for the ability to read her thoughts. What did she make of this mess, of him and their relationship. Could he ask her without dragging her back into the depression she had just left behind? Or would the questions prompt her return to the half-life she lived for the past six months?

He drummed his fingers along the steering wheel then stopped when he noticed her staring at his hands. She recognized his quirks. Did she know he words for her?

"Sam? I need to tell you something that I didn't say back at the Firm."

"What is it?" Her voice was soft but held emotion, unlike the monotone voice he fought to forget.

He felt her inquisitive eyes on him and he didn't dare look at her, afraid he would reveal too much. "Rex told me I have twenty-four hours to present a solid defense for Davi," Heath said, his voice thick as he fought back a more emotional response. "If Davi isn't to blame, then who is?"

"Not me."

"I'm not suggesting that. You're not capable of the evil necessary to end another's life."

"It's not your responsibility to find out who the culprit is," Sam said. "You need to defend Davi, the DA needs to prove his guilt."

"When have you ever known me to sit idly while my client is in the hot seat?"

"I admire that trait in you. You're always willing to go the extra mile for one of your clients."

Heath momentarily swelled with pride. "You're my wife, it's obligatory you believe in me." It was a different thing to hear Sam compliment him. It felt good.

"The truth is, I'm afraid this is going to lead us to Rex. If he's the culprit, then what do I do?" Heath asked. "What happens?"

"You don't know that for sure. What about other possibilities? Let's take it one step at a time. Once we have more information, then you can think about what you would do if Rex is involved. Stay present until we have a clear picture."

Heath nodded, his self-doubt diminishing with her steady presence. He could do this. "I missed this, us. You were always my sounding board."

"Well you know what they say, behind every smart man is a smarter woman," Sam said with a smile.

Heath chuckled. "Do you ever regret not finishing your law degree?" Heath asked, changing the topic.

"It wasn't meant for me," she said. He watched her tuck a strand of hair behind her ear, a small shrug. "I enjoy talking about these things with you but the reality is I would fold under the late hours, the public speaking, ugh." She shook her head. "You can take it. Give me an old library stacked with books any day of the week."

"What of your job, Sam? Any regrets?" They were almost to the restaurant.

Heath waited until he was certain she wasn't going to answer then he heard a soft "Yes." She continued. "I miss getting up every day with a purpose. When I worked, there were always students or patrons needing me. I felt useful and enjoyed it." She shifted in her seat and looked at him, her hand touching his arm. The warmth of her touch seeped through his shirt, all the way to his core. "Not that I mind our life. I miss helping people, I miss feeling like I have something to contribute beyond being a good housewife or faux socialite."

Her words wounded him though she meant no ill intent. "Why tell me this now? I thought you loved our life. Throwing parties and going around to different galas. You always appeared content."

"I feel like something inside of me is awake, something I had buried deep down. Do you remember the dreams I used to have? Of the lake?"

He nodded, recalling the terrors she would wake from, sweating and scared.

"I had the dream again. It's been years since the last time. I don't know what caused it to return but I somehow think it's related to Bailee Talson."

"Of course the dreams are related. You found a deceased woman. Did I force this change in you?" Heath questioned. Did he push her too far?

"No, my actions are my own. Only I can claim responsibility just like only you can claim responsibility for your actions. What Rex did has no claim to who you are, remember that. Don't lose sight of who you are." She squeezed his arm.

Heath allowed her words to sink in. Was he blaming himself for Rex's actions? He felt betrayed. If Rex, his mentor, was capable of the unspeakable, what did that make Heath capable of? Could he be corrupted? Was that his new path? The distance from Sam was jarring him. The silence grew between them as they both were lost in thought.

He shoved those thoughts away too. Focus on the present, deal with emotions later.

"We're here," he said, winking at Sam, hoping she didn't see through his façade. Heath parked outside the restaurant and climbed out of the car to open the door for Sam. She smiled up at him with trust in her eyes. If only he was worthy.

They found a different hostess behind the podium near the entrance. "Excuse me," Heath said, "I was wondering if Willa was working today. My wife and I like to sit in her area. She was wonderful last time we dined here."

"I'm sorry sir, Willa is unavailable. I would be happy to seat you in Jo's area on the patio."

Heath looked over the hostess's shoulder to the bar, hoping to see a familiar face and finding none. "I think we would be happy with a table inside."

"Absolutely, follow me this way," the young hostess said as she led them to a small secluded area near the back of the restaurant. As many times as Heath had been here, he never noticed this area.

"Now what? Why did you tell her we would take a seat when Willa isn't here?" Sam said sitting across from him.

Heath waited until they were alone and leaned toward Sam, his voice quiet. "I want to think about the next step without having to drive around town. Plus, being able to admire your pretty face is a bonus."

Her lips quickened into that smile he loved. She tried to suppress it but he was confident he could ease the smile out of her. Sam was back but she certainly wasn't the old Sam he used to know. The woman across from him appeared confident, more in control than Sam had ever been. He loved her dearly but she had almost felt like she was an extension of him, a half to his own. Now, she was her own person. Isn't that what he loved about her before? Her confidence and independence? When had she lost it? He hoped whatever demons she was battling wouldn't change her for good.

"We should move on to our next stop and come back here later tonight," Sam said. "It's a bust."

"We're running out of time." Heath glanced around the restaurant. A gentleman in a button down shirt and slacks caught his eye, chatting with a waitress. "Bet you that man over there is the manager of this restaurant." The man leaned into the waitress, whispering in her ear with a hand on the small of her back. Heath frowned.

Sam turned to look at the man. "I wonder if he was the manager hitting on Bailee Talson?"

"We need his attention...Agh!" Heath cried out as a wet coldness spread across his lap. He jumped up, out of his seat in a poor attempt to brush the worst of the liquid off of his pants.

"Oops," Sam said, "my hand must have slipped." She gave him an apologetic look before turning toward the man. "Excuse me, sir!" she called out, her hand waving frantically in the air.

Heath sat back down, using a napkin to absorb the worst of the water. "Nice move. Though we need to discuss why I'm the one who's always the victim?" Heath questioned, cocking an eyebrow in her direction.

Sam shrugged. "You're a better actor."

The man approached the table, a swagger to his step that made Heath cringe. He didn't want this man anywhere near Sam. He curled his fist and plastered on his fakest smile.

"Ouch!" Heath yelped at the sudden pain in his ankle. He looked over to see Sam giving him a dirty look. What was wrong with him? He tried to look friendlier. This man could be an ally and Heath didn't want to push him away.

"What can I help you with?" the man asked Sam. Heath watched the man's eyes roam over Sam's body, not bothering to spare so much as a glance toward him. What game was she at?

"Excuse me, sir, I can't believe I did this again for the second time today. I'm such a klutz. I was hoping you would be able to have one of the lovely waitresses refill my water glass for me." Sam pointed to the water spilling over the edge of the table. "I accidentally spilled water all over my husband." She batted her eyes.

"Certainly," the man said. He flashed Sam a look venturing close to a leer. The manager picked up the water glass. "I would be happy to do that for you." Heath couldn't believe her audacity.

They watched the manager walk away to refill the glass. "Sorry, it was the best I could think of," Sam said.

Heath playfully narrowed his eyes before grinning at Sam's quick thinking.

The manager returned with refilled glass and pitcher of lemon water a minute later. He placed both on the table in front of Sam with a flourish. Heath held his tongue despite the primal urge this man brought out in him.

"Thank you so much!" Sam flashed the manager a smile. "You know, I don't remember seeing you around here. Did you take over management of this restaurant?" Sam said as she twirled a finger around a stray piece of hair.

"Yes, I did. I'm Devon. I was hired four months ago when the new owners took over. They were looking for someone with a bit more...experience in running a restaurant than my predecessor," he said, puffing out his chest.

Heath stifled a groan, this was too much. He was just about to send Devon the manager away when Sam redirected him.

"Sounds like you have a lot of experience to be running a fine establishment such as this, especially with being so young." Sam glanced around then dropped her voice to a whisper. "What are you going to do with all the rumors about the young lady who worked here that went missing? I'm sure you have a lot of guests wondering about what happened to her."

Devon's nostrils flared at the mention of Bailee Talson. "I try to keep all of the gossip out of the restaurant. It's bad business having reporters outside spreading such lies about our establishment. Bailee Talson was a troubled young woman who ran with the wrong crowd. She likely got caught up in something and before she knew it found herself in over her head."

"Such a tragedy," Heath said, his eyes focused on the man in front of him. What did this guy know?

The manager shrugged oblivious to Heath's tone. "As you can understand, we have an image to maintain. It's no good for business to have that type of clientele hanging about, let alone working here."

"What do you mean? Did she bring her personal life into work?" Sam questioned.

"There were a few times she showed up to work not completely put together like she should be. She used to be one of my best employees, then all of a sudden, she no longer wants to pick up any shifts. She asked me to cut back her hours." The man turned up his nose. "I have a business to run, I can't allow my staff to pick and choose when they want to work."

"I understand. It must be difficult managing so many employees," Sam said leading him into more questions.

"It is." Devon nodded in agreement. "I had no choice. I made the difficult decision to let her go."

Sam flashed Heath a bewildered look. Something wasn't right with the story as they knew it.

Heath changed his perspective on the man, looking at him differently after his admission. "I thought Bailee Talson never showed up for her scheduled shift? That she was a no call, no show?"

Devon shook his head, a frown marring his face. "Those reporters write whatever they want to in order to sell a story. I told them and that Detective Hart the truth, I had to let her go. She showed up late for the third time in a week. I told her to pack up her locker and leave. I don't have time for that type of behavior here."

"Rightfully so," Heath agreed quietly, his eyes meeting Sam's, imploring her to continue the conversation.

Sam continued. "The other rumor going around is you had a special relationship with Bailee."

Anger flashed across Devon's face. "Listen, I don't know what those reporters are writing but I wasn't going to allow her to use me!" Realizing he said more than he intended, Devon straightened his necktie then leaned in toward the table. "It's true we had a consensual relationship, but we never had sex, just flirting. But I could tell she was only using me to get better shifts. Then, out of nowhere she turned cold. I pursued her but she wasn't interested."

"Anything happen after? Lingering bad feelings?" Sam questioned.

"Nothing. She proved she wasn't interested and I have a reputation to uphold. I'm not going to be seen as the man chasing after her. Not long after she started acting erratically."

Despite the manager being a creep, Heath could tell this was the type of man who wouldn't let a woman cloud his ambition.

"Do you remember what you were doing the night Bailee went missing?" Heath asked.

"The same thing I told the detective. I was here until close then went home alone. I opened the next morning and wanted to be here early for prep."

"Thank you so much for taking care of us but I'm afraid we have to get going," Sam said.

"You're leaving so soon?" Devon questioned.

"We're running late for our appointment with our realtor," Sam said.

"Next time you're in the area make sure to stop by, I will make sure our chef prepares a special menu for you. Just ask for me."

"We will," Heath said and shook the manager's hand. "Thank you. You have no idea how much you've helped us."

Heath placed his hand on Sam's back to guide her out of the restaurant and further away from the creep. Once they were back in the safe confines of their car, Heath turned to Sam. "Please don't ever do that again."

"Do what again?"

"Flirt with another man in front of me," Heath said through gritted teeth. "It took all my patience not to jump out of my seat and punch him."

"I won't, I promise," Sam said. "I didn't mean anything. I acted to get his attention, that's all." She took out her phone to check the time. "Twenty-two hours to go before your time is up. What's next on the agenda?"

"Meeting up with Willa is a bust. Devon will recognize us and question our motives for meeting with her instead of him when he just made such a grand offer to us."

Heath started driving south of the restaurant, toward the center of town. "If what he is saying is true, I think our next best step is to find out what happened after Bailee Talson was fired. We can check to see if she also disenrolled from her classes at the college."

"Do you think she would have?" Sam said.

"Maybe, but we only have twenty-two hours left and I'm hitting a roadblock. We need to change up our process to include her life outside of the restaurant, going all the way back to before her disappearance."

Sam nodded her agreement. "Did you notice how he said he didn't like the reporters around but he was more than willing to talk about her disappearance to us, just regular customers?"

Heath agreed, "I wondered that too. He likely is just a man spurred by a woman he was interested in and didn't take it well. Probably fired her to save face."

"There's only one way to find out," Sam said as they drove to the college hoping to discover more about the hidden life of Bailee Talson before her death.

CHAPTER SEVENTEEN

HEATH SAT, impatient, outside the admissions office, waiting while Sam tried her hand in obtaining information on Bailee Talson's transcript. After twenty minutes, she exited the college building with a slight slump in her step.

"No luck?"

"None at all." Sam sat beside him. "I tried the concerned older sister act."

"For what it's worth you don't look a day over twenty-three," Heath said wrapping an arm around her shoulders. "I asked Tyler to take a look into Bailee Talson's file to see if any information has been uploaded about her college transcript or academic profile." Heath zoomed in on the text on his phone so they both could read, the white light illuminating their faces as they huddled closer together.

"He discovered she was a communications major from 2017 through 2019 when she disappeared. She lived in off-campus housing with a roommate," Heath read aloud from his phone. "If you remember, Theo mentioned Bailee was reported missing by her roommate."

Sam looked at his phone to follow along. "That's all the information gathered during the investigation?"

"That's what it looks like. The DA likely thought she had everything they need to proceed with charges and didn't waste additional manpower."

Heath raked a hand through his hair, thinking through all the details they had so far. "By all accounts Bailee Talson was described as a good girl from a lower middle-class family trying to better herself. She was likely awarded a grant or scholarship with GPA requirements to maintain her financial aid."

"If something caused her to start missing classes, her GPA might drop and she could lose her scholarships," Sam added.

"Exactly!" Heath said as he stood and paced around the small area. "If she lost her financial aid then she would need to make up the difference. she'd pick up additional shifts at her job to make up for the lost aid. It would be a heavy burden to replace the financial aid and pay her share of the rent for the apartment while still purchasing necessities like food."

Sam continued the thread of thought. "But we have multiple witness accounts saying she cut back her hours at work. Maybe she hoped to improve her GPA?" Sam countered. "She could've hired a tutor."

"That's possible but...let's try another angle. Think about it, a small town girl from finds herself here. Charleston College is in a wealthy area. If she found herself surrounded by peers with money and privilege...what do you think she would want to do?"

"She would try to fit in, be more like her peers so she wasn't an outcast."

"What if the something that caused her to drop her grades and stop picking up shifts was really someone?"

Sam nodded. "Someone with money."

Heath looked at her. "Yes, someone who told her they would be able to provide for her. She wouldn't need to finish school or even worrying about working."

Sam whistled. "Are you thinking a Cinderella story? Girl meets her Prince Charming who is ready to sweep her off her feet?"

"I was thinking more a sugar daddy but we can go with Cinderella story for the romantics at heart," Heath said with a wide grin.

"But Bailee Talson didn't strike me as the type of girl who would be willing to share herself with just anyone," Sam said. "She would have to be in love in order to do that. If it was love, she would've gushed about the new guy to her girlfriends or coworkers."

"How would you know what she was like?"

Sam fidgeted with the hem of her shirt. "It's just a feeling I got when I talked with her. She seemed like a sweet girl."

"When you talked with her? What are talking about?"

Her face scarlet, she stammered, "Um, uh, I just had a feeling. You know? Like a feeling in your gut telling you something. In her photo, Bailee reminded me of my sister. Sweet, naïve. I would hate to know something bad happened to her."

"Sweet girls are capable of doing bad things," Heath reminded her, mentally filing away the reaction Sam had to Bailee. Maybe it was just lingering trauma he needed to find her help for.

"Not her. Just play along with me, all right?"

Heath shrugged. "Let's find her girlfriends, roommate, anyone who can help us shed a light on who this mystery person is. Just keep my suggestion in mind."

"I will." Sam toyed with the hem of her shirt. "You're right. She has a motive. I still don't think it would be for power."

"No," Heath thought aloud, "but someone powerful could have been protecting her."

"Do you think she got caught up in something and needed protection?" Sam said.

"There's only one way to find out," Heath said. He turned toward her and held out his hand.

"Oh, how romantic," Sam said as she took his hand and got up from the bench. "Spending quality time with my husband by helping him solve a case that could potentially cost him his job and our livelihood while I sit behind bars."

"Well, when you put it that way it does make it seem morbid." Heath squeezed her hand. "I promise we'll figure this out and when we're done here, we'll go on that getaway."

"I'm holding you to it," Sam said.

"I know you are." *Me too,* he thought.

She returned the squeeze. "I found a new dress I think you'll like."

"Hopefully we won't eat any spicy noodles this time."

Sam gave him a playful smack on the arm.

"How much time do we have left?" Heath asked her.

"Twenty hours to go."

Heath sighed. The weight of this case burdened him like no other before. There was still so much they didn't know. He was too far over his head to stop now. They would see this through to the end. "Let's go find our roommate and see what gossip Bailee shared with her friends." Heath hoped she was a chatty type.

***

"EVICTED," Heath said in disbelief as he stood outside the door of Bailee's last known address, the apartment she shared with another college student. "You've got to be kidding me!"

The apartment building skirted the edge of town, far enough away from the college that transportation would be required. The exterior was kept in modest repair, a few crumbling bricks here and there while the interior was a span of white walls and dark brown carpet. Sparse decorations, nothing extravagant, but more importantly, the building appeared clean and safe. The perfect place for an apartment for someone needing to keep housing cost low in the city.

They were running around in circles. Every single step forward, they tumbled back further from their goal.

"The date of eviction was three weeks ago," Sam said as she looked over the pink sheet of paper printed with bold, black letters taped to the front door. "She was reported missing around the same time."

"Evictions take time. Our girl wasn't holding up her end of the deal," Heath said as he looked up and down the hallway. Her money problems likely began a lot sooner than what Heath originally thought.

"Nor was her roomie by the looks of it," Sam said.

Heath agreed, "They both must have been just making barely enough to keep this apartment afloat between them."

"Did you hear that?" A scratching noise caught Heath's attention at the end of the hallway. He turned toward the sound, glimpsing movement from the end of the hallway.

Beside him he heard Sam inhale loudly, then whisper, "No, it can't be." He glanced back to her, finding Sam's face drained of color. He wasn't sure what spooked her but he needed to find out who was just in the hallway with them.

"Excuse me!" Heath called out as he quickened his pace.

Sam followed behind him and he waited for her to catch up. Heath placed his hand in front of her. "Stay behind me," he said, positioning his body in front of her. Goose pimples broke out over his skin as his senses heightened. He didn't see the person again but his body tensed, waiting.

A door shut. They ran straight ahead toward the end of the hallway where a window loomed. Heath ran up to the window and looked out, noticing there were no stairs. The hallway split into two directions, each ending with fire exits. Along the right hallway, a child of about eight years old stood, her knees dirty and a red juice moustache stained her upper lip. Another child, much younger, clothed in just a diaper and shirt stood next to her.

The older child pointed toward the fire exit the opposite way. "She went that way," the young girl said.

"Stay here with the children." Heath motioned to Sam. "See if you can find Mom or Dad."

He ran down the hallway and pushed open the heavy door of the fire exit, the sign warning of alarms a falsehood. Heath exited the apartment building onto the small, rickety fire escape.

Instinct told Heath to look down between the open grates of the floor. Near the bottom of the fire escape he saw a slight figure climbing down the remaining flight of stairs.

"Hey!" Heath shouted as he started to descend the stairs after the unknown person. "Stop! I just want to talk to you!" His heart pounded in his chest as he finished climbing down the last set of stairs and dropped to the ground.

He stood, looking around to find himself in the back alley of the apartment building. Large dumpsters scattered the alleyway, overflowing the area with garbage bags and foul smelling liquid ran on the ground toward sewer drains. The woman was at the end of the alley, near the sidewalk where an intersection led back toward the college. Cars, bicycles and people passed by. He needed to reach her before he lost her in the crowd.

Adrenaline kicked his body into a full-fledged run, this time he would catch her. His strength and speed were no match for her as he quickly reached her heels. "Please, stop!" he said urgently, "I can help you!"

The woman turned around, her face half hidden beneath a baseball cap worn low over her brow, her blonde hair stuck out in a low ponytail. He reached out a hand to her, his palm open. She stared at his hand then his face, her features in shadow from her baseball cap except the streaks he saw on her cheeks. "Come back with me and we can talk, please."

"It's too late," she rasped, then turned and ran straight into the intersection.

Heath swore time slowed as the young woman stepped out. He braced himself for the worst.

A car slammed on its brakes, the tires squealing as it just barely missed the woman in the baseball cap. The driver hung out the window cursing at her. She looked around in panic as if realization of what she had just done washed over her. The woman turned and ran down the street, pushing people out of her way and dodging baby strollers. Too soon she was out of Heath's sight.

Heath stopped to catch his breath, hands on his knees as his heart beat rapidly. He sent a silent thanks to whoever was watching over the young woman.

He needed to reconvene with Sam. They were short on time and losing options fast.

CHAPTER EIGHTEEN

SAM LISTENED PATIENTLY while Health reconstructed what transpired after he left her at the apartment building with the children. Thankfully, they were fine. Mom was home in the apartment, busy cooking dinner. The two children heard noise outside the door and ventured out to investigate. A few words later, the children were safe inside with Mom and Heath had returned to her side, albeit out of breath and shaken by what happened.

They reconvened at the sandwich shop on Charleston College campus for lunch and more importantly, so he could fill her in on the details of his unsuccessful chase.

"I can't believe the young woman was so frightened of you she dared walk out into traffic to get away," Sam said. She remembered the rising panic she felt right outside the apartment door, before Heath saw the woman. Sam wished she'd seen her too. Maybe she would've recognized her but instead her panic gave way to an image of Bailee's ghost, standing before her. She froze then disappeared, not before Sam was filled with terror. So much for wanting to call upon Bailee's ghost. Sam had the chance and froze.

"I didn't say anything to her that would've spooked her.

She probably thought I wanted to hurt her." Heath covered his face with his hand.

Sam placed her hand on top of his other hand. "You didn't do anything wrong. She ran away because she didn't want us to discover why she was there. She was okay, right?"

Heath nodded, the color finally returning to his face. When he had met Sam back at the apartment complex, his face was robbed of all color and he refused to talk until they reached the restaurant.

"You know I'm not the type of person to chase after a woman? I would never harm her or anyone for that matter."

She nodded her head in agreement and stroked his hand. "I know you're not capable of that. So why did you run after her?"

Heath looked out the window before he spoke. "I chased after her because she appeared guilty, like she was snooping around while we were at the apartment. I offered to help her but she said it was too late. Too late for what?" Heath tilted his head, directing his gaze toward her. "Before I first saw her, you said 'oh no.' Why?"

Sam leaned in, closing the gap between them until she could see the gold flecks in his brown eyes. "It wasn't the woman." Sam took a deep breath and closed her eyes, knowing she couldn't keep her secret from him any longer. His possible reactions to her confession scared her. Her honesty could push him further away. She needed to take this step if she were to fix their marriage and find peace for herself. "I thought I saw Bailee Talson standing next to the other woman." Sam held her hands up in front of her. "I know it sounds crazy. It wasn't the first time I thought I saw her."

She looked at his face for reassurance but what she saw on his face was pity instead. He stroked her arm, his brown eyes never breaking from hers.

"I understand how you must feel with her disappearance

and murder. You found her just as you were coming back to me, to life. Normal people would shatter beneath that type of horror. This type of case wasn't something I would want you involved in."

Sam pulled away from him, her attention drawn to her hands. Heath corroborated her worst fear, something was wrong with her and Heath thought so too.

The more she shared, the more he would pressure her to see a doctor.

No, she had to keep this to herself for now. Play along with him until she saw the case through. What she did recognize with the visit to the apartment, was each vision of Bailee brought a rising panic, similar to anxiety attacks she used to have.

Was it connected to Bailee? Her visions, the panic, the changes in temperature? More importantly, they weren't any closer to finding out what happened to Bailee. It had to be connected. How could she use this to her advantage to help them find out what happened?

Heath kissed her forehead, bringing her back to reality. He picked up the remnants of their shared lunch and threw it in the garbage. "I think it's about time I go back to the office to see Tyler. I can fill him in on the details of what we discovered and find out if he recovered data from your thumb drive. I'll drop you off at home along the way."

Sam stopped in her footsteps. "What do you mean?"

"We're too deep into this case. It certainly isn't what I imagined. I refuse to let you get hurt."

"We've been over this already. I'm helping you with this case." She placed her hand on his chest, she could make out the throb of his heartbeat against her palm. "I'm not leaving you to do this on your own. I told you I would help and I intend to keep my promise."

He back-peddled, raking a hand though his hair. Heath covered his face with his hands and rubbed his face before grabbing her by the shoulders. "Sam, if something terrible happened to you I would never be able to forgive myself. You're already under immense stress from what you went through." He pulled her against him and whispered in her ear, "It's not normal to see dead people, Sam. This isn't some type of movie or TV show."

The warmth from his hands sunk through her shirt. She wanted his touch and more.

No, she wouldn't be pushed away this time. She shook off his hands. "I understand it's not a movie. A woman is dead. A woman I found. I feel somehow responsible. It's stupid." She pressed on, fighting through her thoughts. "This is our life, our livelihood. Don't turn me back when you need me the most," Sam said making her case, determined to stay by his side, to see this case through and bring closure to Bailee. "I'm not sick. I don't know what I saw. The visions…are related to Bailee Talson's death. I can't explain it. It's just a feeling I have."

"Fine. This is your last chance. If things start to take a turn then we're both getting out as quickly as we can and leaving the rest up to the professionals."

"Aren't you the professional?" Sam teased him, taking a step towards him and tipping her head back to look in his eyes.

He gripped her hands. "The trained police force, Sam. You know, Theo. I don't know why I do this to myself. Do you know any other attorneys that chase down suspicious people in alleyways with their wives in tow?"

"Nope, I only know of one and he happens to be standing right beside me." Sam gave him her biggest smile.

"The next time I get the crazy idea I want to take on a special high-profile case, remind me the little ones will do."

"You just need a firm hand to guide you, that's all," Sam said as they walked back to the car. She hoped the ride back to the Firm was uneventful. Yet, she had the strange feeling they were beginning to uncover something meant to remain hidden.

THE LARGE CROWD of reporters once gathered around the Firm had dwindled to a few sporadic news agencies. The other agencies likely back at the station to splice together a video feed for the evening news.

Heath placed his arm around her and pulled her tight against him, as if to block her from view. "We'll go in the front entrance this time."

They ignored the pleas for comment and walked into the Firm. Just as the building bustled with activity a few hours earlier, it was eerily silent now, their footsteps loud on the wood floor.

Maggie was nowhere to be seen, the receptionist desk empty.

They found Tyler behind his computer monitors, behemoths that took up the space of his desk, leaving only a narrow sliver for his keyboard. His head was tilted in concentration.

"The A-Team has returned. Or is it the B-Team?" Tyler offered in greeting, his eyes focused on his monitors. His fingers glided easily over the keyboard in quick strokes. Every now and then Tyler would touch the screen of one of the computers.

"Did you discover any new leads?" Tyler asked without breaking from his task.

"Not exactly. We stopped by Bailee Talson's apartment, hoping to meet with her roommate. There was an eviction notice taped to the door and Heath chased away another woman who was near the apartment," Sam said as she sat at one of the empty chairs near Tyler.

Sam didn't want to steal her husband's thunder but she

knew he would take the long way to the point. Tyler had to be in the know so they could compare notes and make a plan of action.

Tyler looked from Sam to Heath and back again. "Is this the same Sam who walked out of my lab a few hours ago? 'Cuz I know that girl would never have volunteered information about her husband's case."

Sam shrugged. "People change."

Tyler looked at her with a smile. "Indeed they do. I sure hope your husband is ready for the change."

"Her husband is standing right here. How about you include me in your conversation next time."

Tyler gave Heath a slap on the back. "Sorry, man, I'm just trying to take it all in." Tyler returned to his desk. "So, a woman was snooping around the apartment? Was it the roommate returning for a few things or someone else?"

Heath stood by Tyler, reviewing one of the monitors closest to him. "I don't know. My guess is it was the roommate returning for a few items before the landlord changed the locks. Do we have a description of the roommate?"

"Dark hair, average build and height. Does that match what you saw?"

Heath shook his head. "No, the woman had blonde hair and was slim."

"Well, hopefully this can be of more help." Tyler handed a paper to each of them. "It's a copy of Bailee Talson's autopsy report. Her body had some bruising around the neck inflicted pre mortem and...she had been sexually active before her death."

"Cause of death?" Heath asked.

"Poison," Sam whispered, looking up from the paper. "Who would want to poison a college coed?" Slouched in her seat, the emotions of hearing about Bailee's autopsy weighed heavy on her. Sam stared at Tyler's monitors when she noticed a familiar name.

"Tyler, do you mind enlarging that report?" Sam asked, pointing to the section of the screen.

"This one?" Tyler expanded the section of the file.

"Is that Bailee Talson's police report?"

"Yes, it was sent over in the discovery this morning along with the autopsy. I reviewed everything but I didn't find anything out of the ordinary."

Sam stood up and walked toward the computer screen. "Do you mind if I have a look?"

Tyler stepped aside for Sam to get a closer look. She took over control of the keyboard and mouse. Sam wasn't sure what she was looking for except for Theo's signature at the bottom of the report. Nothing grabbed her attention until she read through the report again. This time she opened her mind and allowed her intuition to guide her.

"They found a watch with Bailee's body?" Sam recalled her meeting with the ticket attendants at the train station. Hadn't she made up the watch as a reason to talk with the women? Or did she? Sam attempted to visualize the watch again. Nothing. A chill ran down the length of her back and Sam turned to look at Heath and Tyler, trying to disguise her unease. "We need that watch. Tyler could trace it back to the manufacture. If it was an expensive brand, we could trace it back to the purchaser."

Both men looked at her with amusement. "Are you sure your wife didn't get her law degree behind your back and start her own practice?" Tyler kidded.

Heath kissed the top of her head. "Nope but she's always been the smarter half of our team."

Sam smiled at the compliment then faltered. Sam didn't say the next words, knowing they both realized what she was thinking. Rex had been seen with Bailee before her disappearance. Was he helping Davi cover up his crime?

"I'll see what I can do," Tyler said.

Heath exhaled and Sam thought she saw his shoulders slump. "Any luck with Sam's thumb drive?"

"Nothing yet. I'll take another stab at it and let you know."

"Thanks. I'm going to tell Rex about what we discovered," Heath said. "Hopefully, he'll be forthcoming with more details."

"I'll look for Maggie to see if she can help me go through Rex's appointments to create a timeline of his activity. We can meet back in your office after you talk with Rex," Sam said.

"I didn't see Maggie in the office today," Tyler said as he and Heath huddled around the two computer screens.

"I know where to find her. Good luck." Sam left the two men to figure out how Heath would confront Rex with as little fallout as possible.

It felt good to contribute to the case, despite the possibility of Rex's involvement and the implications that would have on Heath and her. Maybe she should look into going into some sort of law? Sam shook her head. Wishful thinking on her part. Heath would just have to live with her being his shadow for now, as long as he had a job.

Sam found Maggie in the library, just as she thought. Maggie stood on the edge of a ladder attached to the enormous bookshelves. Sam loved this place just as much as she loved the library at her old job. The smell of the books, both old and new, wrapped around her like a warm blanket on a chilly fall morning. Gosh, how she missed her job!

"Sam, I didn't expect to see you here."

"I didn't expect to find myself here either. I couldn't sit at home. I felt trapped."

Maggie jumped off the ladder, her dress gave a flourish as her feet hit the ground. "I wouldn't expect anything less from Heath Crenshaw's wife," Maggie said.

Sam frowned at the comment.

"I'm sorry." Maggie placed an arm around Sam. "I didn't

mean it the way it came out. I know you're more than just a wife."

Sam managed a smile. Maggie meant no harm by her words. She of all people knew what it was like to be brushed to the side as an accessory despite her own accolades.

"There's nothing to be sorry for." Sam returned the hug.

Maggie nodded at Sam, the air cleared between the two women. They had always got along well and Sam realized how much she missed the other woman.

"I suppose you're looking for something to help out the case?"

"That's right. I need to check Rex's appointment book?" Sam asked her voice hopeful. "Heath and I discovered a lead I would like to research before presenting the information to him."

"Good luck." Maggie opened up her hands in defeat. "My attempt converting Rex to the digital life failed. He's stuck with his antiquated little black book of dates. He mentioned to me his agenda went missing. I had to order him a new one." Maggie rolled her eyes.

Defeated so soon? She sat down in one of the chairs in the middle of the room, her posture slumped. "I'm not sure what to do now," she confessed to Maggie. "Are you sure you don't have anything?"

"It's not your responsibility. That task belongs to your arrogant husband."

"You're right, I just hoped I could help him out."

"Sometimes just being here as support is all the help you can provide. It may not seem like much to you but it means everything to the person you're here for."

She thought over the bit of advice. Maggie was right, it wasn't Sam's case or her responsibility to find Bailee's killer. Good luck telling that to the weird compulsion she felt. If it was Bailee at the apartment then she still needed help. Her continued ghostly presence had to mean she needed Sam to be her advocate. Ghostly presence. When did she accept she saw ghosts?

Sam stood up suddenly as something Maggie said stuck with her. "Could you do me a favor and look again for Rex's agenda? Maybe it will turn up somewhere unexpected."

"Sure, I'll let you know if I find anything."

"Thanks, Maggie. I appreciate the advice too. One of these days we need to meet up for lunch again like we used to."

Maggie smiled, her round face lit up. "I'd like that. You should go get some rest, you look tired."

"I will. If you see Heath, let him know I needed to run an errand near the college."

"Will do. Now if you'll excuse me, I need to find that damn agenda book and refill the cases. The interns are incapable of doing anything intelligent when Rex is around."

Sam's stomach rolled at the mention of his name. She hoped Heath achieved what he set out to do. If so, then they would have an answer to his involvement and be able to move on to the next task.

She left the library and walked toward the entrance of the building. Heavy in her thoughts, she didn't see the woman until she was right on top of her.

Too late Sam threw up her arms as they collided. She braced herself for a fall that never happened.

"I'm sorry about that," Sam said as she steadied herself, one hand out in front of her and the other on the wall. Her eyes squinted at the woman. "What were you doing in that office?"

The young woman looked over her shoulder. "Oh, I was, I was just given some files to take to Attorney Crenshaw. I didn't realize he wasn't in there."

Sam eyed the woman up and down, taking her measure. Young, likely one of the semesters interns.

"You can give me the files. I'll deliver them to him." Sam held out her hand for the file.

"That's okay." The woman pulled the files close to her chest. "Maggie told me I was responsible for these files. I don't want her to think I'm incapable of a simple task."

Maggie's presence appeared to precede her. "All right then, have a nice day," the young woman said as she backed away from Sam. She turned to walk down the hallway, back toward the library.

"You too," Sam replied, watching the young woman leave. She entered Heath's office to grab her bag she had left earlier and jotted him a quick note before locking the door behind her.

Sam realized it was time to face her visions once and for all.

CHAPTER NINETEEN

HEATH BREATHED DEEPLY and steeled himself outside of Rex's office, a last minute mental prep before confronting his friend and long-time mentor. No matter the outcome of their conversation, Heath refused to allow the implications to sway him from his future. He would be going home with his wife tonight. The Firm and the outcome of the Davi case did not define him, just as Sam sought to prove her own worth outside of their marriage, his worth existed outside of his confines as a defense lawyer at the Firm.

His hand hovered in front of the door. How many times had he entered this room to debate with Rex? Was he ready? Heath squeezed his fist and knocked.

"Come in!" a deep voice boomed from beyond the door. Heath walked into a darkened room, the only light a sliver of gold shining from between the curtained window.

"I hope you returned to give me an update on the Davi case," Rex said, his profile lit by golden rays.

Heath remained near the door, hesitant to take a step further into the room. The absence of light played tricks with Heath's vision and he felt a heaviness in the air. His steps forward hesitant, he closed the door gently before speaking.

"We've come across a new perspective I think you may find intriguing."

Rex took a sip from the glass in his hand, his head inclined toward Heath. "We?"

"Yes, Sam is assisting in her own way."

"Of course. She's an intelligent woman. You would do well to remember she won't want to stay in your shadow for long." Rex turned back to face the window. "Indulge me then. What new information did you and…Sam discover?"

Heath steadied himself then launched into his hastily prepared speech. "Sam and I reviewed the Davi case files again, finding the lack of information unsettling. We required additional interviews with new witnesses." He walked to the small bar on the far side of the room and poured himself a drink from the crystal decanter. "We wanted to ensure the statements were concise and complete."

Watching Rex's back, Heath raised his glass to his lips before stopping "We discovered a witness from the restaurant Bailee Talson worked at who states she saw the deceased woman get into a red antique car one evening before she disappeared."

"Did she?" Rex said. The softness of his voice at odds with his stiff back, Rex's easy demeanor gone.

"Yes. The irony is the witness said you were the man in the car. You were the man Bailee Talson met with."

Silence.

A heavy weight pressing down on Heath. He pushed on, despite knowing he should wait, force Rex to speak first. "Why would you be involved with Bailee Talson but not disclose your involvement to the team? Do you understand how much time we spent on this case when you could've told us from the onset you have a personal involvement with the dead woman?"

Heath walked around the desk, closing the distance between himself and Rex. The need for answers must've weighed on Rex. He turned, his blue eyes meeting the hurt in Heath's brown eyes. "A young woman is dead, your friend is charged with her disappearance and murder, yet you said nothing about your involvement with this woman. Why?" Heath demanded, not backing down.

Rex's expression changed, pain flitting across his tanned skin, a mirror to Heath's own troubled countenance. He'd admired and respected him since they first met, with Heath often attempting to emulate this man. Was his respect misplaced? The admiration then as well as now? Did he have the same poor judgement?

"You need to tell me the truth," Heath demanded. "I need the truth."

Rex sipped his drink. "Do you remember when I asked you to join me here at the Firm?"

"Yes." Heath shrugged. "You told me the work would be hard, the hours long and my wife would grow to hate you."

"What else did I tell you?"

"There would come a time where I would second guess everything I learned in law school. Learning to follow my gut instinct would provide the best for my clients."

"Has that happened yet?"

"Yes." Heath met Rex's stare. "Why am I here, standing in front of one of the most powerful men in Midnight Harbor, asking him why he is keeping secrets from his staff and friends."

"You need to be able to use your gut instinct in times when research and evidence points you in another direction, to wade through what may be false, seeking the truth." Rex walked away from the window toward the bar. Heath could smell the scent of bourbon in the air and doubted this was only Rex's second drink of the day. "It seems I am able to give advice, however, I rarely act on it myself." Rex stared into his glass before throwing back the remainder in one swallow.

He poured himself another drink while Heath gave Rex

time and the opportunity to tell his side and give reasons for the betrayal.

"Davi sent the girl to me after he spoke to her. He told me she had information we might find useful."

"What did she say to him?" Heath questioned. "Davi said he never met with her beyond the initial request for a meeting." Rex shrugged off Heath's question.

"She mentioned she needed to get out of a tricky situation. She explained a select group of women were providing escort services to powerful businessmen in Charleston and the surrounding area, including Midnight Harbor," Rex said. He glanced up from his drink to meet Heath's eyes.

"Around this same time Claudia confided in me. She heard a rumor from one of the women at the salon she frequents in Charleston. The woman must not have known Claudia was an attorney because the woman bragged about a way to make easy money. Claudia ran with it. She wanted to investigate the rumor further to see if there was a connection to anyone in Midnight Harbor."

"So that's what you and Claudia have been working on for the past few weeks? A rumor from a salon and waitress?"

"Why get anyone else involved? It was too early in the investigation for us to take the risk, even with you. We couldn't use the information without a contact in the police force. Claudia couldn't get anyone to give us the time of day."

"What happened?" Heath said urging Rex.

"As luck would have it, Bailee Talson agreed to meet with us. She talked at length about how she was recruited into the program by another woman. An alarming number of women from the local colleges were involved."

"That's it?" Heath said.

"No, Bailee was in a difficult situation, she wanted to leave the escort agency but didn't have the funds to survive on her own. She felt isolated. Her parents were hours away and she recently lost her scholarship. She was evicted from the apartment the morning she met us. Claudia agreed to take on the case pro bono if Bailee would stand against the owners of the escort agency. I contacted the DA for assistance. We thought we could trust her. Apparently not."

Heath watched Rex sit in a chair, his eyes glassy.

"What happened to Bailee after you met with her?" Heath said as he sat across from Rex.

"I never heard from her again. Neither did Davi or Claudia."

Heath reflected on the information Rex divulged. "I wonder what spooked her into dropping contact?"

"I wish I knew. If I had any idea of what would happen to her I would have personally seen to her safety. I didn't think she was in immediate danger."

The entire case had become convoluted and too many of his friends and colleagues were involved in the game of hidden agendas and buried half-truths. Concern rooted and spread, a fear Bailee's case was mishandled, ultimately leading to her disappearance and subsequent death. How was he going to find her justice and protect Davi if those he trusted were involved? Heath bristled at the implications this case would have on his future and on Sam. How had he allowed his position at the Firm to create a wedge in his relationship with her? Heath knew his next move. It was clear to him now. A decision he made before he knocked on Rex's door.

"Davi won't face issues in court," he said to Rex. "Tyler and I ran over the discovery files again as well as the statements from witnesses to be sure we have a solid case. Davi has an alibi in Kerri Reid which has been vetted. I updated Nathan on the case before I met with you."

Heath clenched his fists at his sides. "Just answer me one thing. Were you ever going to tell me about your involvement?"

Rex sighed. "I was going to tell you when the time was

right." Rex stepped toward Heath. "This is so much larger than just Davi and Bailee Talson. This goes far beyond their reach. If I crack this case, the Firm could become one of the most sought-after practices in the South."

Heath let out a mirthless laugh. "I see. When were you going to tell me Davi was the pawn for a larger case?" Heath placed his hands in front of him. "How I am to provide for my clients when the owner of this firm is keeping secrets?"

"I needed you on this case because I knew you would be relentless in your search for justice for both Bailee Talson and Davi. My faith in you never wavered."

"Then why didn't you involve me from the beginning? I've wasted so much time and manpower on this case when you withheld information all along."

"I knew you would be able to discover the information to move forward with Davi. Once everything had settled, I intended to bring you onboard with Claudia to handle the larger case."

"Davi was brought in for questioning today for something he is innocent of!"

"You think I don't realize my mistakes!" Rex's voice boomed, echoing off the walls of the room. "He was my best friend in college. He trusted me to help him!" Rex's face strained.

"You didn't help him, you failed him." Heath ripped his security badge from the chain around his neck and threw it at Rex's feet, back peddling toward the door. "You failed us all."

Heath walked out of Rex's office, his steps echoing on the hard wood floors of the hallway. There was no turning back now. As he assured Rex, Davi would have a solid case, Nathan would be able to deliver anything Davi required. Heath allowed his career to control him and mold him into someone he knew he wasn't. He wanted to practice law to protect the innocent and disadvantaged, not play games with people's lives. Heath discovered the answer he sought but lost the man he admired in the process. It was a hollow victory.

Desperate for Sam's touch and the comfort of their home, Heath walked toward his office for the last time. He wasn't sure of the path he was headed on, but it didn't matter as long as he had Sam by his side. He'd turned away from her when they needed each other the most. He refused to let anything separate them again.

SHE WASN'T in his office. He discovered a handwritten note left on his desk and swore under his breath as he read her elegant script. When did Sam become so brazen? He checked his phone for any missed notifications. None, only the note told of her absence.

Heath flipped on the television in his office for white noise while he quickly packed the important things he needed in the overnight bag Sam brought, grabbing a few things from his office before he left for good. Sucking in a deep breath, he braced his hands on the desk. He never told Tyler he planned to quit. It was a thought that grew from his gut on the walk to Rex's office. Then bloomed once he confronted Rex.

It was done now. Tyler would learn soon enough. Heath grabbed the remote, his fingers hovered over the off button when he realized the TV was playing a video of Sam. He watched her walk across the sidewalk and assault a photographer videotaping her. Heath pinched the bridge of his nose, this was just the last thing he needed, Sam exploited by reporters on the evening news.

"We identified the woman in this video captured by our field reporter as Samantha Crenshaw, wife of the attorney Heath Crenshaw. Attorney Crenshaw is currently defending Nicholas Davi in the disappearance and murder of young college coed Bailee Talson."

Heath flicked the remote to turn the television off. That woman on screen looked like Sam but didn't act like her. Sam would never behave like that, would she? She occupied her time between the ladies' auxiliary club and dinner parties for friends and family. The reality was Sam had done neither in months. The woman in the video had a certain confidence in her step Sam lacked for a very long time which Heath recognized in her today.

His blood pressure rose as he thought about how long and often the photographer had been following Sam. He accepted the media scrutiny with his profession, especially with a case like Davi's, it was part of the deal with being a defense attorney. They crossed the line by going after his wife.

Heath needed to find Sam before she got into any more trouble. If Davi and Rex were not directly responsible for the murder of the coed, Midnight Harbor had a killer on the loose. Heath wanted Sam back home where she would be safe. He had to find her before it was too late.

The door opened as he placed his hand on the doorknob. Maggie stood on the other side, her petite frame blocking his way out.

Heath stifled a groan and walked back into his office. Maggie let the door shut behind them with a thud.

"Where do you think you're going?" Maggie said, her voice underlaid with steel.

"I'm leaving to go find Sam."

"That's not what I meant. Why did I have a file transfer come across my desk updating Nathan to lead attorney on the Davi case?"

Heath tried to walk past the petite powerhouse. "Because he is the lead on the case."

Maggie moved to block him. "Why did you transfer the case into his name?"

"I don't have time for this, Maggie. I need to find Sam."

"When I saw her earlier she said she was running a quick errand near the college."

"You spoke with her before she left? How long ago was it?"

"Probably about thirty minutes ago. She wanted to know if I had any information on Rex's meetings for the past few weeks. You know Rex lost his damn agenda book." Maggie placed her hands on her hips. "Now, answer my first question."

Heath looked Maggie in the eyes, forced himself to meet her steady gaze and sighed. "I quit. I transferred the case to Nathan to take over in my place."

"You just can't quit in the middle of a case!" Maggie said, her eyes wide. "Nicholas Davi was brought in for questioning last night. We need you to lead the case in court."

"Davi has a solid defense and alibi. The only thing that would help him further is if the police apprehended the killer or we had a confession on tape."

"We need you here." Maggie's shoulders slumped.

Heath placed a hand on her arm to reassure her. "I can't work here anymore. I wish I could tell you more. I'm sure you'll find out sooner or later why I left."

"You didn't even give me a chance to talk to you about the intern."

"You're just going to have to talk to Rex yourself. There's nothing I can do about it now. I can't go back in there to talk to him."

Maggie stepped aside, letting Heath walk past her. "All right, but you better stay in contact with me."

"I will."

Heath left his office, thinking about how he walked these hallways nearly every day for the last five years, first as an intern, then as an attorney. Was he really leaving for good? Hard to think of a life beyond the Firm. He dreamed of becoming senior counsel and a partner someday. Now, those dreams would never be.

Sam reminded him of the man he strived to become. If he stood beside Rex, he would allow himself to become complacent. Already on the path to becoming a person he didn't recognize, he refused to go any further. There was a difference between honesty and loyalty.

Heath Crenshaw reached the entrance of the Firm without so much as a look back and strode through the front doors, into the unknown.

CHAPTER TWENTY

SAM STOOD in front of Bailee's apartment building shortly after leaving the Firm, certain her answers would be here. Earlier, the unknown woman distracted them, preventing a look inside the apartment. Instinct propelled her, whether by a personal compulsion or ghostly influence, this place beckoned her return. Maybe Bailee's personal belongings contained a psychic imprint. A figment of her left behind. Sam hoped the remnant could help induce another vision.

Dim lights in the hallway flickered, creating diluting shadows along the length of the hallway. Two slips of tape held the pink eviction sign to the front of the door, the edges curled from wear. The door handle gave way with little resistance. Was the door unlocked earlier? She shivered, wondering how many other people had already been in this apartment before her.

Don't even think about it, she told herself.

A sense of déjà vu washed over her, reminiscent of the last time she hesitated before a doorway. Funny how doorways could hold one prisoner but with the right intention, open to new revelations. A prisoner of her own making no longer,

Sam gave a keen glance in both directions before slipping into the darkened apartment.

Sam brushed off her hands, taking inventory of the room. White walls and clean floors leading to a sliding glass door which opened onto a small balcony. Two hallways branched off to either side of the living room, ending in bedrooms.

In the first bedroom on the right, she discovered no furnishings. Not a piece of clothing or personal effect left behind linking the previous inhabitant to the room.

Clothing and makeup had been strewn about the second bedroom, making a mess of the floor. The bed had been stripped haphazardly and the contents of the dresser dumped onto the floor.

A familiar pull, or what she thought a sixth sense, that told her this was Bailee's room. Based off what she saw of her surroundings, Bailee was either in a hurry to leave or someone had been here after she went missing. What could they have been looking for to leave such a mess?

Whatever it was must have been important. The unknown woman! Was she the one who made this mess? If so, she needed to speak with Heath for a better description of the woman. They needed to find her to discover why she was here and what she was looking for. Or had already taken.

A torn picture on the floor, half hidden by clothing, caught Sam's attention. She bent down and picked up the photograph, recognizing Bailee in a red cocktail dress. Her arm was in the crook of a man in a tuxedo but the direction of her gaze told the viewer her attention was on the person missing from the picture.

Whoever the person was, Sam couldn't tell. The tear marred the photograph, taking the identity of the mystery person with the missing piece. All except a slender bare arm. Someone didn't want their identity known. But that look from Bailee...Sam knew it well. Had seen it in the eyes of her husband as he held his body over her when making love.

That was the look of desire and unabashed need. Bailee wanted the person missing from the photo.

Is this what the unknown woman took? Sam searched for other photos when her heart rate increased. The temperature dropped causing the hair on Sam's arms to stand straight as a chill crept down her neck. Recognizing the symptoms now as the precursor to a vision, Sam looked around to find her.

Bailee. Sitting cross-legged on the edge of the bed, wearing the same clothes Sam remembered from before. Almost translucent, the pretty blonde stared at the photograph. Sam couldn't tell but it looked like she held a gold watch in her hands. Was that the watch from the police report? "My mistake in kindness was deceit," she crooned.

Fighting against her panic, Sam stood. "Deceit? Whose?"

"I only wanted to be free." Bailee's voice sounded like a hundred whispers.

Sam reached out to the woman. "Free from what?"

A door creaked, the noise echoing through the still apartment. Frantic, Sam stepped back from Bailee, torn between hiding or talking to the woman, afraid she would never see her again. A quick succession of clicks from the living room.

"You're running out of time…death arrives at midnight." The translucent figure of Bailee rose above the bed then dissipated into a swirl of mist. Having lost her chance, Sam looked around for a place to hide when a force pushed her toward the closet. *Here.*

Sam patted the ground for an object to defend herself, her hand connecting with a half-empty perfume bottle. She curled her first around the bottle. At least she could throw it at the person as a distraction, to buy herself a few seconds to escape. If it came to that.

She huddled into the corner of the closet at an angle where she could peek through the slanted shades and closed the door quietly behind her. She slowed her breathing, listening as footsteps increased in volume until a shadow crossed the closet door. Her vision blacked out, Sam held her breath and waited while the person stood on the other side of the closet door, blocking any chance of Sam sneaking away unnoticed.

The closet door creaked. Sam covered her head with her arms, rolling up in a fetal position in the corner. The creaking stopped, the door left cracked open. The shadow moved, light returning to the closet when Sam heard a grunt and thud followed by scuffling footsteps. The darkness once again covered the slates of the door, blocking her sight to the struggle beyond.

Sam clutched the perfume bottle high over her head, ready to smash the bottle into the intruder's head. The closet door creaked open, revealing the angry face of her husband.

"What the hell are you doing here alone?" Heath said, reaching down to help her out of the closet. Sam grabbed hold of Heath's hand, his warmth covering her own cold hands as he yanked her into a standing position.

She looked past Heath at the body being held down on the floor and recognized the man as the photographer who harassed her outside of the restaurant. Though she confronted him, she wondered why he continued to follow her now. Sam tore her gaze from the photographer, recognizing Theo restraining the man. He was casually dressed in jeans and button-down shirt, the sleeves rolled to his elbows. A police badge hung from a chain around his neck.

"I...I came back searching for any information," Sam said, stuttering over her words.

Heath's hands and eyes traveled over her body, checking for any injuries. Satisfied, his eyes flicked over her lips before meeting her gaze. She licked her bottom lip, wanting to feel the press of his lips against hers. She thought better of it and lowered her gaze. Heath stepped back from her, his face set in stern lines. "Why would you do something so reckless?"

Sam flinched at his words, at the anger she recognized in his tone. She certainly didn't intend for trouble. How would she know that creep followed her. She wanted justice for the young woman who had been killed. How would Heath understand when he didn't believe her visions of Bailee? He had no right to treat her like this.

"I'm not hurt. Scared and curious why this guy keeps following me. I acted impulsively without thinking about the consequences," Sam said, looking back at the photographer. She hid her trembling hands by crossing her arms over her chest. "I should've brought someone with me. I won't make the same mistake again."

She felt Heath's eyes travel over her, searching for any hidden hurts. Having found none, Heath turned his attention to the photographer. He strode over in a few steps, leaned down and grabbed the man by the front of his shirt, lifting him in the air before slamming the man against the wall. Sam stumbled back in surprise, her hand reaching out to steady herself and found Theo standing next to her.

Heath held the man firmly, the fabric of his shirt bunched around his fist. "What do you think you're doing following my wife?" Heath pinned the man against the wall. Theo stood beside Sam, ready to intervene, his eyes on Heath and the photographer.

"I'm just trying to make a living," the man responded, struggling in Heath's grip.

"Why don't you try to make an honest living for a change instead of chasing down people when they're most vulnerable?"

"Drama sells, you should know that. Nobody wants to hear about the beauty queens and new store openings. They want to hear about the murders, and missing persons, especially when local celebrities are involved."

"Local celebrities," Sam whispered, her mind racing back toward Davi and Bailee. She walked forward until she was face to face with the man who had invaded her privacy. "How long have you been following me?"

"Since the night he won." The photographer nodded at Heath. "He just won that fraud case and the new agencies were desperate for any information. I thought if I couldn't get to him, maybe something on you would sell."

Heath made a noise resembling a growl. She placed her hand on his bicep, offering him comfort as well as seeking it for herself. She needed to feel the strength in him to help balance her and push away the intrusive thoughts threatening to grip her.

"Who else has seen your pictures?"

"No one. Except the video of you attacking me yesterday. I sold that video to the local station for a nice sum of cash. I needed it. You broke my camera. I needed a quick replacement."

"Was the memory card damaged in the old camera?" Heath asked.

"No, the memory card is fine. It's here in my replacement." The man nodded toward the camera.

Heath let go of the man's shirt and grabbed the camera from around his neck. Sam leaned into him as Heath flipped through the pictures.

"Hey you can't do that, that's mine!"

Theo stepped forward, creating a barrier between the two men. "From my perspective, your camera is evidence. I hope you weren't stalking this young lady."

"Watch me." Heath gave the man a cocky grin while he continued flipping through the images.

Sam watched in silence at the images changed from the previous day to the next. Dozens of pictures of Sam flipped past as Heath returned to the beginning.

The first images were of a gala held the same night Heath left dinner early to report for the Davi case. Sam saw Nicholas Davi and Kerri Reid along with a few other local celebrities entering the building, a group of young men and women with them.

The pictures progressed to images of her that same evening then to Josie standing at the front door of her house. A few photos of employees of the Firm flashed by, a picture of Rex and Davi leaving the firm. A picture of Kerri Reid again, this time entering the firm followed next by Nicholas Davi. More pictures flashed by until finally they came upon images of a young woman carrying a pile of folders in one arm, leaving the Firm.

"Stop, she looks familiar," Sam said.

Heath stopped and zoomed in on the picture. The woman's head was covered in a paisley scarf and large sunglasses perched on her nose. Sam noticed the woman wore a tailored jacket. Sam recalled the woman from the train station. Could this be the same woman? Sam saw the glint of an ID badge hanging around her neck.

"That's the intern I bumped into earlier today. I saw her leaving your office," Sam said to Heath, tugging on his sleeve.

Theo perked up at those words. He kept his eye on the photographer but directed his attention to Sam and Heath.

"She was leaving my office? That's the new intern Maggie has been complaining about. She told me she had a bad feeling about her."

Heath continued flipping through the pictures until he landed on one of the woman standing in front of a black car with tinted windows.

"Who is she talking to?" Sam said.

"I'm not sure but we need to find out," Heath said, handing the camera over to Theo.

"I'll call for backup to take this one in," Theo said. "Go ahead without me."

Sam gave the photographer one last dirty look before she turned to leave the apartment.

They exited Bailee's apartment together and she grabbed Heath's arm, stopping him from walking away. "Are you thinking what I'm thinking?" Sam asked.

Heath patted her hand and dug out his phone from his jean pocket and immediately started texting. "I think you could use a coffee to help soothe your shock over that dipshit in there. And it's time I talk to Maggie about her intern problem."

CHAPTER TWENTY-ONE

MAGGIE RESPONDED IMMEDIATELY. The intern vanished. Nothing left behind to indicate when she left or when she intended to return.

The possibilities of what the intern was up to ran through Sam's head as Heath drove them toward the Firm. Silent with both hands on the steering wheel, his eyes never left the road. Sam relished the silence between them, using the quiet intermission to reflect on the incident at the apartment building.

Being truthful to herself, a part of Sam relished Heath coming to her aid with Theo. It was a disgustingly romantic ideal, a knight saving the damsel, but she didn't seem to mind today. Heath's aggressiveness today aside, he was not a violent man, choosing to avoid conflict with wit or charm, but this case had pressured him into facing his own demons. She wasn't surprised his control snapped back at Bailee's apartment.

She admitted she had a propensity for finding trouble. She knew her limitations and she had crossed the boundary of what she knew herself capable of because that sixth sense, that pull was increasing in strength.

Sam never should've left the Firm alone. Despite her limitations, the pull persisted in guiding her toward discovering the person responsible for Bailee's murder. And look what happened when she followed that instinct. She saw Bailee again. They were on the right track.

Death arrives at midnight.

Sam recalled Bailee's haunting words, searching for meaning.

Heath's voice broke through her daydream, "Here we are." His voice quiet and hollow. She didn't like hearing his voice take on that inflection. She must've lost track of time while thinking. Expecting to see the Firm, Heath had pulled into the driveway of their home instead.

"I don't want to come home. I thought we were going to the Firm to confront Amanda, the intern?" Sam said turning toward Heath. "She knows something about Bailee. I know it."

"Like you sensed Bailee's ghost?" Heath shook his head, his voice still hollow. "Maggie said she isn't there. Even if she were there, I can't allow you to go with me. Don't you understand the significance of what happened today?"

Heath pivoted in the driver seat to face her, his face haggard. Her handsome husband looked exhausted and... vulnerable. A side she rarely saw in him. It made her feel guilty that she brought out that side he never showed anyone but her. He trusted no one but her with his heart.

The guilt gave way to indignation when she thought of his presumptuous action against her. "Since when do I need your permission to do anything?" Sam narrowed her eyes, feeling her cheeks turn hot. "I know it was stupid to return to the apartment without help. I just...I needed to see it for myself. I can't explain it. It's like a feeling or sixth sense is telling me where to go and I can only follow along."

"Stupid, you think your actions today were stupid? You could have been hurt or killed!" Heath got out of the car and slammed the door behind him, the impact shaking the car.

Sam jumped out of the passenger seat, her stride purposeful as she trailed behind him toward their home. "I wasn't hurt. All I need to do is take some additional defense classes at the local gym. Then I will be better prepared next time." Sam thought about it for a minute. "I could also learn to shoot and get a license to carry."

Heath spun around on her, raking his hands through his hair. "Are you kidding me! Do you even hear yourself right now, Sam?"

"Yes, I've had the entire time from the apartment to here to think about it. Bailee needs me. You need me. I need this."

"You're not training or taking martial art classes, or learning how to shoot and you most certainly are not getting a license to carry a weapon!" Heath stormed into the house, the door swinging open behind him.

Shocked at his outburst, Sam sputtered before pursing him. "How dare you tell me what to do. I've supported you these past five years while denying myself what I want! To discover who I am? I can't continue to live in a shell preoccupied with frivolous parties when young women are being killed in my town, especially when I'm connected to them."

Sam stood in the foyer and recalled her conversation with Josie and interrogation from Theo in this same space. Heath had to understood what this meant to her, she had to make him understand.

"I can see her, Heath. Bailee asking me for help."

Heath turned to face her. "Where is this coming from? Ghosts? They're not real, just figments of your imagination you've created to protect yourself from the trauma you experienced. You know who you are. You're my wife, Samantha Crenshaw. When have I ever denied you anything? Everything I have done is for you, for us, to make our lives better! I have sacrificed in order to build my career so we could have the life we wanted. Now, you tell me that's not who you are? Who the hell are you then? Someone who make reckless decisions, wants to carry a gun and run around town chasing after ghosts?"

Heath turned his back to her. "This isn't my Sam. If this is the person you really are, I want nothing to do with her."

The words hammered into Sam's chest. She watched him walk away as the pressure in her chest broke. Sam gasped and her eyes stung, the threat of tears eager to run a trail down her cheeks. "How dare you turn this around on me. After everything, how dare you! I don't even understand what's happening with me. I see a dead woman, Heath, is that what you want to hear? Sleeping, awake, it doesn't matter my state of awareness, I see her and she needs me."

Sam ran up the oak staircase of their house into the nearest bedroom, slamming the door behind her. She locked the door and leaned back against the frame as her eyes burned from unshed tears.

She slid down the length of the door onto the floor, her knees curled up to her chest. A sob broke from inside her and came out in heaving gulps escaping from the place she kept her heart buried. She cried for herself and Bailee, for her lost job and past self she no longer recognized. Most of all, she cried for Heath, the man she loved who no longer wanted her.

Sam heard Heath cursing from downstairs. His words wounded her. Taking his anger out around him instead of bottling it up as usual.

Wiping away her tears, Sam recognized the pale pinks and white furniture of the room she was holed up in.

The nursery.

The embodiment of her failures as a wife, as a woman.

She sobbed harder, of all the rooms to take refuge in. She wasn't sure how much time passed, the heaviness a burden on her chest threatening to suffocate her. Not until her legs ached and the stabbing pains from sitting forced her to stand did she walk into the middle of the nursery.

The bright airiness of the room was a stark contrast to the dark anger and pain swirling inside Sam. She looked around her at what could have been. So many hopes and dreams had gone into the creation of this room. So much love. She recalled the afternoon Heath spent building the curved wooden crib, cursing at each misstep as he fumbled over the shoddy directions.

Sam ran her fingers over the white lacquered wood, imagining how things would be different if she never lost their daughter.

In the time after she returned from the hospital without their baby, she allowed herself to be consumed in her grief, turning their shared loss into her own failure. She allowed her grief to turn into a depression that slowly erased her light and existence into never-ending numbness.

Standing in the room, Sam realized it wasn't until the death of Bailee did she feel a desire to be involved in an activity. That she felt something to grab onto and be useful again. Something that told her she mattered and she wasn't broken because of her loss.

Sam had used the investigation as an outlet for her grief and a way to heal the festering wound. Now that she finally found a purpose, Heath, the one whom she should trust and love with all her being, threatened to take it away from her.

No, she wouldn't be a dazed passenger in life anymore. Her loss, her sorrow, it consumed her until she was an empty husk. She refused to become that person again, to allow someone to place her in a powerless position. Life was for the living and she wasn't finished yet.

Heath didn't want her. Fine. She'd go on without him. After she discovered who killed Bailee. For now, she needed to make it work. They were so close. Making her decision, Sam used the bathroom sink to splash cold water on her face. She stormed downstairs, braced herself to face Heath's residual anger.

She found him in the kitchen, hands braced on the island, his head hanging.

"Listen. You may not want me anymore because I'm not—"

"That's not what I meant." Heath's voice cracked.

She held up a hand. "I'm not finished. We can figure out the details later. This is what's going to happen. We're moving forward like grown adults would to figure out where the intern went so we can question her. Afterward, we can discuss the future. I'm coming with you and no words or cursing will stop me."

Heath's face told her he hated everything she just said. The shrill ringing of a phone stopped him from speaking. Heath clicked the call over to speakerphone and in that moment, Sam knew she had won him over. "Hey, Maggie. I hope you have good news."

"I looked all over the Firm for our nefarious intern, who I warned you about by the way. She's not here and I discovered she only partially completed her time sheet. I'm not sure when she was here or not."

"Okay, I get it, I was wrong," Heath said, placating Maggie. "Do you have her phone number? Maybe we can call her to talk."

"No, Rex has her contact sheet and he's been in his office all day brooding."

"Maybe she knows we're on to her. She likely went back to her dorm room or apartment to get a few things if she's going out on the lam." Sam spoke up from beside Heath.

Heath shook his head in disbelief. "First, you're acting like law enforcement, now you're using their terminology?"

Sam shrugged off his remark. "Thanks for checking, Maggie. Do you know where she lives?"

"I'm not privy to that information. Only contact information and she is one of the summer interns from Charleston College."

"Thanks. Any luck with Rex's appointment book?" Sam asked.

"No, it's still missing. Damnit! I gotta go, Nicholas Davi is here and he looks pissed!"

"Thanks for checking," Heath said as Maggie disconnected the call. Heath's expression failed to remain neutral. His mouth twitched into a small smile. "So, what's next, detective?"

A tease she normally would've enjoyed, Sam turned up her nose at the jab. "You're not going to let me live this down, are you?"

"Oh no, I'm going to enjoy every minute of this."

She let him have his moment of brief satisfaction by giving him an eyeroll. This was going to be harder than she thought. Working beside him, knowing the words were said but not resolved. She could do it, would do it. "We may not know where she lives, but we know Amanda is attending Charleston College. I wonder if she is involved in any extracurricular activities?"

Heath rubbed the stubble along his jaw. "I never asked her, I didn't have the opportunity to speak with her after we ran into each other." He closed his eyes for a moment then opened them. "Hold on," Heath said, "I remember she dropped her keys along with files she was carrying when I ran into her."

He closed his eyes again and Sam swore she could see him mentally sorting through images in his mind. "I can see Greek letters imprinted on a keychain attached to them." He opened his eyes. "The intern is part of a sorority. I saw the Greek letters on her keychain when she dropped them."

"Do you remember what the letters looked like?" Sam said, amazed again at his ability to mentally sort memories.

Heath looked at Sam with a pained expression. "Really? Do you have any idea how many of those damn events I

attended? You have the letters all over your college memen-
tos. It's your sorority, Alpha Delta Pi."

Sam gave him a weak smile in return. She reached for his
hand then thought better of it. If he saw the gesture, he didn't
mention it, instead settling for words. "Where to, Sherlock?"

"Charleston College. We have an intern to track down."

CHAPTER TWENTY-TWO

THE DAYLIGHT of afternoon faded into early dusk by the time Heath and Sam arrived at Charleston College. They parked next to the unmarked car driven by Theo, a few blocks down from Greek Row, where most of the sororities and fraternities stood.

Theo climbed out of his car, looking at Heath and Sam then shook his head and grinned.

"You realize it's not proper procedure for you to be this involved in a case," Theo said to them. "Certainly not one as contentious as this."

"To hell with proper procedure," Heath said. "I'm not employed by the Firm any longer. We'll be witnesses if anyone asks."

"Fine. I'll ask around. Try to find Amanda without being too forthcoming."

"If I initiate the conversation, maybe she'll talk," Sam said.

Theo shook his head. "No, it's too risky."

Sam pushed on, "It's just a bunch of young women. I'll ask the first few sisters if they know where we can find her."

"What am I thinking going along with this? I'll mic you. If you get nervous, give me the signal, I'll handle the rest." Theo dropped a small bag on the hood of his police cruiser, pulling out a mic set. "Please don't do anything stupid."

Both men turned their eyes toward Sam. She furrowed her brow and crossed her arms over her chest, giving both men a dirty look. "Leave it to me. I wasn't Midnight Harbor's former darling for nothing. Let's go see what we can find out about this intern and what she was doing handing over those files."

The sorority house for Alpha Delta Pi was easy to locate amongst the grouping of sororities located along Smithson Way. Each house proudly displayed their allegiance with sorority letters embroidered on flags or painted on the front door of the houses. Pretty flower pots decorated the large, airy porches.

The Zeta Sigma Chapter of Alpha Delta Pi gained affiliation with Charleston College in 1979. Shortly afterward, a founding sister acquired and redesigned one of the homes to accommodate the growing sorority. This particular sorority was a chapter of the larger organization, one of the first secret societies for women. It also happened to be where Sam pledged during college.

Heath hung back with Theo as Sam played her part of big sister visiting the house of her little. The ploy may not have worked on the college administrators, but hopefully it would with unsuspecting coeds.

Time ticked by in what felt like hours as Heath watched Sam walk toward the house from their vantage point a few blocks away. Theo sat next to him on the bench, relaying instructions to Sam via the discreet mic he attached to Sam before she left. The device wasn't much but it allowed for them to hear everything Sam said in the house.

"What do you think we'll gain from this plan?" Heath said, breaking the silence between the two men.

"Motive and why the DA is blinded by quick justice without a proper investigation...among other things."

"Nicholas Davi told me Fabian is running for office," Heath offered. "It would sure look good to nab a high-profile celebrity."

Theo snorted. "Of course she is." He looked at Heath. "It's not just a motto. I take my job seriously to serve and protect. Something in my gut tells me more is at play with this case. I want to find the person who did this to that young woman. She deserves justice. I'm determined to find it for her."

Heath nodded in agreement. "That's the same reason I went into law. I wanted to defend individuals who had the cards stacked against them. To provide them with a source to achieve justice." Heath was glad to find they still shared a common ground. After everything Theo had seen, he still appeared the ever-hopeful youth, wanting to do good works for his town.

Theo pointed toward the houses. "What about Sam? What's her stake in this?"

Heath sighed, he couldn't tell Theo about Sam's secrets when he didn't even understand it himself.

He had been nasty with her. Said things in his hurt he could never take back. Words he didn't mean. Furious at his behavior but not wanting to ignore Theo, he opted for shared knowledge, hoping it would be enough.

"Justice. She's brilliant and loyal. She chose me to give her loyalty. Sam gave up her career in law school so I could pursue my own career as a defense attorney. She said she would wait. Time passed and she never reenrolled. She supported me every step of the way. I think she finally grew dissatisfied with her current life path, wanting something more than what the life of a housewife could offer her."

"So, she highjacked your case?"

"Something like that." Heath chuckled. "I just want her to be happy, be safe.I don't know what I'm thinking going along with her plan."

"She has an innate sense, almost if she knows something

we don't. I know it sounds crazy. How else would she have known where to find Bailee? Heath, the body was hidden in the grass stalks, far away from the side of the road."

Heath met the questioning look in Theo's eyes. "You would be surprised to learn what I used to find crazy is becoming the new norm," Heath said, taking his eyes from Theo's gaze. "I can't give you the answer you want. Only Sam can and only when you're ready to accept this world may not be all we thought it was. Aside from that, my concern is for her safety. She isn't trained to be involved in cases like this. She doesn't even carry pepper spray."

"Hopefully, it doesn't come to that," Theo said, understanding in his voice. "All I need is her to gain some additional information from the sisters so I can track down the intern for questioning. If there is a moment where we think something might happen, I move to get her out. I don't like this but it may be the only chance we get."

The detective's words were little comfort. He was going to have a long talk with Sam after this was over. To offer his apology and, if she wanted to pursue this way of life, then she needed to put in the work to ensure her safety. She was untrained, untried and too confident in whatever gift or curse she gained. It made for a deadly combination.

Heath glanced up to see Sam's figure disappear down the street between groups of students. The two men huddled around the speaker, quietly listening through the static to hear the outcome of Sam's arrival at the sorority.

A terrible sense of foreboding flooded him. Heath looked to his left and right, up and down the street. The normal liveliness one would expect from a row of college houses had nearly doubled in volume. Young men and women crowded the streets, overflowing onto the lawns of the houses.

"Where did this crowd come from?" Heath said, looking around.

Theo slapped the side of the speaker. "I'm picking up a lot

of interference from the crowds. I can hardly hear where she is."

"Sam, are you there?" Heath said into the mic.

They waited, listening to crackles of static from the small speaker.

"I'm still here." Sam's voice, clear and loud, broke through. "There are a lot of students around. I think there is some sort of block party going on tonight."

Theo looked at Heath. "That would explain why there are so many students around in the street, it's Greek Preview Night."

Heath rubbed at the stubble along his jaw. Of all the nights for the colleges to have the drunk coeds walking around, this would be their luck. He needed to get Sam out of the crowd.

"Sam, forget it, this is too risky," Theo said into the speaker. "You should turn around before the crowd gets any larger. We'll meet you in the middle."

"No way. I'm going ahead. I need to find out some background on the intern before we move ahead."

"No, Sam, please come back. At least meet us so we can accompany you."

"I'm sorry, Theo. Not when I'm this close."

"Sam, baby, tell us where you are. We'll meet you so you're not alone," Heath pleaded.

"I just turned right down Winnow Street. I'm only about a block or so away from the house."

"Okay we'll be right there. And don't do anything until we meet you there."

Heath and Theo ran down the street, dodging between students when they heard Sam from the other end talking to someone. They stopped under a tree, hidden from the street view of the gathering students.

"Hi, my name is Samantha. I'm a fellow Alpha Delta Pi sister and alumni from the Class of 2013. I was wondering if I could take a look inside the house to see how much has changed since I pledged here?"

"Oh no," Heath said, hunched over and breathing heavy. He stood up and motioned to Theo. "We need to go now."

Voices cracked over the speaker. "Sure, Amanda will show you around. Didn't you say you have a few minutes before you head out? Come on inside, we're happy to have you here."

Heath exchanged glances with Theo. "Hell's Bells," he groaned. "Sam ignore our warning because she was just granted the VIP tour…with the intern as her guide."

CHAPTER TWENTY-THREE

SAM THOUGHT she knew what she was doing. When she stepped over the threshold of the Alpha Delta Pi house, she doubted her decision. What was she doing here, eager to speak with one of the sorority sisters? Was she crazy? No, she knew she wasn't. The hope to gain more information about the intern, Amanda, and her motivations caused Sam to became caught up in the moment. The compulsion propelled her forward, despite objections from Heath and Theo.

Amanda stood in front of her, a sweet, serene look plastered on her face. The same look she used when Sam ran into her at the Firm. The same face Sam recognized to be false. She saw the shocked expression only moments before the sorority sister, Tammy, made introductions.

Sam had a feeling this woman standing before her was the missing link in the case. Was Amanda the killer? She didn't know but she had to think of a plan that would allow her to maintain her cover and keep a friendly tone with Amanda until Heath and Theo arrived.

With nothing left to do but move forward, Sam held out her hand in greeting. "Hi, it's nice to see you again. I remember you from the Firm. I had no idea you were a sister too." She kept her tone even and friendly, despite the nerves threatening to turn her knees to gelatin and her voice a quivering squeak.

The young woman eyed Sam up and down and feigned surprise. "Oh, that's right. You're Attorney Crenshaw's wife. It's good to see you again. Especially so...soon after we last met." Amanda smiled and clasped Sam's hand in a firm shake.

"I'll let you two get better acquainted. Let me know if you need anything," Tammy said as she patted both women on the arm before turning away. She turned back on the heel of her pink platform pumps, the exaggerated movement swung her long ponytail. "Don't forget to show her the new library. It's a gift from one of our alumni." Tammy gave a wave before disappearing into another room deep within the house, leaving Sam and Amanda alone.

They were still surrounded by other sisters and potential pledges. Sam raked her brain trying to think of something to fill the awkward silence growing between the two women.

"Well, I guess the first floor is the best place to start. Follow me this way, I'll show you around." Amanda placed her hand on Sam's shoulder and guided her past the other sisters gathered in the room. Playing along with the other woman, Sam allowed the guidance around the house, even though the other woman's touch sent her heartbeat racing.

"Over here you'll find our formal sitting area for greeting alumni and guests of honor." The room was styled tastefully with an ornate rug covering the restored wooden floors. The furniture and decorations were simple, tasteful additions to the room.

"Through this hallway is the dining room with a walkway directly into the kitchen. The sisters alternate chores throughout the week."

"Ow," Sam cried out as Amanda's grasp tightened on her shoulder.

"Sorry," she said her hold loosening. "We'll take the stairs here to the second floor where the library is located."

Amanda led Sam up the staircase to the second floor, careful to stay close to her. Once at the top, she steered Sam toward the doorway to their left which led into an expansive library, furnished with small desks, sofa and chairs for studying or casual reading. Sam's lips twitched into a smile, the library was breathtaking. "Wow, this is a new level of amazing," she managed to say.

"Yeah, it is pretty nice, isn't it?"

Momentarily distracted, Sam composed herself and thought of a way to swing the balance of power in her favor. She needed this opportunity to learn more about this woman, her motivations and reason behind the picture of her beside the dark town car. "How long have you been part of Alpha Delta Pi?" Sam asked.

She walked away from Amanda to admire the books lining the shelves on the other side of the room and lifted her brows in appreciation. The rows were neatly organized, a mix of classics, genre fiction and academic resources. Maggie would be impressed.

"I pledged when I was a freshman. I knew it was the sorority I wanted to join long before I even received my acceptance letter." Sam turned to face Amanda who was now standing in the room. "Here is a painting of our founding sister," she said gesturing toward the wall. Both women came to a stop in front of a large marble fireplace. An ornate, golden frame cased an oil painting of a matronly woman, her gray hair carefully coiffed, and a shrewdness shined in her deep-set blue eyes.

Amanda pressed on, "I was impressed by the number of women who were able to launch careers in lucrative areas once they graduated from Charleston College. I have no doubt the sorority helped the women find those jobs via networking."

"Alpha Delta Pi has a strong network in place for providing long-term support to their sisters."

"I've heard. The sisters also have another factor in common."

"What would that be?" Sam asked, turning toward the other woman.

Amanda stared right back at Sam. "They usually come from upper class families looking to milk connections to establish their children amongst society."

Sam noticed the turn in the young woman's tone and her expression close enough to a leer. Where before Amanda spoke lightly, a bitterness laced her tone. Sam reminded herself to tread carefully. She had no knowledge of this woman's character or motives. With the turn in temperament, she quickly discarded her goal in discovering Amanda's motive. Her new goal? Get out of the house as quickly as she could without raising additional suspicions. If she could gain additional information while doing so, all the better. But she wasn't going to risk it.

"Wealth tends to gather in similar places. Midnight Harbor and Charleston are expensive towns to reside in."

Amanda ignored Sam's remark. "If you would follow me, I'll show you the third floor and some of the rooms up there." Amanda turned her back to Sam. Glancing down at the desk near the painting, Sam noticed a letter opener next to a pile of stationery and pens. She careful slid the opener into her pocket as she followed the woman to the second set of stairs back near the end of the hallway, away from the library.

Sam wiped her sweaty palms on the front of her shorts. Sam felt sick, her stomach rolling over in knots. She had the distinct feeling like she should abandon the rest of the tour. Taking the stairs one at a time, Sam reached the top of the landing to find a series of doors along the length of the hallway.

"Over here," Amanda called to her from near the end of the hallway. "I have something I want to show you."

Sam walked into the room and startled when she felt a hand clasped around her upper arm. Amanda grabbed her arm from inside the room and pulled her in before shoving her to floor. Sam hit the floor with a thud, her teeth rattled in her mouth from the impact. She pushed herself up into a sitting position, giving herself a moment to recover from the shock before she attempted to stand.

Amanda's figure towered over her, blocking the door out of the room. The once sweet face that greeted her now peered down at her with a malicious sneer, the light glinting off an object in her hand.

"Enough with the act. Why are you really here?" she demanded. Amanda tightened her grip around the object in her hand.

"I don't know what you're talking about. I wanted to reconnect with my former sorority. I read in the newsletter there were some changes to the house. I wanted to see them for myself."

Amanda sliced her arm through the air in a cutting motion as if to silence Sam. "Cut me the crap. I know you're not here to reconnect with anyone."

The intern remained in front of the doorway. The only other way out of the room was through the window behind Sam. The room they were in was on the third floor. She would break a leg or worse if she jumped. Sam couldn't chance going out the window. She needed to find a way to get past Amanda without inflaming her further.

Sam decided bluntness would be the best way. Despite her initial sweet impression, Sam decided Amanda was anything but demure. "I saw pictures of you leaving the Firm to meet with a man in a dark car. Who were you meeting with?"

Amanda walked slowly over to Sam so she was merely a few inches from her. "What else did you see?"

"I didn't see anything else."

"How long have you been with your husband? Have you ever wanted for anything in your life?" Amanda's tone hinted at a deeper emotion.

Sam noticed the tension in the room and changed her tactic, trying to reason with the woman for now. It had certainly been a horrible idea to come here. She was trying to play the hero, something she was not.

"My husband and I are college sweethearts. We married soon after graduation."

"How nice for you," Amanda sneered. "I was the poor girl. I had to work for what I wanted. Nothing ever came free; everything had a price."

Amanda circled around behind Sam. Not wanting to provoke her, Sam strained not to move. With Amanda standing behind her, the path to the door opened. All she needed was to distract the other woman before she could make a run for it.

"I'm sorry you had a difficult childhood. It sounds like you were able to turn it around into something great for yourself."

"Are you kidding? I sacrificed so much to be accepted into this college. I chose to pledge to this sorority to gain a foothold into the lifestyle I knew I was destined to be a part of."

"You're proof hard work pays off. You've done well for yourself," Sam said. She needed to keep the intern talking, keep the discussion positive. She could no longer hear Theo's voice in her ear. She glimpsed the mic on the ground and silently hoped they were almost here.

"It wasn't enough. I had the grades and scholarship but I wasn't born into this lifestyle. These girls, they're used to living in houses like this. They have cars and allowances and European vacations their trust funds pay for. I don't. I tried desperately to fit in. To keep with the lifestyle of clothes and hair and nails and shopping. I was still found wanting. Soon, I was dipping into the money I had for college. I needed to replace it, quickly."

Sam let the realization sink in, Amanda knew she was cornered. Whatever game she played was ending and she needed to keep Amanda engaged now that she was so close to revealing her motive. "What did you do? To keep up with the other girls?"

Amanda walked back around to Sam and smiled. "One night at a party I met another girl like me. She told me all about how I could overcome any obstacle with her help. I could pay off all my debt, pay for school while still having enough to live the lifestyle I wanted."

"What did you do when she offered you help?" Sam asked.

"I accepted her offer. She took me under her wing, introducing me to people who were looking for strong, confident, beautiful women to provide companionship to high-profile clients."

"You're an escort," Sam said in disbelief.

Amanda shrugged as she began to pace in front of Sam. "Yes, you could say that. I started meeting clients so they had arm candy for a gala or dinner."

"What does that have to do with the town car outside the Firm?" Sam asked. She might be able to make a run for the door, if it wasn't for what Sam recognized as the object Amanda was holding, a syringe. Sam wasn't a fighter, but in this instance, she would do anything to reach that door.

"It was great money. I attended parties with people who would be able to influence my career."

"People like Nicholas Davi?" Sam questioned trying to piece together the other woman's story and relation to Davi and Bailee.

She nodded. "But it wasn't enough, I wanted more. I asked for additional clients when my mentor recommended I begin to offer...additional services to my clients in exchange for a higher pay rate."

"You started sleeping with them?" Sam inferred.

The intern shrugged her shoulders again, not fazed by the implications of her confession. "The acts varied. The more intimate the act, the higher the pay. But the best money? It came from clients who wanted information. Secrets and ideas people shared between the sheets, not thinking a lowly escort would know what or who they were talking about."

"The person in the town car...was that one of your clients?" Sam asked then remembered Amanda clutched folders against her chest. "Those files...you were meeting to give him information about the case...you took the files and were the one feeding information to the media about Nicholas Davi!"

"Yes, I took the files. I wanted out. I was tired of sleeping with old men. I met a client who told me he had a job for me that would allow me to live the way I wanted as long as I left the area after the job was completed. He wanted any information I could find out about Nicholas Davi."

"You sold out the Firm for a payout?" Sam tried to keep her tone neutral. "What else did you do? Were you involved in the disappearance of Bailee Talson?"

"Selling out? No, I was taking advantage of my position. Like Rex Brown doesn't release information to the media on his own to cultivate an image of his clients. I was only doing what the wealthy do, but to my own benefit. I had nothing to do with Bailee Talson, but I'll let you in on a secret." Amanda leaned down to whisper into Sam's hair, "I wasn't the only college girl who was recruited into the agency."

Sam glanced up at Amanda and allowed the information to lead her to the next question. "Is that how you know her? Through the escort service? Was Bailee an escort, too?"

Amanda smirked and shrugged. "I don't know who recruited her. We're told not to speak with one another unless the circumstances demand it. I met her at a dinner party held by her client. She told me she used to be a waitress and couldn't keep up with her rent payments and tuition."

"Who was she there with?" Sam questioned, thinking back to Davi and Rex. They both attended gatherings the night of Bailee's disappearance.

"I'm not telling you who was there."

"What happened? Did you see her again? She stopped showing up to work according to the staff at the restaurant."

"You're full of a lot of questions this evening," Amanda said, grabbing Sam by the hair. Sam struggled in the other woman's grasp. Amanda pulled on Sam's hair harder bringing tears to her eyes. "Don't worry, you'll just feel a pinch," Amanda said as Sam watched her raise her arm, the syringe in her hand.

Sam cried out against the woman's hold. "You killed her! You killed Bailee!"

"No, I didn't kill her, I didn't do anything like that. Don't you understand? You can't leave. They own you. They tell you what to do! I couldn't leave. The only thing I could do was find a way to get out!"

"The missing files from the Firm. Who did you give them to?" Sam said, the question lingering in the air. "Who killed Bailee?" Sam continued to struggle against the other woman. She felt something sharp push against her leg.

The letter opener. If she could only get her hand free, get to that letter opener, she could use it to break free and run.

"I don't know who killed her. He paid me to get the files, I didn't think it would go this far and someone would get killed. I just wanted a way out. I thought when I tipped off Davi, I could force him to pay up to keep his name out of the papers. Instead he went right to Rex. I had to do what I needed to break free."

Sam struggled against the woman, trying to get a foothold

to maneuver her body out of Amanda's grasp. "Nobody owns you. You have a choice. Let me help you."

"You can't help me. No one can help me!" Amanda's hand raised back to jab the syringe into Sam's neck.

One quick movement and the weight of the letter opener slid into Sam's palm. With all her might, Sam spun and stabbed outward at the other woman. Pain blossomed down Sam's arm as the letter opener made contact with Amanda's leg.

"Bitch!" Amanda cried out and staggered, loosening her grip on Sam's hair. Sam wrestled free and leapt up, racing toward the closed door. A loud crunch ripped through the air and the door swung open, revealing Theo and the barrel of a gun pointing directly at her.

"Hands up!" Theo cried out. She raised her arms, dropping the letter opener.

Heath stepped out from behind Theo and looked from Amanda at the window to Sam with her hands in the air and shook his head. "I hope this isn't becoming a habit, Mrs. Crenshaw," he drawled before catching a sobbing Sam in his arms.

CHAPTER TWENTY-FOUR

"THANK YOU," Sam said, accepting the hot coffee from the woman. She wrapped her chilled hands around the white Styrofoam cup, inhaling the aroma as the steam wafted up into her face. She blew on the drink and sipped, pleasantly surprised at the taste. The coffee would never replace her favorite café's, but the administrative assistant of Midnight Harbor's Police Station made a decent cup of coffee.

After the fiasco with the intern, Amanda, and almost getting stabbed with a syringe containing who knows what, Sam and Heath followed Theo back to the police station for statements and processing. She was grateful for the brief respite between Theo's questions and Heath's kisses and reprimands, each man redirecting her attention away from the case in their own way. The constant hovering of both men over her like hens guarding their eggs could irritate the calmest person. She was ready to call Josie for backup before she snapped.

Sam stretched and grimaced at the pain in her shoulder, convinced she pulled a muscle from the maneuver she did turning and stabbing Amanda with the letter opener. Who would've thought she had the guts to do it. She moved into a more comfortable sitting position when Heath entered the interrogation room and sat in the chair next to her. She wasn't going to let him dominate the conversation and spoke before he even had a chance to blink. "Did you get the confession from Amanda? About the missing files and blackmail?"

Heath rubbed at the stubble on his jawline and Sam's eyes followed, wanting to plant kisses along the way to his spot behind his ear despite the unsettled feelings between them. "Theo recorded everything thanks to the mic line you were wearing."

Relief washed over Sam before she remembered poor Bailee and her reason for being at the police station. "Amanda didn't murder Bailee. That means the killer is still loose in Midnight Harbor. I need to hear the recording. I know there is something in there I'm missing that could help us."

"Right now, your only job is to rest and recover. Theo will handle everything from here," Heath said with a wave of his hand. "I'll see how much longer we have to stay."

The wait felt like eternity until Heath returned. "We're free to go. Theo will follow up in a few days' time."

Heath helped her up, leaving the blanket on the chair and placing his jacket around her shoulders. "I'm taking you home. No yelling, or trying to get me to go anywhere else. Got it?"

She nodded, too weary to fight. The drive home was a blur as Sam dozed off and on. Heath helped her inside, tenderly attending to her. He carried her to bed where she must've slept for what seemed like days but was mere hours.

When she awoke, she found him in the bed next to her, propped up on his shoulder, staring at her.

"Hey, sleeping beauty." He hesitated before grabbing her hand, his warmth soaked into her, erasing the coldness threatening to devour her heart. Words had been said between them. Awful, hateful things they couldn't take back.

Heath's hand moved to her shoulder then to her face. "I

don't want to lose you," Heath said, his voice husky. "I'm sorry for what I said. I reacted out of anger and…fear. I want you to understand my point of view. I can't allow you to continue down this path. It's not safe. I don't understand what caused this change in you. You were never reckless, never cared about my work beyond the concern I exhausted myself. Where is this coming from, Sam? Why can't you just be like your old self? Give the ladies' auxiliary a call or go to brunch with Josie. If you want I'm sure I can put in a call to the library at the college to see if they can take you back on a part-time basis."

"Please, Heath, just stop." Sam pulled away from him. "Stop talking about the old me. The old me may have been all those things on the outside, but inside, I was lost, unfulfilled and…lonely. I devoted my life to being the perfect wife, perfect host, and perfect employee. It's utterly exhausting to face that life again. I can't go back to that. I can't just sit back anymore while it feels as if someone else controls my life."

Sam turned over in bed thinking back to the agreement and room she took refuge in. She was afraid to face him. The thought manifested and before she could stop herself, she spoke her deepest truth. "If it wasn't for losing our baby then I may still be that same woman. But I'm not her. I'm not perfect," Sam said as a sob escaped her, renewed tears streaming down her face and the taste of salt on her tongue.

"If I was perfect then I would be a mother right now." She sucked in a breath. Her truth was free. "I'm not any of those things. I'm just a woman who wanted a baby so badly with the man she loved. Not only did I lose the baby but now I'm losing you too." Sam covered her hands over her face, muffling her cries. She steadied herself then continued, wanting to release the hurt. "If I was perfect then I could have saved her." There it was. Now he knew what she kept buried inside for so long.

Sobs wrecked her body as Sam finally gave voice to the

feelings she had kept hidden, deep inside herself. Sam turned to look at Heath, her words coming from her heart. "I will never be that woman again. Life is too precious for me to not have a purpose to live for besides being your wife. I love you but if I am unable to be a mother, then I need to find meaning where I can. More than what the old me did to stay content. It's all so frivolous when life isn't guaranteed."

"Sam, why did you never say anything to me about the way you felt? Do you think I don't grieve as well?" Heath moved toward her, wrapping his arms around her so her head rested against his chest. He held her chilled body against his, trying to wash away all the hurt she hid away from him for months.

"Damnit, I knew you were grieving. Anytime I tried to talk to you or engage, you would push me away. I turned to the next thing available to me which was my work. If you wouldn't let me emotionally provide for you, then I thought at least I could provide for you financially, in hopes you would see there is more to our life than a baby It's the cave man in me."

Sam dried her tears on Heath's shirt as he stroked her hair back from her face. "We have each other. When you returned from the hospital, you left a part of you behind. I saw only sadness in your eyes and part of me grieved at what we lost. I used my work to hide away from my grief and sadness since I didn't want to burden you. Then each day became another then another, until I worked all the time. I told myself I was furthering my career but in truth, I wanted to bury any feelings of inadequacy. I hoped to make partner so I could show my worth and finally spend time with you, travel like we always hoped."

Heath sighed before he continued. "Each day and week turned longer until we became more strangers than lovers. I don't want you to be the old Sam if you're not happy but I only know her. I want you to be happy with me and your choices. I want to be the one you choose every day, every time." Heath took her face in his hands. "Maybe we'll never have children, but we'll always have each other and that's enough for me."

"You dummy, you're the only man I have ever wanted. I love you." Sam kissed his hand. "I need you to understand, I need to be more than just Mrs. Crenshaw, I need to be Samantha first, I need to just be Sam." Heath wiped away her tears, nodding his understanding. "Which means I make choices based on what is best for me. I'm not asking you to like them, and I'm certainly not asking for permission. You're not my keeper. I need to find myself and figure out this... strange supernatural sense I have."

Heath pulled her mouth against his, kissing her deeply. When he was done, their lips swollen, he whispered into her ear, "Whatever you want, Sam. There will be rules for both our sanity and safety." He kissed her again. "Just don't expect me to join the Midnight Harbor Auxillary in your place."

CHAPTER TWENTY-FIVE

SAM'S HEART soared at the words Heath spoke. The way he kissed her, held her...she knew it came from his heart. The hurt was deep from months of separation. Though she could feel the pain slowly melt away with the increased attention Heath lavished on her.

Their lips met in a passionate mix of stranger and comfort, desire and need. Sam's hands pressed against Heath's chest, tracing a path over his firm muscles. Her hands needed to roam over his body and relish in the hardness of his muscles and softness of his skin. She ached with a need deep inside her, desperate for the touch of his hands and lips. His cologne smelled crisp and clean, reminding her of better days on the horizon.

Heath pulled back from her, his breathing uneven. Dark brown eyes gazed into hers, seeing the hurt and loneliness in her grief she kept hidden from him and the rest of the world. He brushed back Sam's hair and grazed his fingers over her face, tilting her chin up.

"I want you more now than I have ever wanted you before," Heath said, his gaze shifting to her lips. His hand moved down her arm and gently cupped her breast, running his thumb over her nipple. His face broke into a wicked grin as her nipple hardened under his touch.

Her sensation heightened, a tremor ran through her, from Heath's touch along the length of her body, ending in the space between her thighs. Sam ached for his touch and wound her fingers through Heath's hair, pulling his head down for another kiss as she moved against him, relishing the feeling of his hard body against hers beneath the layers of clothing separating them.

Boldness overcame her and soon her hands roamed over his chest, loosening the remaining buttons of his crisp shirt until she yanked open his shirt, revealing his tanned muscular chest. Heath slipped his arms out of the shirt. "I see you're as impatient as always, love," he murmured in her ear, sending another bolt of shock waves down to her core.

"I'm trying to understand why there are so many buttons on your shirt," Sam said and loosened his belt while his hands made quick work of Sam's shirt, revealing a pink satin bra.

He laughed. "So easy to tease." His hands cupped her breasts gently before undoing the clasp of her bra, letting the pink scrap of satin drop to the floor. He hooked a finger in the belt lip of her shorts and drew them down the length of her thighs, his hand leaving behind an ache as his dark blond head followed the path his hands made.

Sam gasped, feeling the brush of Heath's teeth as he used his mouth to pull down her pink panties. "A matching set." Naked in front of her husband, any vulnerability hidden now laid as bare as her body and soul before him. Sam pushed herself up on her elbows and cocked an eyebrow at him, her head held high, never taking her eyes off of his.

Heath pulled her to the edge of the bed, kneeling in front of her, his hungry eyes lingering over her from head to the tip of her toes, basking in her openness, her beauty. "This reminds me of the first time I saw you naked," Heath said as he ran his hand up her inner thigh. "I couldn't believe my luck. I had the hottest babe naked in my dorm."

The tug of nostalgia from the long ago memory pulled her close. This moment did feel oddly reminiscent of the first time she was with Heath. "I seem to remember there was some awkwardness on your side," Sam teased. She recalled the vulnerability and shyness then. Now, she had the confidence to take control of what she wanted.

Sam locked her eyes with his. "Make love to me right here, right now."

Heath stood quickly, grabbing her hips and throwing her legs around his waist. He spun her around their bedroom, his hungry eyes staring right into hers and threw her back onto the bed. Sam laughed as she landed, sinking into the softness of blankets and pillows. She rolled over onto her hands and knees, arching her back so Heath was behind her and gave him a saucy smile from over her shoulder.

He stalked toward her. Lowering himself to his knees, one hand grabbed her hip as he used the index finger on his other hand to stroke her between her thighs. Sam threw her head back and moaned. Not soon enough his tongue replaced the touch of his fingers and worked magic as Sam's hips moved, urging for more.

The need inside her grew until an explosion of sensation rocked her body, a moan escaping her lips. Before she caught her breath, Heath continued the strokes until another wave of completion washed over Sam.

"Heath," she whispered.

He stood, both hands on her hips, kissing a path along her back. He flipped her over, covering his body with hers, and eased her legs open with a knee. She wrapped her legs around his hips. "I missed you. I want you to know, nothing will ever keep me from you again."

She pushed herself up from her elbows easing Heath's pants off with a combination of her hands and feet. Right now she needed him. Sam stroked him before guiding him into her. A rake of teeth against her neck and his breath hitched as he moved ever so slowly against her. "Sam," he whispered, biting her earlobe.

Not wanting to rush the moment, Heath and Sam rocked against one another, their rhythm slow and steady. Whispering words into each other's ears, only interrupted by kisses. When they reached the edge of a crescendo, Heath sped up and with a moan, took Sam's mouth against his, relishing the feeling of oneness as they clung together. Reaching the peak, Sam moaned his name and they tumbled over the edge in unison.

CHAPTER TWENTY-SIX

HEATH'S EYES lingered on Sam's prone body while in bed, their arms and legs intertwined. He saw her as a changed woman from the one he married five years ago. Wasn't he also a different man from the one she married? The seasons of life were inevitable, it was how they weathered the coming storms that mattered.

Sam needed acceptance as she grew into her new skin, just as she pushed him to be the man she knew he could be. Heath recognized his weakness. Sam had been hurting yet he turned his back on her, not able to be the rock she needed when he should've been her anchor in the storm. He refused to fail her again.

Heath understood now, Sam sacrificed in her journey to support his. He would no longer stand in her way. He would support her while she embarked on her own journey to realize her potential.

He hugged her close, the scent of her wrapping around him in a comforting cocoon. Pleased she was doing something she found passion in, just as he found passion in helping others. He tried not to think about Rex and his former position with the Firm. He made the decision that was honest to him and withheld his integrity. He would find his own way in time.

His phone buzzed from the nightstand. He answered the call, placing it on speakerphone. "Hey, Theo. What's up?"

"I'm wondering if you could swing by the police station with Sam. I have the recording from the confrontation with Amanda."

"I don't think now's the best time," Heath said.

Sam grabbed his arm and pulled him back down into the bed, her gaze lingering on his deep brown eyes. "Listen to me, Heath, I need to hear that recording."

"Sam—"

She held up a hand, cutting him off. "Please. Let him know I'm ready."

"Why do you have to be damn adorable when you're asserting your dominance?" Heath grabbed her hand and kissed it. "Fine. We'll be there in fifteen minutes." He disconnected the call and raised his eyebrows. "Are you going to go in your birthday suit or something else?"

Sam smacked his arm playfully.

"Or you could stay here like the dutiful wife?"

"I'll take my chances with the recording."

"Damn, if I didn't try," Heath said rolling her on top of him and making her fast lose interest in any recordings.

Much later they returned to the interrogation room with Theo, a handheld speaker in tow. Theo thumped the speaker on the table and gave her a hard-eyed stare. "One listen, okay? No theatrics, no running off to be the hero. I'm only doing this because you asked. Got it?"

"Yes," Sam murmured demurely despite the adrenaline coursing through her, pushing her into motion. Since when did she embrace the fight mode rather than flight? She would have to think on it later.

Theo hit the play button and the three of them huddled around the small black speaker, captivated by the exchange between Amanda and Sam. When the recording finished, Sam stared at the table and tapped her finger in thought. What was it Amanda said again that caught her attention at the time?

"Theo, do you still have the camera from the photographer who stalked me?"

"Sam, I allowed you to listen but I'm not going to placate you with participating in this charade." He turned toward Heath. "Take her home. I'll call with any questions."

Heath gently grasped Sam's elbow, guiding her toward the exit. "Theo, please. Let me help. I…" She stopped herself from blurting out her secret and looked up at Heath's face. He shook his head in a silent *no* before pushing her toward the exit. She turned and looked at Theo, bent over the speaker, fiddling with the buttons.

What could she do to make him understand she could help him? Bailee spoke to her at the apartment about time running out. Was this it? Was Sam's time finally up? Not believing it for a minute, she needed to think fast. Recalling the police report from Tyler's computer she pushed forward with the strange knowledge she learned from a supernatural source.

"I know Bailee was found with a watch. A woman's watch. Gold with diamonds." She closed her eyes, forcing herself to remember the image she received before and the vision of Bailee holding the watch. She pushed out beyond that image, trying to think of Bailee's body lying in the field to take her to that special place where she could connect and Bailee could influence her. "The media reported you found it with the body. But that isn't true, is it?"

Theo's head snapped up, his eyes held hers.

Darkness surrounded her. Panic. Running but feeling so tired, her legs so heavy.

Sam sucked in a breath, forcing herself to fight her own panic as the thoughts and emotions of Bailee coursed through her, using her as an outlet.

Stumbling. Falling. She's behind me. Struggling. Not this way. No, not like this. A hand slipping a watch off her wrist into a purse.

"You found it in her bag along with her phone. But you can't crack her phone." Sam gasped and grabbed her forehead as a vice grip tightened around her head, erasing the image of the watch from her mind.

Her kindness, her deceit.

"How do you know that?" Theo took a step toward her then stopped when Heath pushed her behind his back.

Sam placed her hand on Heath's back, the muscle beneath his shirt coiled and tense. She stepped beside him, her arm wrapping around his waist for support. "Because I saw it, just now."

Heath exhaled and glanced down at her, a sad smile on his face and nodded his head in resignation.

Sam walked over to Theo and gently touched his arm. She lowered her voice to a bare whisper. "If I confide in you, do you promise me what I tell you will never leave this room?" She heard the door shut and glanced back to catch a glimpse of Heath leaning against the doorframe, blocking the exit.

Her eyes searched Theo's, begging him to trust her and keep her secret. He nodded his head. "Yes, I'd like to hear what you have to say. You would be surprised at what I've heard. I've come to think nothing could ever shock me anymore."

He motioned toward the table and chairs. Sam followed him, taking the seat across from him. She dropped her hands in her lap and crossed her fingers and relayed the story of how she received the image of the watch at the train station, omitting the details about Bailee's ghost.

Sometime later, after much pacing on Theo's part, he said

to her, "So, you're able to see things? Images related to Bailee's death?"

Sam shrugged. "I'm not sure. The watch I saw in my mind is the same one you found. If you just let me see those photos, I'm sure I can help you piece together the night of Bailee's death."

Theo looked from her and wiped a hand across his face. He turned to Heath, still leaning against the doorway. "What say you, Heath? Ready for another adventure?"

"It would seem my wife has caught a case of Nancy Drew syndrome. I'm afraid the only cure is enabling her relentless pursuit and preventing myself from gaining any more gray hairs."

Sam uncrossed her fingers and stretched her hand out, easing the cramp from holding the position for so long. She smiled, knowing they were both unable to resist playing the hero.

They gathered around the small laptop Theo smuggled into the room along with the flash drive from the photographer's camera. He loaded the pictures onto this laptop and started from the beginning.

"Amanda said she met Bailee at a dinner party. They worked for the same escort agency but never met before that night. She was evasive with the timeframe," Sam said closing her eyes and trying again to call forth her sixth sense. Pain shot across forehead again. She pinched the bridge of her nose.

Nothing. The pain was almost too much now. "What if we start from the beginning of the camera roll?"

Theo followed her command and soon images flashed across the monitor again, beyond what Heath had shown her at Bailee's apartment. The images began with a picture of none other than Rex Brown standing beside Nathan Lee, both men wearing tuxedos. Heath gestured to the laptop monitor.

"I remember Rex and Nathan attended the same charity gala and were called in from the event. They arrived at the Firm still wearing their tuxes. We need to go further back. Sam found Bailee's body the night after. The coroner said Bailee died prior and was dumped in the field."

Another series of images flashed of people coming and going in evening wear from outside the conference hall before transitioning to another location entirely, Magnolia's, a banquet hall and restaurant. The people in these pictures were also dressed up and it wasn't long until Sam caught a flicker of recognition in one of the photos. "There," she pointed her finger, "Nicholas Davi and Kerri Reid."

Theo enlarged the image of Davi and Kerri, her arm was linked in his, her head thrown back in laughter as they walked up the steps into the restaurant. He clicked the mousepad and the image moved to the next one then another. It wasn't until a few pictures later Sam whispered, "Bailee," and pointed to the image of the young blonde woman walking behind another couple. From the photo she appeared to be alone.

Heath inhaled and leaned back in his seat. "This confirms she was there with Davi. Damnit! That son of a bitch lied. He's been playing us!"

Sam shook her head. "That's only speculation."

Theo bookmarked the image then flicked to the next, showing the gradual decline of attendees entering Magnolia. The images changed to show people leaving the restaurant. Theo clicked though until one caught their eye, Davi and Kerri, arm in arm again with a laughing Bailee following closely behind them. Davi looked straight ahead while Kerri had her head turned back toward Bailee, like they were sharing a joke between friends.

"Well this just took an interesting turn,"

"He said he left with Kerri to attend another party. He

never said Bailee joined them," Heath said as he looked at the next picture of them climbing into a darkened limousine.

"I think it's time you gave your former client a call," Theo said.

Heath swore and pulled out his phone, punching at the screen. He stood up and walked away, the phone up to his ear then pulled it away and looked at the screen. "No, no no. My battery just died!" He walked away from them, head in his hands.

Sam's gaze lingered on the picture, trying to make sense of what she saw. Bailee climbing into the limousine, Kerri was smiling, her hand on the roof of the limousine, Davi standing behind her, his hand on the small of her back. She analyzed the picture, picking apart the pieces until she saw it.

"Theo, zoom in to this area here." She pointed with the tip of a pen. Theo zoomed in on the area of Kerri's hand on the roof. "Do you notice anything in particular with Kerri's arm?"

Heath heard and walked back over to the table. He leaned down to look and swore again, this time with increase adjectives. "The watch. Kerri Reid is wearing a gold watch." He paced around the table. "When I met her, I noticed a white band of skin around her wrist. I thought it odd, especially for a woman like her who appeared to be put together. She must have lost it."

My mistake, her deceit. The words Bailee crooned to her reverberated in her mind.

"We need to find out if the watch belongs to Kerri," Theo said. He turned to Sam. "Thank you for your help. I'll show this to the chief and check if Kerri Reid called in a lost watch." He stood and started walking toward the door.

"Theo, I can help with Kerri," Sam said, fidgeting with the hem of shirt.

"You've done enough. Go home and get some rest. I'll call Heath if I have any questions."

"Kerri Reid offered me a job," she blurted out, avoiding Heath's gaze.

"What?" Both men turned in unison, the same word spoken by both with measured volume.

"I met her at the book signing and Josie told her I was the unofficial town historian. She offered to meet with me about a project she was working on and hired me on the spot."

"You didn't think to tell us this?" Heath asked, his eyes narrowed and voice softened.

"I didn't think it would be important. Everyone was looking at Davi. What would Kerri want with Bailee, she's just a college girl?"

"I'll be the one to figure it out," Theo said from her side. She could only see his profile but noticed he held Heath's gaze. "Sam, go home. That's an order. If you don't comply, I'll have you arrested."

Sam sucked in a breath, looking from Heath to Theo. They didn't understand her compulsion and likely never would. They didn't understand cutting her from involvement in the case was like eviscerating her in half.

She closed her eyes against the threat of tears. When she reopened them, Heath held his hand out to her. "Let's go home, baby." He gave her hand two squeezes and pulled her up. They walked out the police station together and out of hearing range from the front door, Sam rounded on Heath. "You know what this means to me. How could you let Theo push me out of the investigation?"

Heath placed her arm in his and pulled her close, so they walked side by side toward the parking garage. "Quiet. We don't know if the camera was recording in the room."

She furrowed her brow and glanced up at Heath's face for understanding. He gave her his signature cocky smile. What did she miss?

"How well do you think you can portray a bored society wife visiting her new employer?"

Sam's face broke into a wide grin. She squeezed his arm linked in hers. "I think I could convince a few people." She turned away from Heath and thought about the image they portrayed. Another perfect Midnight Harbor couple, out for a stroll. If only those around her could foresee what they were about to do.

CHAPTER TWENTY-SEVEN

THE RED DRESS slid up her hips as Heath's hands lingered on her shoulders, adjusting the straps of the dress in place. He kissed her neck and pulled the zipper up slowly, then leaned against her, pressing his body into hers and whispered in her ear, "If I don't get the chance to take this dress off you, I will be a very unhappy husband."

Sam eased back against his chest, feeling the warmth of him along the length of her back. His arms clasped her around the waist and she watched him in the full-length mirror behind her. Heath's face was darkened with stubble, his eyes weary and hair wilder than she'd ever seen. Despite his appearance, his brown eyes shined with a ferocity she knew existed within him. He wouldn't let anything happen to her.

She turned in his arms and kissed him, biting his bottom lip before pulling away. "An appetizer for what's to come."

Heath brushed her hair away from her eyes and kissed her forehead before swatting her on the butt. "Go on, Nancy Drew, redeem your husband and bring justice to the citizens of Midnight Harbor. Or something noble like that," he said, waving his hand in the air.

She rolled her eyes, trying to hide the smile and grabbed her purse from the dresser. What type of person was she, smiling at the thought of confronting a possible killer? A tape recorder peeked out from one of the inside pockets of her purse. A brief pause at the mirror to check her lipstick before she walked out the door for her performance of a lifetime.

The drive to her destination was slow due to increased traffic for the upcoming weekend. She thought she saw a sign for a spring festival of some sort. There was a time not too long ago she would've helped organize the event. Now, she braced herself for what she was about to do, digging deep within herself for the courage and strength to see this through.

Once at the hotel, a quick stroll through the lobby and she was riding the elevator to one the top floors. The doors opened, revealing a lush carpeted hallway with soft cream and pastel pink tones swirled throughout the carpet and wallpaper. Small tables with various knick-knacks and vases of silk flowers lined the length of the hallway, the light from the scones casting a warm glow.

Sam paused outside the room the text message indicated and knocked on the white door. Her hand hung in the air when the door flung open, revealing a disheveled Lilliana, Kerri Reid's personal assistant. Dark circles ringed the skin below her big doll eyes and her translucent skin was red and blotchy, like she hadn't slept in days.

"Hi." Sam extended her hand to Lilliana in greeting. "It's nice to see you again."

Lilliana looked at Sam's outstretched hand and took it into her own. Her eyes widened as Sam passed the woman a small folded paper.

"Is Kerri available? I'm here to drop off the reading materials I mentioned in my text message."

Lilliana nodded her head and moved aside. Sam entered

the hotel room and was momentarily in awe of the spacious suite. No expense too great for Kerri Reid.

"Lilliana dear, who is it?" Kerri called out from inside the suite. Sam walked into the living room area and found Kerri clad in a silk robe. The fabric drooped elegantly off her shoulder.

"Oh, Samantha! What a surprise. I was expecting someone else for tea." Kerri stood and walked toward her and took her hands. "Please join me." Kerri practically dragged her to the small table set up near the fireplace. A tea service had been laid out complete with small sandwiches and pastries.

Sam sat in the chair adjacent from Kerri. She placed her purse on the ground and spared a quick glance to see Lilliana sulking near the door.

"Pray tell what do I owe your visit?" Kerri poured tea from the porcelain pot into Sam's cup before her own. Sam glanced around and took notice of the open bedroom door. A suitcase sat on the bed and clothing flung about in disarray on the bed and desk. She noticed more suitcases were lined up against the wall.

She turned back to see Kerri drop a spoon of honey in her teacup before doing the same to her own.

Sam gave Kerri her best smile. The same one she practiced in front of the mirror her last year of college, when she realized Heath's intentions to make her his wife. His ambitions far outweighed her own, and she prepared herself to be a society wife, perfecting her smile with grace despite the circumstances.

"I brought over a few books I thought you would find interesting. For your next project."

"How delightful!" Kerri blew on her tea before sitting the cup down again. She reached out to take a scone off the tray when Sam noticed the whitened band of skin around her wrist, just as Heath had told her.

Sam met Kerri's eyes from across the table and motioned

to Kerri's wrist. "It looks like you lost something. A bracelet or maybe a watch?" She wanted to smack herself as soon as the words crossed her lips. Damn, so much for subtly.

Kerri's eyes crinkled as a small smile lifted at the corner of her lips. "How observant of you, Samantha. I did in fact lose a sentimental watch not too long ago. Lilliana has been searching all over Midnight Harbor for it."

Sam pulled a small photograph from her purse and placed it on the table in front of Kerri. "Is this it?" The gold link watch appeared duller in the photograph than Sam imagined it being in her mind.

"That's it! Wherever did you find it? Lilliana will be so pleased to know she no longer has to haunt around Midnight Harbor for it." Kerri bit a small piece of the scone and chewed.

"Does the name Bailee Talson sound familiar to you?" Sam asked, picking up her teacup. She tried to keep her hand from shaking and took a small sip.

"Of course. Isn't that the poor girl they found dead in the field?" Kerri *tsk*ed. "I heard she was running around with the wrong crowd. Bad things happen to people who get in over their heads."

Sam matched Kerri's gaze and placed another photograph on the table, this one of Kerri, Bailee and Davi. "Do you mean, your crowd, Kerri?" Boldness was never a character trait anyone from Sam's circle would attribute to her personality. Maybe it was a mistake on her part, but Sam felt the need for bluntness in her conversation turned interrogation. Sam sipped at her tea again to busy her hands and waited for Kerri to respond.

Tilting her head, Kerri made a show of looking at the picture of the trio getting inside the limousine. "I may have forgot a piece of information from that evening."

"Forgot or omitted from your statement?" Sam placed her

tea cup down on the saucer, the porcelain clinking. She jabbed at the photo. "This woman is Bailee Talson. This photo is one of the last times she was seen alive before she bought a train ticket at the station from an attendant named Robin." She moved forward in her seat and reached out to take Kerri's hand in her own. "Please, tell me what you know of Bailee. What happened between this photo and when she was dropped off at the train station?" Her voice broke on the last word as she pleaded.

Kerri pursed her lips before placing her other hand on top of Sam's. She pulled away from Sam and leaned back in her seat, crossing her legs at the knee. "I know Bailee. I made her acquaintance at a charity gala in Charleston for one of my favorite non-profits. She was there as a date for an old friend. We started talking and quickly found we had a lot of interests in common."

Sam blinked as a fogginess settled into her head. She took another sip of tea, hoping the caffeine would keep her awake as Kerri shared her secrets. "Then what happened? Why is she leaving with you and Davi in this photo?"

"I saw her again a few times after that night, at other events in the area. We always sought out each other for conversation away from the other attendees. It wasn't until early this year she made it clear she wanted to be more than just friends."

Sam's mouth dropped open and she quickly closed it. "You mean, you and Bailee…were lovers?" Her brow furrowed as she mulled over the implications of the relationship.

Kerri toyed with the handle of her tea cup and batted her eyes at Sam. "Yes, Bailee and I were lovers. We had a relationship up until the night of this photograph. My dear friend, Nicholas Davi, escorted me that evening, which she took offense to. Bailee wanted us to be open in our relationship. That night, I explained to Bailee I could no longer see her. I was going to be traveling with my book tour and didn't have the time to devote to her like she wanted."

"She didn't take the breakup well?"

"Of course not. She cursed at me, screamed and begged me not to leave her. I couldn't handle it so I left her alone at the place we stayed at. Nic had been called away and left long before our argument."

"Why didn't you just say so during your statement with Heath?" Sam said, weariness creeping into her despite the revelation Kerri shared. "Nicholas Davi is being charged with her murder but…you said he left the two of you alone. Kerri, your watch was found with Bailee's body. What happened?" Sam questioned.

"She must have stolen it from me before I left. Probably to blackmail me into staying with her."

Sam tried to think through the building haze in her brain. It became difficult to keep her eyes open and focus. There was something she was missing in Kerri's story. "You have to go to Detective Hart and tell him your story," Sam pleaded. "He can help you clear Davi's name."

"No, that's not how this is going to go."

"What?" Sam questioned, feeling the increasing pressure of a headache forming. "What do you mean?"

"I'm sorry, Samantha. I truly wanted our collaboration to work out but I'm finding your sudden obsession with me and Bailee Talson unsettling. It's best I speak with Detective Hart and your husband before you hurt yourself or someone else."

Sam sputtered, and stood, her legs leaden with weight. She plopped back down in her seat. "What do you mean? You offered me a job as a consultant."

"Dearest, my little visit was to encourage you to look away from Bailee's murder. My Lord, are you persistent with playing detective. Then Lilliana saw you at Bailee's apartment. How do you think it would've looked if she was caught by your husband?"

She stood and walked around to Sam's chair, placed her hand beneath her chin and tilted her head up. "Samantha, I loved her but there was no way I was going to allow her to go public with our relationship. My fans couldn't handle it. My agent, my manager, no one would accept it. I couldn't let her do it and ruin everything I've built."

Sam looked into Kerri's eyes. "You killed her because you didn't think people would accept her as your lover? Who cares what other people think? I'm sure your fans would've loved her. You never gave her a chance."

Kerri's beautiful face twisted into a macabre mask. "She was going to expose us." Kerri released Sam's chin and walked away toward the mantel of the fireplace. "I took care of her so she would never tell about our relationship. Money, clothes, everything she could possibly want. She wanted more. The night she went missing I met her at the train station. We talked over tea and she agreed to come back to town with me."

Sam's eyes widened. She recalled the poison that killed Bailee and the foggy feeling she was now experiencing. "You poisoned her with that tea."

No. She glanced down at her cup. "You poisoned me!"

"As I said, your obsession has gotten out of hand. You killed yourself in front of me because I wouldn't give in to your demands. Such a pity. I'm sure your husband will be devastated to learn about how you unraveled since finding Bailee's body."

"No, no...I'm not going to allow you to do this. Lilliana, she went for help."

"Lilliana is mine to control. She does what I say."

Sam watched Kerri rake her fingers along her neck before tearing a piece of her robe. She couldn't allow this woman to win. Kerri picked up a bottle of pills from the mantel and walked toward Sam.

Sensing Kerri's intent, she leapt up, knocking over the tea

service from the table and staggered toward the door. She struggled to move forward, each step more difficult than the last until she was only a few feet from the door.

Her peripheral vision darkened, threatening to slowly disappear until she was blind. Sam forced her eyelids open but her body weight was too heavy for her to carry any further. She stumbled again then sank to the floor, her vision overcome by darkness.

CHAPTER TWENTY-EIGHT

HEATH'S HEART pounded in his chest as he raced down the hallway of the hotel, pushing guests out of his way.

"We're going to make it," Theo called out from in front of him. On their way out of the elevator, the woman Heath recognized from Bailee's apartment stumbled into them. She babbled on about Kerri and Samantha until Theo quietly handed her over to another officer. His priority was to find Sam before it was too late.

Hotel guests and employees cried out as the men rushed past them, desperate to reach the women. Heath focused on the figure of Theo ahead of him. They were going to make it. His labored breathing became a mantra, forcing him to focus, one step at a time.

Theo didn't need to kick open this door. Instead, they discovered the door wide open with Sam in a crumbled heap near the door, Kerri Reid hovering over her. "Ms. Reid, step away from Mrs. Crenshaw!" Theo cried out.

Unable to bear the sight of her on the floor, Heath rushed toward Sam's crumpled body. Kerri backed away and held up her hands. "Thank goodness you're here. I tried to stop her—"

"Don't waste your breath. Lilliana told us about Bailee and Sam," Heath ground out.

Theo moved quickly, incapacitating Kerri. "You're under arrest for the murder of Bailee Talson." He bent her arms behind her back and handcuffed her while reading her rights. The click of the cuffs a satisfied sound.

Heath dropped to his knees before the body of his wife and ran his hands over her face, checking for any hurts. Her chest rose slowly, her breathing shallow. "Hang in there, baby," Heath sobbed. "The paramedics aren't far behind us." He rested his head against Sam's forehead, her skin clammy and cold against his own. He silently thanked Theo for phoning in the additional help as a precaution.

He relaxed a small measure at the whine of sirens from nearby. "Hold on, baby," he said, pulling her into his embrace, comforting them both by rocking her slim body in his arms. He dared a glance over at Theo and Kerri. She was secured in handcuffs, a blank look on her beautiful face.

Where he expected theatrics, yelling or pretend anger from her. Instead, there was the quietness of defeat and maybe the final realization of her actions. He noticed her skin was paler than he remembered. He met her eyes and flinched, squeezing Sam tighter against his chest. Kerri's eyes bore pure malice.

"What the hell did you give her?" Heath asked her, his voice desperate.

"I don't know what you mean." She smirked, taunting him.

"I'm not sure what she gave Sam but I have a feeling it's some sort of poison or narcotic," Theo said to the paramedics. They swarmed the room, one of them pushing a stretcher.

Heath relinquished Sam's limp body and watched as a paramedic placed on oxygen mask over Sam's face.

Seconds seemed like minutes while the paramedics worked on Sam. Heath saw her reach up in an attempt to remove the mask from her face. Heath grabbed her hand and squeezed. "I'm right here. You're going to be fine, baby."

Sam turned her head toward his voice, her hand clammy and cold just like her forehead was. She managed to give him a light squeeze in return.

Heath stepped back to allow the paramedics to load Sam up on a stretcher to carry her out toward the ambulance. He followed close behind, out of the hotel into a crowd of guests gathering outside of the building. Lucky for him, he didn't see the familiar flash of a camera, an all too common disturbance in the past few weeks. And a silent partner in his investigation.

Another set of paramedics rushed past him into the hotel to assist Theo with Kerri. Heath watched Sam loaded into the back of the ambulance and jumped inside to sit beside her. There was no way he was going to let her out of his sight again.

The paramedics slammed the back door of the ambulance closed. Heath watched Sam's face for any progress. Her eyes remained closed, her breathing shallow yet steady.

He looked out the back window as the ambulance pulled away, sirens blaring. He saw Theo pushing Kerri inside his car and gave a wave. For once he was where he was supposed to be. Heath looked at Sam again. She looked so small on the stretcher. He reached out to brush a stray hair away from her face before placing a kiss on her forehead. He finally understood what Sam had been trying to get him to think about before.

There were certain things in life worth fighting for. Things which could not be replaced, bought, bartered or sold.

Heath's fight had been in the courtroom, defending his clients, adding another win to his résumé to earn respect and praise from his peers. But in his haste, the woman who meant the most to him was pushed aside for his career.

Heath settled in for the ride to the hospital, a guardian

over his wife. He was done fighting for others. He understood now his fight was for himself and the woman he loved.

ONCE THE AMBULANCE reached the hospital, the hustle of the emergency room quickly became a blur as Heath raced through corridors after Sam. Rooms, nurses, stretchers, all passed by him in a blur as he breathed through the sterile, alcohol smell of the hospital. As desperate as Heath knew it was for the doctors to provide Sam with the care she needed, he was wont to let her out of his sight.

He watched doctors push Sam into a separate room. A doctor held up his hand, barring him from entrance. "I'm sorry, Mr. Crenshaw. You can't enter."

A nurse or caseworker took ahold of his hand, whispering kind words as she ushered him into a small waiting room. Health glanced around the room to find the space occupied by a middle-aged woman, a family and a few other people. A spattering of chairs and end tables were placed at thoughtful angles and groupings so families could find some small privacy in the room while they waited for word of a loved one.

The only seat Heath could find was next to the middle-aged woman on the bench. He sat down next to her, a small smile played on her lips. The traces of time and a life well lived lined the corners of her eyes and her mouth, only enhancing her natural beauty. Her gray eyes took in his ragged appearance. Health combed his fingers through his hair, trying to straighten it. He must look a mess. He ran a hand over his face, trying to regroup his emotions.

"Waiting for your love?" the woman asked him, her voice gentle. Heath turned to respond and was caught watching her fingers made quick work of her knitting, the marled blue yarn twisting around her needles. He felt her steady gray gaze studying him.

"Yes."

"Me too," she replied, letting out a sigh. "This is the second surgery my husband had in the past month." The woman stopped her knitting and looked down at her hands resting in her lap before glancing up at Heath again. "My husband is a few years older than me. He had a terrible fall not too long ago. He's here now because he had a horrible pain in his stomach. As it turns out, his appendix almost burst. The damn fool."

"How awful. I'm sorry he's experiencing ill health. I hope he makes a full recovery." Heath managed to keep his tone polite. All he wanted to do was pace around the room like a caged animal. He didn't think he could wait here as patiently as this woman.

"Thank you. Since his fall, everything seems to be going downhill." She smiled again at Heath. "We've been together almost thirty years. I raised our children while he worked in the factory outside of town. We've had a good run of it. He drives me batty but I couldn't imagine this life without him by my side."

Heath mulled over her words. Sam was his everything, too. They had been together since college, she had stood by his side through law school and countless hours studying for the bar exam. Just as this woman had stood by her husband, quietly in the background but a steady rock to him for close to thirty years.

"I hope you have many more to share together," Heath said.

"You too. Don't grow old, it's a bitch." The woman laughed, her eyes watery with unshed tears.

Heath smiled at her frankness but took her message to heart. Life was too short to not spend time with those you loved.

They spent the next few hours in deep conversation, sharing details about their lives. The woman told him her story of how she met her husband and all the travels they shared before they settled down to have children. Heath in turn told her about Sam and her dedication to him, about how they met in college and were married shortly after. The two of them sat on the small sofa in the waiting room and made quick friends, opposites in appearance but familiar in heart.

The conversation was soon interrupted by the appearance of a surgeon in scrubs, her face sweaty. "Ellie?" The surgeon noticed the two of them sitting together and held out her hands, a somber expression on her face. Heath held his breath as he prepared for what was next.

"Your husband experienced a few complications during his surgery...he is slowly recovering. He will need to spend time recuperating but is expected to make a full recovery."

Heath exhaled and flashed his favorite cocky smile to his new friend. "Good luck, Ellie. I'm sure your husband will be driving you crazy before you know it."

She turned, giving Heath's hand a squeeze. "I hope your Samantha does well, too. I'll pay you a visit when she recovers. I can't wait to meet her. And remember, she needs a bit of pampering and ice cream. Every girl needs ice cream."

Ellie left with a wave and Heath stared after, alone in the room, waiting to hear how Sam fared. The other occupants had left long ago.

Heath must have dozed off because he was awoken by a hand on his shoulder. He looked up to see Rex standing in front of him.

"This seat taken?" Rex motioned to the seat beside Heath.

"No." Heath stretched out his legs and straightened his shoulders. This visit was unexpected. He wondered if Theo had called him.

Rex sat down next to Heath and handed him a coffee. "I'm

sorry to hear what happened to Sam. She's a force to be reckoned with."

"That she is," Heath replied. The two men sat in silence, reminiscent of the days in courthouse when they worked in tandem, the silence an indication of trust, and interrupted only when one of them made a discovery. The silence never awkward then, just as it wasn't awkward now. Despite the words and animosity that simmered earlier between them, Heath and Rex had a friendship that ran deeper than either of them ever imagined.

Rex leaned his arms on his thighs, the coffee cup held between his hands. He bowed his head then turned his gaze to Heath. "I'm not good at these types of things. I never meant to keep secrets from you. I was...obsessed. I wanted the chance to break the lead on a story which would shake Midnight Harbor to its core. I thought I was doing the right thing by keeping you at arm's length. I thought I was doing the right thing by assigning you to lead Nic's case. I failed to imagine what the consequences of my actions could be. I'm sorry, Heath."

"Thank you for your apology and explaining your actions. It's not like you to become wrapped up in cases. You have a way of keeping yourself at arm's length so you don't use emotion to make decisions," Heath said.

Rex rubbed his hand over the dark stubble on his face and sighed. "I've been...distracted the past few weeks. When Nic approached me, I was already involved in handling the investigation of the escort service. We were unaware of who and what else was involved in the case. We kept a low profile while Claudia followed up on leads."

Heath nodded. "You kept pertinent information from me."

"I did. For that I am sorry. I should've brought you in from the beginning."

Heath saw movement from the restricted door. A doctor in

scrubs stepped into the room, his pace slow as he walked toward them. Heath felt his heart hammering in his chest.

"Mr. Crenshaw?"

The doctor smiled at Heath. "Your wife is resting. She did very well. We had to pump her stomach and give her some IV fluids. I expect her to make a full recovery. I can take you back to see her now, if you would like."

"Yes, I need to see her." Heath stood to follow and felt Rex's hand on his shoulder.

"Good luck, Heath."

Heath gripped the hand on his shoulder and turned toward Rex, pulling him into a one-armed hug. "Thank you."

Rex slapped Heath's back and pulled away, leaving behind something in Heath's hand. As Rex walked away, Heath stared down at his security badge for the Firm and a small thumb drive.

"Are you ready?" the doctor asked, breaking Heath's concentration on the objects in his hand. Heath glanced up to see Rex exiting the waiting room.

"Yes, I am," Heath replied.

Whatever Tyler discovered from the thumb drive could wait. The most important thing to him lay just ahead.

CHAPTER TWENTY-NINE

BEEP...BEEP...BEEP...

Numerous machines beeped around her. Sam squeezed her eyes shut, groaning at the constant noise pounding at her ears. She slowly opened her eyes. Her mouth was dry with an unfamiliar taste on her tongue. She coughed and found her throat raw. Sam closed her eyes before trying to sit up in bed.

"Ugh," she moaned.

"Take your time. There's no hurry," a voice murmured to her left. She felt warm hands gently ease her back onto the bed. She recognized that voice.

Heath.

She rubbed her eyes, pushing away the grogginess like spiderwebs spun in her head. The last thing she remembered was her struggling with Kerri. She turned toward the voice, her eyesight finally settling to normal. She looked at Heath, at the worry lines bracketing his mouth, his lips in a firm line.

"Heath, we need to call Theo." She tried to ease herself out of the bed and fell back with a groan. She felt like a truck hit her, every muscle hurt, even her hair felt sore.

"Don't worry about that just now. You need to focus on rest."

"What happened? Kerri...she, I..."

Sam moved into a sitting position, grimacing against the pain in her muscles. Taking a deep breath to steady herself. "Did you get a confession? Did Lilliana find you?"

"Lilliana found us waiting for her thanks to the note you slipped her."

Her eyes lingered on Heath's familiar face. She'd been afraid she would never see him again.

"We need to talk." His brown eyes were dark with anger.

Sam mentally braced herself for the scathing lecture she was about to receive. She feigned a yawn. Maybe she could evade this conversation for a little bit longer. "I'm really tired, Heath. Let's wait until I have a chance to sleep."

She waited a few minutes before peeking at him.

Heath moved his position so he was just a few inches from her, a determined look on his face. Sam groaned, covering her face with her hand. "I know what you're going to say"

"Good. I'm not falling for your ruse, Sam. I'm going to say what I need to whether you want to hear it or not and you're going to listen."

"Could I have a drink first? Maybe a martini?"

Heath didn't smile at her poor attempt at humor.

Sighing, Sam looked into his eyes. Those amazing brown eyes always conveyed his confidence and warmth. Those same eyes were one of the reasons he stole her heart the first time they met.

His fingers gently grasped her jaw, tipping her chin up to meet his gaze. "Do you understand how close you were to not being here, alive, in this hospital bed?" The softness in his voice almost undid her.

Sam knew she was in bad shape. Machines beeped around her and she caught glimpses of nurses flurrying about the room. Somewhere, deep inside, she vaguely remembered making some terrible decisions which may have led to her waking up in this room.

"No, I don't. What I mean is, yes, I understand I made terrible choices." She held up her hand, the IV pulled against her arm. "Listen. I never thought I would end up getting hurt. I just hoped to a get a confession or some useful information from Kerri. I didn't expect the situation to spiral out of control."

"I don't know what I expected to happen." Heath slumped back in the chair next to the hospital bed and covered his face with a hand. "I take full responsibility for going along with the asinine plan to allow you to question Kerri. It was irresponsible of me and I'm sorry."

"You don't have to apologize." Sam tried swinging her legs over the bed and opted against it. "I wanted to go there. I wanted to question Kerri. I pushed back against you and Theo even though I had no authority or reason to believe I was qualified. I needed answers for Bailee," Sam said, hoping she was able to convey the urgency in her voice. It was her decision.

"I need to apologize, for a lot. I get your drive to find out what happened to Bailee from your involvement with her."

Sam moved to pull away but Heath held tight to her hand. "Listen to me when I say, you don't need to put yourself in danger to find the answer you seek. I handle research for my cases to the best of my ability. When I can't, I hire private investigators to handle any independent research for me. I use my connections in the police department."

Heath released her hand, his touch grazing over her fingertips. "Connections who are trained professionals to handle escalated issues and police procedures. Professionals...to keep me safe." Heath sat on her bed and threaded his fingers through her hair, his thumb tracing along the bottom of her lip. The touch sent a flutter down to her toes despite being stuck in a hospital bed. "To keep you safe so this same exact situation wouldn't happen."

She felt it all in that moment: guilt, embarrassment, anger, sadness. Health was right. She was reckless in her investigation. She owed him the truth. If this was a turning point in their relationship, he deserved her honesty.

No more secrets or avoidance. No more meekness.

Sam took Health's other hand into her own. "I'm sorry too. I wish you could feel what I do so you understood how sorry I am. I didn't mean for any of this to happen. I only wanted to help. I never meant to get so involved in the case. For it to consume me." Sam let go of Heath's hand. "She needed justice." Sam placed her hands over her heart. "More than that, I felt like the part of me I placed aside so I could support your career finally could stretch her wings to attempt something other than cooking or planning another dinner party."

Heath stared straight into her eyes, the intensity of their brown depth warmed her. "You've always been my partner in life. Nothing has changed. If you wanted to try a career or get a new job all you needed to do was tell me. I'm sorry I wasn't there when you needed me." Heath kissed both of her hands. "This idea, to think you have the experience needed to be a private investigator? It's crazy."

She saw the hurt in his expression, in his eyes. The pain she caused him from being distant for so long mixed with a new fear for her safety. She knew what he was going to say next. She prepared herself for the disappointment.

"Just when we started to rekindle our love, you're almost taken from me. I couldn't bear to live this life without you. The only reason I've become what I am is because of your support. Please know I support you in whatever adventure you choose. Just think it through before you jump into the next adventure. Promise me you will think about the consequences of your actions and prepare yourself, and me, for it," Heath said, a smile slowly spreading across his face.

Surprised at his response, Sam was at a loss for words. That he supported her was all she could hope for. Tears welled behind her eyes and he pressed his forehead against hers. "I love you, Samantha Crenshaw, whether you want to be a nosy neighbor, party planner or librarian. You make me a better man. You made me realize I already have everything I always wanted."

Heath bent his head to capture Sam's lips in a kiss, their mouths meeting in a soft brush of lips. She let the rush fade, waiting until she was free from the hospital to show him what she felt. For now words would have to suffice. "I love you too, Heath Crenshaw."

A man cleared his throat. "Excuse me. Heath, Sam?"

They turned to see Theo standing in the doorway, holding a bouquet of colorful flowers. Sam smiled. "Hi, Theo. Please come in."

Heath stood to shake the other man's hand then walked to stand by the doorway, allowing Theo to sit closer to Sam.

"These are for you," Theo said as he offered the bouquet to Sam.

"They're beautiful. Thank you."

"You're welcome, I'm happy to see you're doing well."

Theo sat down in the empty chair beside her hospital bed. "I'm grateful for what you did back at the sorority house and with Kerri. I should've never allowed you to help." He looked between Sam and Heath. "I have a feeling nothing I did would've stopped you from helping."

Sam laughed, then winced again at the pain in her stomach.

"I'm not sure what came over me. I'm sorry for encouraging your participation. This case...was too close to home," Theo's voice was soft.

"Thank you. You're right. You wouldn't have been able to persuade me differently." Sam knew it was too soon, but she had to know what happened. "Were you able to get what we need to convict Kerri?"

"With the recording from Amanda, the photographs and

Lilliana's statement, I'll be able to bring justice to Bailee and her parents."

Sam thought of the intern responsible for causing trouble but not responsible for the death of Bailee Talson. "How is Amanda?" Sam asked in earnest.

"She'll be fine. You stabbed her just enough to draw a good deal of blood but no major damage was done. She'll be well soon enough to face the consequences of her actions." Theo looked at her with a stern look. "You were a tremendous help in this case, Sam. I hope you take precautions in the future with your...ability."

He placed a business card on the bed. "This card is mine. If you ever need me...in a capacity beyond what could be considered, uh, normal." He winked at her before placing another business card on the bed beside his own. "This one is for a former colleague who is available for specialized training, if you find you need it. She's tough but kind."

Sam managed a small smile and caught Heath looking at her. He shrugged his shoulders. "Thank you."

"What happens now?" Heath said from the doorway.

Theo leaned back in the chair. "I'll need to review the recording again to make sure we didn't miss anything from Amanda's confession. We know she is responsible for blackmailing Davi. She likely used her position at the Firm as leverage. As for Kerri...she maintains her innocence. I'm sure the DA will take care of her. After all, she did confess to Sam."

"I understand this is beyond the scope of normal police procedure but maybe I could help you. I might be able to recall something to assist you in the investigation," Sam offered.

Theo looked at her for what felt like ages before nodding. "I'll let you know if I need anything." He stood to leave. "A pleasure as always. I hope when our paths cross again it's for better circumstances. Take care." Theo gave Sam's hand a squeeze.

Heath walked Theo out of her room, closing the door before returning to her bedside. Heath picked up the business cards and raised an eyebrow. "Your first official police contact?"

Sam smiled as she looked at her husband. "Did we make the twenty-four-hour time limit?" She winked at him.

"The hell if I know." Heath broke out in a bright smile that quickly faded as he held out something by a thin ball chain. Sam recognized the name on the small badge. "Your security badge for the Firm. Why?" Sam questioned.

"Rex stopped by to give his well wishes for your recovery...and to say he was sorry."

"What are you going to do with it?"

"I don't know." Heath placed the security badge next to the cards on the bed. He held up a small thumb drive between his thumb and forefinger. "He also gave me this."

Sam took the small file from Heath's hand, her fingers brushing over the blemish marks marring the surface. "Tyler. He did it. What do you think could be on it?"

"I'm not sure. Understand viewing the file comes with responsibility. Once you commit to this, there's no going back."

She turned over the thumb drive in her hand, debating the possibilities. She dropped the drive on the bed next to the cards and badge. She knew Heath loved his job and had worked hard to get where he was. "Heath, your decision is your own. I'm proud of you for standing up for yourself and against Rex. I know how much his friendship means to you. I support your decision and will be by your side no matter what."

"And I will with you too. Just so long as you prepare yourself accordingly," Heath said.

He wrapped his arms around her, pulling her head against his chest. She buried her face in his shirt and smiled. They had been through hell the last year. There were times she thought she lost herself and him. But in the process of finding herself, she found her love for her husband and he for her. They had reclaimed one another just as they had nearly five years ago during their wedding vows.

"Here's to our future," Sam said as she held up the two business cards.

Heath returned her smile with a slow grin. "You know, I can picture you wearing a pair of handcuffs at your hip."

"I bet you would. Get over here and kiss me or else you can say goodbye to your fantasy." Sam leaned toward him and met his lips with a hungry kiss.

"What a cruel woman you are," Heath whispered against her mouth before trailing a line of kisses down her jaw. He pulled back and held up the thumb drive and security badge, "Shall we take a look to see what's on this file, Mrs. Crenshaw?"

Sam laughed at his teasing tone, "Absolutely."

CHAPTER THIRTY

THE WARMTH of the sunny spring day eased the goose-bumps on Sam's arms. She walked carefully over the grass path, her eyes on the tombstones standing still as soldiers in a row. Up ahead, beyond the weathered stone soldiers, she saw where the emerald green grass was overturned, the brown earth a marker for the recent grave.

Sam placed the small bouquet of sunflowers on top of the upturned earth, the grave marker a small black plaque until Bailee's parents could replace it with the angel statue they planned. She met with Bailee's parents after Kerri's charges were announced. They were a lovely older couple, lost without their daughter but comforted by the love of family and friends. And finally, kneeling in the grass, Sam understood why she felt compelled to place herself in danger to bring justice to Bailee.

By placing Bailee at rest, she honored her own daughter whom she never grieved for. A daughter who she finally allowed herself to grieve for as she circled closer to Bailee's killer. A daughter whose life was taken in a twist of fate, with no notice or fanfare, just like Bailee.

"I hope you find peace," Sam whispered. A warmth

spread over her from the top of her head, along her shoulders and down her legs until every inch of her felt wrapped in kindness and love.

In that moment, Sam knew she had accomplished what she set out to do. She gave Bailee her justice and released her own lost little girl.

She stood, brushing the dirt off her knees and thought she saw a translucent figure beside the grave before a flash of light blinded her, taking the figure with it.

Her mouth quickened into a smile. "You're welcome."

Sam retraced her steps through the cemetery to the car until the familiar sight of Heath's long, muscled frame and bronzed hair caused her to break into a run.

She launched herself at him, wrapping her arms around his neck and legs about his waist.

"Better?" Heath nuzzled her neck.

Sam nodded, inhaling his scent deep into her lungs, washing away all the sadness and grief.

"Good. Now prepare to be amazed with your handsome husband's ability to secure a one-week vacation in Key West."

Sam slid down Heath's front, a seductive promise of what he could expect on their overdue vacation. "It's about time. I thought you had forgotten about your promise."

"Never. I was momentarily occupied with your recovery."

"Allow me to momentarily occupy you with the thoughts of me wearing your favorite dress while sipping margaritas."

Heath shot her a cocky grin. "Maybe you can show me what you meant to do that day before the Spicy Sauce Incident. Sauce not included."

Sam hit his arm then laughed as he grabbed her and brushed his lips over hers in a sensual promise of nights to come.

THE END

AUTHOR'S NOTE

Thank you for reading about Sam's journey discovering herself and her newfound abilities. She holds a special place in my heart. I hope I did her story justice.

If you enjoyed reading about Sam and Heath and the town of Midnight Harbor, please subscribe to my newsletter. You'll be first to know of new books will be released in the series along with access to exclusive excerpts and sneak peeks, only available to subscribers.

ACKNOWLEDGMENTS

This book has been a two-year journey from concept to publishing. My story would never have been created if it wasn't for the encouragement and support of my husband, Dan.

I would also like to thank my developmental editor, Jade Hemmings. Your early critique helped me see a new possibility in my story. Thank you to DJ Hendrickson for the expert copyediting and feedback. Sam and Heath's story came alive with your help. Finally, thank you Natasha Snow Designs for creating a drool worthy cover from the few descriptive sentences I gave her.

ABOUT THE AUTHOR

Jessica Lynn lives in Pennsylvania with her loving husband, two rambunctious boys and sweet pups. A lifelong reader, Jessica Lynn is drawn to stories of adventure, romance, fantasy and mystery.